THE DOGS OF WINTER

BOBBIE PYRON

ANDERSEN PRESS · LONDON

This edition first published in 2013 by

Andersen Press Limited

20 Vauxhall Bridge Road

London SW1V 2SA

www.andersenpress.co.uk

2 4 6 8 10 9 7 5 3

First published in 2012 in the United States of America by

Arthur A. Levine Books, an imprint of Scholastic Inc.

The right of Bobbie Pyron to be identified as the author of this work

has been asserted by her in accordance with the

Copyright, Designs and Patents Act, 1988.

Text Copyright © Bobbie Pyron, 2012

British Library Cataloguing in Publication Data available.

ISBN 978 1 84939 521 2

Printed and bound in Great Britain by CPI Group (UK) Ltd, Croydon, CR0 4YY

For Ivan Mishukov,
and all the invisible children,
everywhere

PART ONE

PART TWO

PART ONE

Chapter 1

DREAMS

I dream of dogs. I dream of warm, soft backs pressed against mine, their deep musky smell a comfort on long, bitter nights. I dream of wet tongues, flashing teeth, warm noses, and knowing eyes, watching. Always watching.

Sometimes I dream we are running, the dogs and I, through empty streets and deserted parks. We run for the joy and freedom in it, never tiring, never hungry. And then, great wings unfold from their backs, spreading wide and lifting the dogs above me. I cry out, begging them to come back, to take pity on this earthbound boy.

It has been many years since I lived with the dogs, but still I dream. I do not dream of the long winter nights on the streets of Russia; seldom do I dream of the things that drove me from my home. My dreams begin and end with the dogs.

Chapter 2

BEFORE

Before *he* came, I watched my beautiful mother.

I watched her at the kitchen sink, her pale hands dipping in and out of steaming water as she washed the dishes, humming.

I watched her hang sheets from the line on the tiny balcony of our flat, clothes pegs clamped between her teeth. I handed her more clothes pegs, two by two.

'Such a good helper, my Mishka, my little bear,' she always said.

Before, I sat in my grandmother, Babushka Ina's, lap, and listened as she sang the old songs. She rocked me back and forth, back and forth.

Every morning Babushka Ina walked me down the hill to my school. My mother had to get to her job at the bakery long before the sun rose. At school, I sat at the wooden table and practiced my letters. I learned to sound out 'cat' and 'rat' and to not watch the birds out of the windows.

In the afternoon, my mother and I walked back up the long, low hill to our home. Babushka Ina cooked my favourite cabbage soup while I practised my letters and listened to my mother hum.

Before, it was Babushka Ina who slept with my mother at night. I had my special bed in the sitting room. My mother read to me every night from my book of fairy tales.

This is the way it had always been: me and my mother and my Babushka Ina. This was the way I thought the world would always be.

Chapter 3

AFTER

One warm spring day, my mother waited for me outside the school yard. Her eyes and nose were red.

She dropped to her knees and hugged me to her.

'What is it?' I asked.

'She is gone, Mishka,' my mother sobbed. 'Your babushka is gone.'

I did not understand why my mother cried so. Sometimes, Babushka Ina took the train to The City to visit her cousin. Once, I had even ridden the train with her.

'She has gone to The City,' I assured my mother. I patted her cheek.

'No, Mishka,' my mother said. 'Your babushka has gone to heaven.'

After Babushka Ina went to heaven, my mother began to forget.

She forgot to wash the dishes. She forgot what day to stand in line for macaroni and what day to stand in line for bread.

She cried and cried at night and forgot to take her clothes off to sleep. She forgot to read to me at night. I crawled into bed with her. I could still smell Babushka Ina.

She forgot that Babushka Ina said it was bad luck to cry in your soup, and that vodka and beer were very bad. She sat at the kitchen table and cried and smoked cigarettes and drank.

She never sang again.

My mother forgot to take me to school, and sometimes she forgot her job at the bakery. Sometimes I went to bed hungry. Sometimes I went to bed alone because she went down to the village at night to meet friends.

I watched her as she sat before the mirror, making herself pretty for a date. Red on her lips, blue above the eyes. 'Which ones, little bear?' she asked, holding up one pair of earrings and then another.

She hummed as she pulled on her red coat with the black shiny buttons. She knelt in front of me, hugging me to her. 'Be a good boy, Mishka. Lock the door. Don't unlock it until you know it's me.'

If I had known *he* would come, I would never have unlocked the door.

Ever.

His shiny trousers and scuffed boots filled the doorway. My mother pushed me in front of her. 'Mishka, say hello.'

'Hello,' I said.

He handed my mother a bundle of flowers, bent down, and pushed his narrow face into mine. 'So this is the little man of the house, hey? He's no bigger than a cockroach.'

His smell made my hand want to pinch my nose.

'Shake hands,' my mother urged, giving me another push. He grabbed my hand and squeezed it, hard.

'Don't worry, Anya,' he said. 'The boy and I will have lots of time to get to know each other.' His smile was big, but did not reach his eyes.

That was how it started.

He took her out. He bought me a radio for company.

'It is a radio,' I said, holding it up for my mother to see. I twisted knobs and held it against my ear. 'I can hear the world talking and singing.'

He snorted. 'You won't hear anyone in Russia singing.'

'Why not?' I asked.

'Because, little boy, everyone's too poor to sing.'

'But we are not poor,' I pointed out.

He threw back his head and laughed. My mother hugged me to her. 'No we are not, little bear.'

Soon he forgot to go home. He stayed with cigarettes and bottles of vodka and his scuffed boots next to her bed.

'You're too big a boy to sleep with your mother,' he said. 'Only little babies sleep with their mothers. Are you a baby, Mishka?'

I shook my head. 'I am five.'

He tossed my favourite blanket and my fairy-tale book onto the bed in the sitting room.

'But my mother needs me with her at night,' I said, twisting the hem of my shirt. My mother would move his boots to the sitting room when she came home from work, and put my blankets back in her room. I knew she would.

When she came home from her job at the bakery, she would bring a day-old loaf of black bread, potatoes and cabbage for soup, and a fresh sticky bun for me.

Instead, she came through the door that night with empty hands and a sad face. 'I've lost my job,' she said.

'You can't lose your job,' he said, his black eyes narrow and hard. 'How will we eat?'

'Can't you—?'

He cuffed her on the side of the head. I had never seen anyone strike my mother. I waited for her to hit him back. Once, in the village, a bigger boy knocked me down. My mother grabbed the boy and shook him by his collar. The boy's eyes grew wide with fear and he ran away as fast as he could. Just like *he* would.

But my mother did not grab him by the collar. She did not shake him until his teeth rattled. She pressed her hand to the side of her face and said, 'I'm sorry.'

After that, they sat in the sitting room and drank and smoked and laughed and fought. He did not like me there, sitting on my bed in the corner.

'He's watching me again, Anya!' he said. 'Why is he always watching me?' He stomped across the room and shoved me off my bed. He grabbed my blankets and my book and threw them into the pantry in the kitchen.

'There,' he said, dusting off his hands as if ridding himself of something dirty. 'This is where you sleep now.' My mother stood behind him, twisting her hands.

I burrowed into the nest of blankets in the kitchen pantry. My book of fairy tales rested on a dusty shelf with the ghostly circles of the canned vegetables we no longer had. After days and then weeks, the beautiful golden fire-bird on the cover of the book was smeared with grease;

on another shelf lay a pile of scrap paper, and my favourite pencil. When I couldn't sleep because of cold or anger, I drew pictures. Drawings of firebirds, a terrible witch named Baba Yaga, houses walking on chicken legs, talking dolls, giants and wolves with wings.

Their voices rose and fell beyond the pantry door.

'Why can't you see he'd be better off in an orphanage?'

'I can't send him away!'

'You can't afford to feed yourself,' his voice said. 'Besides, I don't like him. He's odd.'

'There's nothing wrong with him.'

Glass shattered. 'It's him or me, Anya.'

'No! Please don't ask me...'

Another crash. The sound of shoving, angry feet on the floor. 'You stupid woman!' A slap. 'Don't!' A crash. A scream. A thud. A moan. Quiet.

Chapter 4

THE BUTTON

The cold of the pantry floor pushed its way up through my pile of blankets. I shivered and watched the plume of my breath in the air. I was a dragon. I was a firebird. I was not a man who smelled and shouted and blew cigarette smoke through the two holes in his nose.

I pulled my black radio from beneath the blankets and raised the shiny silver antenna to attention.

'... thousands unemployed, homeless and starving. Alcoholism ripping the fabric of our great society...'

'But I am not homeless or starving,' I said to the voice in the radio. 'I have my mother, my blankets, soup with cabbage.' True, we no longer had bread and sausage with our *shchi*, our cabbage soup. And it had been weeks since my mother had worked. But she still smiled (although less often now) and called me her little bear.

I turned off my radio. I folded first one blanket and

then the other just so. I pulled on the Famous Basketball Player shoes my mother and Babushka Ina gave me last Christmas. My toes pushed against the ends of the shoes. I could no longer wiggle my toes.

I stood in the doorway of the pantry, listened, and sniffed.

Was my mother cooking kasha or was she crying? Was he yelling, calling her a stupid, lazy cow, or was he gone? Sometimes after a big fight like last night, he would leave. And for a short time, everything would be as it should: kasha for breakfast, my mother smiling just a little. 'Come keep me company in the breadline,' she'd say. Or 'Let's practice your reading,' or 'Tell me a story, little bear.'

I heard angry voices shouting from the television. I smelled cigarettes. I peered into the sitting room.

'So,' his voice said. 'The little cockroach finally crawls out of his hole.'

He lay sprawled across the couch, his ugly feet bare, a glass resting on his fat belly.

'Where is my mother?' I asked. My eyes darted from the sitting room to the bedroom and back to his face.

He did not take his eyes from the snowy screen of the television. 'Gone,' he said. 'She is gone.'

My heart thumped and thumped against my chest. 'When will she be back?' I whispered.

He turned from the television, and eyed me for a long moment, like a cat eyeing a mouse. 'Never,' he said.

I waited and listened and watched for my beautiful mother.

I listened for the click of her heels coming down the hall. I watched for the bright flash of her red coat.

When he left at night, I searched the flat for clues. If she took this, it meant she would be back in a week. If she took that, it meant she would be back any day.

Everything was where it had always been, except my mother and her red coat. She was gone. Her coat was gone. She must have gone further to find potatoes and cabbage for the soup. Or she looked for a new place for us to live, far away from him.

Something winked from behind the bin in the bedroom. I got down on my hands and knees, stretched my fingers around the paper wrappers and past empty bottles on the floor. My fingers curled around something hard and smooth. I opened my hand. A button from her coat. I held the button up to the light, ran my thumb across its black, shiny surface. And next to the button was a smear of red. Not the beautiful red of her coat but a dark, sickly red.

I touched it with my finger. It pulsed like a heartbeat. It whispered my name.

'Why are you grubbing around on the floor, cock-roach?'

I tore my eyes away from the whispering, pulsing red and looked up at him.

He kicked at me with the toe of his boot.

I held up the button. 'It is from her coat, her red coat.'

'Bah,' he said. 'So what? Who cares?'

'She loved her coat,' I said, following him into the kitchen. 'She loved the buttons. She would not let the coat be without a button,' I pointed out.

He grabbed a hunk of cheese from the refrigerator. He slammed the door shut. My stomach grumbled. My mouth watered. I clutched the button in my hand.

He looked down at me, his mouth full of rotten teeth and cheese. He cocked his head to one side. 'Where do you think that mother of yours is?' he asked.

I shook my head.

He smacked his lips and belched. I laughed. My mother never allowed me to belch.

'I think,' he said, 'she went to the city.'

I frowned. 'Why would she leave without me?'

He unscrewed the top of a bottle. 'Who knows why

women do what they do. You're a useless little cockroach and she's a lazy, stupid cow.'

I drew myself up tall. I squeezed the shiny black button until it bit into my hand. 'She is not lazy and stupid! You are!'

My head slammed into the kitchen floor and a million stars filled the sky.

Chapter 5

THE CITY

The next morning, he said, 'Get your coat and hat. We're going.'

'Going where?' I asked. 'Are you taking me to my mother?' I picked at the dried blood on my ear.

He grunted and flicked his cigarette into the kitchen sink. 'We're going into the city.'

'But my mother—'

He raised his hand. I jumped back, knocking over a chair.

'Enough about your mother,' he said. 'Just get your coat and let's go.'

I followed him to the train station, one step, then two steps behind. Women stood in the breadlines, bundled in coats and scarves and shawls.

My eyes searched hungrily for the red coat. She would see me stumbling behind this bad, bad man. She would run to me, sweep me away. I would show her the missing button. She would hug me to her. 'My good Mishka. My brave boy.' We would not let him through our door ever again.

A hand grabbed the back of my neck. 'Keep up, boy,' he growled.

My legs told me to run, to run as far and fast as I could from him. His hand tightened on the back of my neck. He shoved me through the train-station doors.

'You know where my mother is in The City?' I asked.

'Sure, sure,' he said.

A large, bright eye winked at the end of the train track – the eye of a large beast racing, snaking towards us, hissing and screeching. I grabbed his hand.

He slapped me away. 'Stop acting like a frightened little girl.'

I almost laughed. It was, after all, just the train.

He yanked me through the train's doors and onto a hard plastic seat.

Once, I had been on a train with my Babushka Ina. She had held me up on her lap so I could see the lights of our little village tick, tick past.

He lit a cigarette and snapped open the newspaper. I knelt down and watched our village grow smaller and smaller.

*

'Wake up.' A hand shook me. 'Come on, kid. I don't have time for this.' He pulled me to my feet and out the door of the train. I followed behind him across the platform, past carts of food – roasted hazelnuts, sausages, whole potatoes wrapped in newspaper – my stomach grumbling, my mouth watering. 'Wait!' I called to the back of his tattered coat. But he did not.

Everywhere inside the station were people. They hurried to the trains, they hurried away from the trains. They carried bundles and bags and satchels. They did not look left, they did not look right. They did not look at me as I called again, 'Wait!'

Finally, he stopped.

'Is this where my mother is?' I asked.

He laughed.

It was as I had thought. She had moved to The City. She had a good job and a warm place for us to live with lots of food and sweet sticky buns. When we walked up the steps to our fine new home, she would throw open the door, pull me into her arms.

And she would close the door in his face, for good this time.

He grabbed me by the arm and pulled me up the steps. I stumbled on one stair, then another, scraping my knee. I didn't care. I would soon be with my mother and all would be as it should be.

We broke into the sunlight, the cold autumn air. Snowflakes wheeled overhead, settling on his shoulders and on the toes of his brown boots. He looked up the street one way and down another. 'Where the hell is she?' he growled.

I looked up at him and smiled. He had brought me to her.

Perhaps he was not such a bad man after all. 'Spasibo,' I said. *Thank you.*

We stood in the falling snow and waited. He smoked a cigarette, then another. I watched for the red coat and rubbed the black button in my pocket over and over with my thumb.

A very dirty boy with no coat or hat or shoes walked over to us. My mother would never let me get so dirty. She would certainly not let me outside without a coat or hat, and especially not without shoes.

The boy tugged on the man's coat sleeve. He held out a filthy hand. 'Please, sir,' he said.

Before I could wonder what the boy wanted from him, the man cuffed the boy on the side of the head. 'Get lost, you filthy little beggar. Go and bother someone else.'

The dirty boy glared at me, then spat at my Famous Basketball Player shoes.

'Finally.' The man flicked his cigarette to the ground and wrapped his scarf around his neck. He grabbed my arm. 'Come on, let's go.'

I trotted beside him, looking and looking for the red coat. For my mother's smiling face, her chestnut hair, her outspread arms that would enfold me like angel wings. 'Where?' I asked, trotting to keep up. 'Where is she?'

'There,' he said.

I stopped dead in my tracks. This woman coming towards us was not my mother. She wore a black coat. A brown scarf covered most of her grey hair. Her arms were folded across her big chest. She did not smile as she looked down at me and said, 'So is this the boy?'

I looked from the unsmiling woman to the man. Perhaps she was my mother's friend. 'Are you taking me to my mother?' I asked.

The woman frowned. 'I thought you said he had no parents,' she snapped. Her eyes were small and hard like the eyes of the witch, Baba Yaga, in my fairy-tale book.

'He's just a kid,' he said. 'He doesn't know anything.'

The unsmiling woman sighed. 'Most of the children

in the orphanage don't know anything, either. At least about their parents.'

Orphanage. The word dropped like a cold stone in my stomach. Once on the television news I saw a story about orphanages in The City. None of the children in those places smiled or had mothers. Mostly they cried. They were almost as dirty as that beggar boy, but not quite.

'I cannot go to an orphanage,' I explained to them. 'My mother won't find me there.'

'Your mother isn't looking for you,' he said.

'She is!' I said.

The woman in the coat that was black, not red, grabbed my shoulder. 'Come on, boy. It's time to go.'

'No!' I jerked away from her hand, a hand more like a claw, a witch's claw.

I heard my mother's voice say, *Run, Mishka! Run!*

I span away from them, looking and looking for the red coat. I saw green coats and blue coats and grey coats and many, many black coats.

He grabbed me, twisting my arm. 'Come on, you brat.'

And then I saw it: a flash of bright red. I tore away from his grasp, ripping my coat from my body. *Run, Mishka! Run!*

I did. I ran as fast as I have ever run towards that flash

of red as it descended down the steps to the railway station. I dashed this way and that through the train station, looking in the crowds of hurrying people for the red coat. Finally, I saw it, standing in a line like a beacon, waiting to board the train.

Gripping the button in my pocket, I pushed through the sea of brown, black and grey, desperate to keep sight of my mother. The wave of brown and black and grey swept me onto the train.

I spotted a small figure in a red coat with chestnut hair beneath a blue scarf sitting near the front. I wound through a forest of legs, touched the red sleeve, held out the button and smiled.

The train lurched. I staggered back against brown and black and grey. 'Watch it,' someone said, pushing me upright.

I looked at the face of the woman in the blue scarf. Her hair was black, not chestnut. She did not smile. The coat was not even red.

She was not my mother.

Chapter 6

THE TRIBE

The train lurched. A voice announced, 'Leningradsky Station.'

I sat up, rubbed my eyes and uncurled myself from the train floor. The wave of brown, black, and grey coats spat me out of the train and carried me along the bright corridor. Was it still day or was it night? I had no idea. In the underground world of tunnels, it never changed.

I followed the stream of people up the long staircase, through the clicking turnstiles, then up the wide steps to the street.

Cold slapped me in the face. Stars glittered overhead in the night sky. I reached up to pull my hat down over my ears. My hat was not there. My coat was gone too. He had pulled it off as I tried to get away.

I thrust my hands into my pockets and looked for anything familiar. I saw no bakery; I saw no butcher's shop where my mother bought bones for the soup. I did not see our apartment building squatting at the top of the low hill.

I shivered in the night wind. I trudged back down the steps to the underground, where it was always daytime and not as cold. I spotted a heat vent underneath a long bench. I crawled under the bench and curled up around the warm air. I splayed my fingers across the grate, thought about the red coat that was not the red coat, and finally slept.

Something grabbed my foot and yanked me from my sleep. 'I've almost got it!' a voice said.

I scrambled back, pulling my foot away, and banged my head on the bottom of the bench. A dirty, narrow face with beady eyes glared at me.

A giant rat had come to eat my foot! I shrank back in horror and tried to make myself as small as I could.

A grimy hand reached for me. It was not a rat. It was a boy!

Another face appeared next to his. A bruise shadowed a dark eye. Its husky voice said, 'Why, it looks like a little bear all curled up in its winter den.' Holding out a hand, it said, 'Come here, mishka, little bear.' The voice and the hand belonged to a girl.

I looked from the girl to the rat-faced boy and back.

She called me little bear. My mother called me little bear.

'Have you seen my mother?' I asked the girl. 'She is looking for me.'

The rat-faced boy laughed. 'Yeah, right. All our mothers are looking for us.'

The girl jabbed him in the side with her elbow. 'Shut up, Viktor,' she snapped. She peered at me under the bench.

'Did you lose your mother on the train?'

I shook my head. 'I lost her before,' I said.

The girl nodded. 'It's been a long time since you've seen her?'

I blinked back tears. 'But she is looking for me,' I said.

The girl held out her hand again. 'She won't find you hiding underneath a bench,' she said. 'Come on out, little bear.'

Four children encircled me. I could not tell their ages or their size. Their mothers dressed them in cast-off clothes either many sizes too big or too small. Still, where there were children, there were adults. They would tell me how to find my mother.

'My name is Tanya,' the girl said. She pointed to the rat-faced boy. 'That's Viktor.'

A girl with a baseball cap and a cigarette tucked behind one ear jabbed her thumb at her chest. 'I'm Yula and I make more money than anybody else.' She pointed to a dark-skinned boy with dreamy eyes, 'Mr Glue Head there is Pasha.' Viktor snickered.

'My name is Mishka Ivan Andreovich and I am five years old.' I stood as tall as I could in my Famous Basket-ball Player shoes. 'I have to find my mother. We live in the town of Ruza.'

Rat-faced Viktor laughed and waved me away like an annoying fly. 'We've all lost our mothers, stupid.'

Tanya glared at him. 'What do you know? Maybe his mother is looking for him. Ruza is a long way from here. If we bring him to her, she'll probably give us money.'

'I don't believe in mothers,' Viktor said. 'There is no mother looking for him, and he's too small to keep.'

I started to ask him how he could not believe in mothers. Everyone has a mother, even mean, dirty children. I started to tell him about the red coat and the black button and how my mother read to me every night from the book of fairy tales, and how everything changed after Babushka Ina went to heaven and my mother began to forget and he came into our house, when a low, lazy voice from the shadows said, 'As always, Viktor, your imagination is limited by your pea-sized brain.' The rat-faced boy flushed. His eyes shifted nervously from side to side.

'He is useful to us precisely *because* he's small.' The voice stepped from the shadows, cigarette smoke streaming from his nose.

The tribe of children fell silent and stepped back from me. I rubbed the black button in my pocket with my thumb over and over.

He flicked the cigarette to the floor and stepped close. He took me by the shoulders, turning me this way and that. 'How old are you?' he barked.

'Five,' I whispered.

He nodded and pinched my arm. 'Small for your age. Even better. And those big brown eyes will grab the ladies every time.'

He wore the coat of a policeman. True, it was torn and filthy. It had no buttons. And his trousers and shoes did not look like policeman trousers and shoes. Still, my mother always told me the militsiya's job is to help.

'I'm lost,' I said. 'And I'm hungry.'

He squinted through the smoke. 'So?'

'I need to find my mother. She's worried about me.'

He spat something dirty onto the ground. 'What do I look like, a policeman?'

'Yes, you do. My mother always told me to ask a policeman for help if I got lost. So I am asking you.'

I gave him my best smile.

The girl named Yula howled. 'Rudy, militsiya!'

The others took up her chant. 'Rudy, militsiya! Rudy, militsiya!'

I turned to Tanya. 'Please,' I said. 'Take me to your home. Your mother will understand.'

She nestled in close to Rudy's side. He draped one arm across her shoulders. With the other, he swept his arm wide, taking in the soaring arches, the grimy pillars and the dirty, tattered children. Some followed passengers off the train, begging, while others were asleep on the cold, hard floor, their arms outstretched, palms up, begging even in sleep.

'Do you see any mothers here?' he asked. 'Do you?'

I looked from Rudy's cruel grey eyes, to Tanya. She leaned her head on Rudy's shoulder, her eyes filled with pity. 'We have no mothers, Mish. This is our home.'

Chapter 7

PRETEND

'Here's what we're going to do,' Tanya said, leading me up the long stairs to the world above the underground. 'We're going to say you're my little brother. My ill little brother. And we need money to buy you medicine.'

I frowned. 'That's a lie. I'm not your little brother. My mother told me to always tell the truth.'

Tanya sighed. 'Haven't you ever played pretend, Mish?'

I nodded, although I had never played pretend with anyone else.

'So that's what we're doing. We're pretending we're brother and sister and you're ill. I bet you're really good at pretending to be ill.'

I clutched my stomach and moaned.

'Good! Good!' she said, clapping her hands. 'Now let's hear you cough.'

I hacked and spat. 'Like that?' I asked.

She hugged me to her. 'Just like that,' she said.

'And if I'm really good at pretending, will you help me find my mother?'

She ruffled my hair. 'Of course, Mishka.'

So there on the streets of The City, on a cold fall day, I performed. I clutched and moaned and coughed and spat. I squeezed tears from my eyes while Tanya grasped at the people, all the people hurrying by. 'Please help us,' she'd say, plucking at a coat sleeve, a string bag. 'My little brother is ill! We need money for medicine.'

Most dropped coins in her outstretched hand without bothering to stop. Soon the coins *clink clinked* in her coat pocket.

One man shoved a note in her hand and said, 'Get him a coat, for God's sake.'

One woman gave us both a yellow balloon with a ribbon on it.

No one asked where our mother was.

By afternoon, I was too hungry to play pretend. 'We have plenty of money now to eat whatever we want,' I said.

Tanya jingled the coins in her pocket. 'We don't use money for food, silly,' she said. 'We use it to make us happy.'

'Food will make me very happy,' I pointed out.

'We steal food,' she said. 'It's easy enough.'

My mouth dropped open. I stepped back, shaking my head. 'I can't steal. Stealing is wrong.'

'Who says?' Tanya shrugged.

'My mother says.'

Her eyes blazed. She slapped the side of my face. 'Wake up, Mish. Do you see your mother here? Do you see my mother here? Or Yula's mother, or Viktor's, or Pasha's?'

I wiped at my wet eyes and shook my head.

Her face softened. She smoothed my hair. 'I'm sorry,' she said. 'But you need to learn. We make our own rules. And our number one rule is to do whatever we must to take care of ourselves. If that means steal, we steal. If that means lie, we lie. Understand?'

I nodded. I touched the bruise blooming on my cheek.

Tanya peered down at me, hands on her hips like my mother did when she was about to tell me what a troublesome boy I could be. 'OK,' she sighed. 'I'll get you food.'

She scanned the plaza. People filled the benches, tilting their faces up to the autumn sun, paper bags at their feet. She pointed at a fat man sitting on the edge of the fountain. 'That man will need a lot of food to fill his big, fat belly.'

I nodded. Surely if he knew I was lost and without my mother and very hungry, he would share his lunch with me.

Tanya pinched my shoulder. 'Here's the plan: You pretend you're playing in the fountain, OK? Pretend?'

I nodded.

'Get close to him and splash him lots.'

'But,' I said, 'that will make him angry and then he won't share his lunch with us.'

Tanya rolled her eyes. 'God, you're stupid. The whole point is to make him angry! Angry enough to chase you. Then,' she said, grinning, 'I'll steal his lunch.'

I looked at Tanya and at the fat man sitting on the edge of the big fountain. The brown paper bag at his feet bulged like his belly.

The fat man fed us well. My Famous Basketball Player shoes were wet and so were my trousers up to my knees. I shivered as I licked the last of the sausage grease from my fingers. With my belly full, guilt crept into my arms and legs like a spider and gnawed at my heart. I fingered the button in my pocket. My mother would slap me for what I had done.

Tanya stood up and stretched. She jingled the coins in her pocket. 'Come on,' she said.

I trotted behind Tanya, following her through the streets, still looking for the red coat. Brown coats, grey coats, black coats. Was that a red coat?

I tripped over something and flew through the air. Tanya dragged me up by my arm. 'Watch where you're going,' she said.

I looked back. I'd tripped over a boy lying on the pavement. Was he pretending to be ill too? A fly crawled across his face. He was missing his shoes. Someone would stop. Someone would brush the fly away from his face; someone would gather him in their arms. But no one did. They walked past him and round him and even over him as if he were nothing at all. As if he were a ghost.

'Come on,' Tanya said, jerking my arm, hard.

A gust of cold wind blew scraps of newspaper down the pavement, and blew the fly off the sleeping boy's face.

Chapter 8

SCHOOL

'Do we go to school tomorrow?'

Viktor laughed and passed the bottle to Yula. She tipped the bottle back and took a long drink. Pasha breathed in and out, in and out of a brown paper bag.

Tanya leaned back against Rudy, her face full of dreams. 'The city is our school, Mish,' she said. She opened her arms wide. 'The whole wide world is our school.'

I puzzled over this. I wanted to go to school. I loved the smell of my classroom: wet wool, warm chocolate drinks and bread.

'But I want to go to school,' I said. 'I am learning to read and write.'

'That's because you're stupid,' Viktor said.

Rudy flicked his cigarette at my feet. 'The schools don't want us,' he said.

'But all children must go to school,' I said. 'It's a law.'

A train rattled to a stop. People poured out of the doors, going this way and that, looking at watches, at signs, anywhere but at us. But I looked for the red coat. I looked for the train with the letters *Ruza* on the front.

Viktor leapt to his feet. His dirty, tattered coat swirled out around him as he span and span. 'We are the law!' he sang at the top of his lungs. 'The streets are the law!'

'The vodka is the law!' sang out Yula.

'Glue is the law,' Pasha mumbled from his cardboard mat.

'Stealing, surviving is the law,' said Tanya.

'Money and only money,' Rudy intoned, 'is the law.'

Everyone nodded.

A traveller from the train threw a half-eaten sandwich in the rubbish bin. Yula and Viktor dashed to the bin, sliding and slipping on the marble floors. Viktor grabbed for the sandwich, knocking Yula to the ground. Yula jumped onto Viktor's back and clawed and screamed, 'It's mine! Give it to me!' Viktor slapped at her like an annoying fly.

Tanya and Pasha laughed. 'Ride 'em, cowboy,' Tanya called.

Rudy blew long streams of smoke from his nose. 'Filthy animals,' he muttered. 'They're no better than dogs fighting in the streets.'

I had seen dogs in the streets during the day, many of them. Sometimes they growled, sometimes they flashed their teeth. None fought each other.

Rudy stood and strolled over to Viktor and Yula, who were rolling, biting, punching on the train-station floor. All the people coming and going, going and coming from the trains streamed past them. Surely someone would tell them to stop. Someone would call the police.

Rudy flicked his cigarette onto the floor. Then he kicked Viktor in the side with his black, pointed-toe boot. 'Get up,' he commanded. Yula grabbed a fistful of Viktor's hair and tugged hard. Rudy's boot toe found her back-side. Yula screamed in pain and rolled away. Viktor grabbed for her leg. Before he could reach it, Rudy kicked him in the bum too. His face slapped the ground. A puddle of blood spread across the cold grey floor.

Rudy picked up the half-eaten sandwich, still wrapped like a gift in white paper now spattered with blood.

He presented it to Tanya and bowed. 'For you, fair princess.'

He sat down next to me as Tanya wolfed down the sandwich. My stomach grumbled even though I felt sick, sick and cold. The red blood on the floor. There had been that red patch on our floor too. I had touched it. I had wondered if it could be – Rudy jabbed me hard in the side with his elbow. He pointed at the bleeding Viktor and the crying Yula with an unlit cigarette. 'That's all the education you need, Mish.'

I crawled to the long bench above the heat vent. I curled up under the bench and turned my back to all the people coming and going to and from the trains. The people who never stopped, who looked through us like ghosts. The people in their brown coats, black coats and grey coats, never red coats.

I turned my back on these motherless children, for children was what they were. None of them, not even Rudy, I would learn, was older than fourteen.

I closed my eyes against the bright lights that lit the soaring marble arches, the grimy grey floor, the cold statues of men on horses, the sad ghost children of Leningradsky Station. I was not lulled to sleep by my mother's fairy tales. I did not feel her kiss good night or the press of her warm body next to mine. I was lulled to sleep by the clacking of trains in the station and the click of boot heels on the hard floor.

Chapter 9

THE PUPPY

And so days and nights and days passed. Tanya and I wandered the busy streets and squares playing the different pretend games she made up to get money and food. She knew many pretend games. Some of the games left me feeling ashamed.

And every evening we all huddled together in the train station. They would argue and swap cigarettes, tubes of glue, bottles of drink that smelled like the bad man. Most of the time Rudy was there, but sometimes he was not. But always, the money went to Rudy. If he suspected you kept money from him, he beat you bloody.

On one particular day, Tanya was too ill to go out above ground. 'You go with Pasha today,' Rudy said to me. He cuffed Pasha hard on the side of the head. 'And keep your head out of the bag and bring back some money. You're behind.'

I trotted after Pasha up the stairs that rose and rose up to the daylight. 'What pretend games do you know?' I asked him. 'I'm tired of Tanya's pretend games.'

Pasha shrugged, squinting in the sun. 'I don't know pretend games,' he said. 'Only girls and babies play pretend.'

'I'm not a baby,' I said. 'I'm old enough to go to school.'

'Yeah, yeah,' Pasha said. His dark eyes scanned the streets. 'I'm almost ten and I know more about things than any of those kids in school.'

He dashed across the street. Against a tall iron gate sat a child with a puppy in her lap. 'Where are the puppies today?' he asked.

'In that burned-out nightclub,' she said.

Pasha grabbed the collar of my jumper. 'Come on. Let's go and get a puppy.'

My heart leapt to the sky. A puppy! I had always wanted a puppy, had begged and begged my mother for one. 'I will be the best boy in the world,' I had promised her, 'if I can have a puppy.'

And always she would say, 'We can barely feed ourselves, Little Bear. How could we feed a growing puppy?'

Now I skipped behind Pasha, singing, 'A puppy! A puppy! I want a puppy!'

Pasha stopped in front of a tumbledown building that smelled like smoke. 'Shut up,' he said. He cocked his head to one side. 'Listen,' he whispered.

We heard soft mewling sounds coming from one corner of the rubble.

'This way,' Pasha said.

I stumbled behind Pasha over broken bottles, charred boards, legless tables and piles of bricks until we found an overturned crate. Inside were two puppies.

'Oh,' I gasped, falling to my knees, not caring about the broken glass. I could not believe my good fortune. Finally, I would have a puppy.

Pasha grabbed a brown and white puppy by the scruff of the neck. The puppy yelped. 'Grab the other and let's go,' he said.

I picked up the other puppy – brown and white like its brother – very gently and held it in my arms. The puppy whimpered and trembled. 'I won't hurt you, little one,' I said into its ear. 'I'll take good care of you for ever and ever.'

'Come on, Mishka,' Pasha called from the street.

I hugged the puppy to me as we crossed the street again to a park. A park would be the perfect place for my new puppy and me, I thought.

Pasha sat down on a sunny patch of cement not far from a man and his cart selling hot potatoes. 'Business people come here for lunch,' Pasha said. 'They always give more money if you have a puppy or a kitten.'

My puppy chewed on my finger. 'I'll use my money to buy my puppy the very best food,' I said.

Pasha sighed.

'And I'll buy her a beautiful collar and a soft bed and a lead so that she'll never leave me.' I kissed my new puppy on the top of the head. 'What should we name our puppies?' I asked Pasha.

A woman dropped two coins at my feet. Another woman dropped a coin in Pasha's outstretched hand.

'Name them?' Pasha snorted. 'We don't name them. We use them to get money, that's all.'

I clutched my puppy to my chest. 'But she's my puppy!'

Just as Pasha said, the park filled with people. Legs walked past, hands dropped coins and even notes on the ground in front of us. The puppy wiggled in my lap.

'I don't care about the money,' I said, sweeping my coins into Pasha's pile. 'I'm going to keep her. I'll take her back to the station and everyone will love her.'

'You better not,' Pasha said. 'Rudy will kill it. Don't think he won't.'

I jumped to my feet and clutched the puppy to my chest. 'I'll keep her, then,' I shouted. 'I won't go back!'

Pasha eyed me for a long moment. 'You'll never survive out here on your own, Mishka. There are people who do terrible things to kids like us.'

The puppy wriggled out of my arms and slid to my feet. I watched as she snapped up a chunk of dirty potato. 'Rudy is a bad person,' I said, not looking at Pasha. 'He beats his friends and he takes our money.'

'But he protects us, Mishka. We're safer with Rudy than out here on our own. We all know that. That's why we put up with his beatings.'

In a voice that was almost kind, Pasha patted the ground next to him. 'Come and enjoy the sun and the puppy.' I looked away, fighting tears.

Pasha sighed. He handed me some coins. 'Here, go and buy yourself and the puppy a potato,' he said.

I scrubbed the tears trickling down my face. I held out my hand. A passer-by dropped three glittering coins into my palm.

Chapter 10

THE MIRROR

Tanya and Yula giggled in the train-station toilets.

'Let's try your hair this way,' I heard Yula say to Tanya. 'This is the way the boys like it.'

Soon, they paraded out of the toilets, their greasy hair piled high on their heads. They wobbled on someone's cast-off, high-heeled shoes. It was the first time I'd seen Yula without her baseball-player hat on and a cigarette tucked behind one ear.

'What're you looking at?' she snapped.

'You don't look like Yula,' I said.

She grinned and twirled. 'I look like a movie star, don't I?'

I shook my head. 'You look like a scarecrow on stilts,' I said.

Before I could blink, she reached out and slapped me to the floor. 'You think you're your mother's precious little

Mishka?' She kicked me in the shin. 'You should go and take a look at yourself in the mirror, runt.'

'I'm not tall enough to see in the mirror,' I pointed out. Besides, I would always be my mother's fair-haired, moon-faced boy. She'd told me that.

Yula kicked off the very high shoes. She grabbed me by the arm with one hand and a wooden box with the other. She pushed me through the bathroom door. She threw the wooden box down in front of a sink, and then shoved me on top of it.

Yula grabbed me by the shoulders and gave me a hard shake. 'Take a good look, runt.'

The boy who stared back from the mirror was not me. This boy in the mirror was filthy. His eyes were eclipsed by dark half-moons beneath. His hair stood up this way and that in ragged, greasy spikes. This boy in the mirror had grey skin beneath the filth and bruises on his too-thin face. The eyes were the eyes of a ghost.

My mother would not know this boy looking back from the mirror if she passed him on the street.

That night, under the long bench over the heating vent, I did not tell myself stories memorised from my fairy-tale book. I did not imagine my mother kissing me good night. I rubbed the black button from her coat over and over and over with my dirty thumb and thought.

If I came to The City on a train from my village, then certainly I could take one back. I had seen trains with the name of my village in big letters on the front. Why, I asked myself, did I think she was here in The City looking for me? How did I know she wasn't back at our flat, waiting and watching out the window for her little bear to come home?

I thought and I thought throughout the night as the trains came and went, as the other children laughed and cried and fought. I thought about going back home. I thought about the warm bed that my mother and I shared and her beautiful white hands slipping in and out of the hot, steamy water in the kitchen sink and the something good bubbling on the stove and her smiling mouth and her voice saying, 'My little bear. My smart, beautiful boy.'

And then I thought about that boy in the mirror, and I knew I had to go.

Chapter 11

RUZA

I sat huddled on the bench inside the rocking, clacking train. I hadn't had to wait long before I saw a train with the name of our village on the front. I just stepped onto it. I didn't even say goodbye to Tanya, Yula, Pasha or Rudy, and especially not Viktor.

I watched all the different coloured coats come into the train and leave the train. Some people read, others slept. One woman smelled of onions and had tired eyes. Another tossed her long black hair. None of them noticed me there on the bench on my way home.

There were many stops on our way out of The City. A few other children rode the trains, most with grown-ups. The grown-ups read their papers or gazed at nothing out the windows. A man in a fine hat collected tickets; he looked through me too. But the children saw me. They looked at me with wide eyes. I made myself small.

And then, at one stop, the doors to the train slid open and in walked two dogs. I sat up straighter.

The dogs sniffed their way down the aisle, their tails wagging. I waited for someone to shout at the dogs, to drive them off the train. But no one did. The people read their books and newspapers, and snored with their weary heads against the train window. No shouting. No chasing.

The dogs finally settled near a child and mother. They circled three times and lay down with a sigh. I watched them as they dozed. I could barely breathe for the wonder of dogs on the train.

When next the train stopped, the larger dog, with fur like a bear, sat up and searched the air from the open train door with his nose. He lay back down and resumed his nap. At the next stop, he did the same thing. But this time, he nipped the smaller dog on the ear. They trotted out of the train door and disappeared into the crowd.

My hunger woke me. I sat up and looked through the train window. We were no longer in The City.

Just as I began to worry I'd slept past my stop, the man on the loudspeaker called the name of my village, Ruza.

I scrambled down from my seat and off the train.

I pushed my way through the forest of legs and bags

and satchels. Surely my mother would be there in the train station watching for me in her red coat with the one black button missing. Surely she had been there every day, meeting every train, watching for her Mishka.

But no one was there watching for me and smiling when she set eyes on her smart, beautiful boy. There was no red coat or chestnut hair.

I walked through the village, past the school and the butcher shop and the fabric shop and across the street to the bakery where my mother had worked. A cold wind blew through my thin jumper. The bakery was dark.

I walked up the long, low hill to the apartment building squatting at the top. Nothing stirred from within or from without. But surely she was there, waiting for me. Watching for me.

I ran up the stairs two by two to the third floor. My heart flew ahead of me.

The door stood ajar. I started to push it open, then stopped. What if *he* was there? What if he was there with his big, ugly feet and rotten teeth and bottles of vodka? The stench of his sweat, the red smear on the floor—

The door flew open. I jumped back.

'Who the hell are you?' A large, doughy-faced woman in a black coat and dirty head scarf loomed in the doorway.

'I am Mishka Ivan Andreovich,' I whispered around my pounding heart. 'I live here. With my mother, Anya Andreyevna.'

The woman snorted and began picking up bottles. 'Then your mother is a pig,' she said.

Anger flamed in my face. 'My mother is not a pig!' I said. 'He is the pig.' My stomach churned at the thought of him. 'He is a bad man,' I said.

She shrugged. 'Whatever. They aren't here now. No one has been here for weeks. I'm stuck with months of no rent and cleaning this pigsty for new tenants.'

'But we live here,' I said. 'She just went away for a while.'

She stood and eyed me wearily. Her face softened a bit. 'She's not here, boy. Do you not know where she is?'

I shook my head.

The woman began stuffing rubbish into bags. 'Some of the neighbours said they heard screams. As you say, he was no good. She may have come to a bad end.'

She straightened, her face closed. 'Whatever happened is not my concern. You don't live here anymore. You'll have to find another place to live. Don't you have family somewhere?'

I shook my head again.

The woman – she was a pig-faced woman – sighed and threw up her hands. 'I don't know what's become of us, living like dogs, leaving our children to run wild.'

'But my mother would never leave me. She—'

The pig-faced woman talked into a bag of rubbish. 'If you were to ask me, which no one has, we were better off in the old days. Things ran smoothly as a train back then.' She tied off the top of the binbag. She pointed a stubby finger at me and shook it. 'Say what you want about Gorbachev and Communism, but since the Soviet Union fell, this country's gone to hell in a handbasket.'

She slung two bags of rubbish over her shoulder. 'I want you gone when I get back.'

I listened to her clomp down the hallway.

I walked slowly from one room to another. Stinking rubbish fouled my mother's tidy kitchen. The refrigerator door stood open. There was nothing except a hunk of mouldy cheese and a half-eaten, sour-smelling sausage. I stuffed them greedily in my mouth as I wandered into the bedroom. Everything was gone... my mother's clothes, the wooden icon of a saint she kept over the bed. Even her smell of cigarettes and lavender – gone.

I went back to the kitchen pantry, where I had slept after he came. Everything was gone there too – my clothes, my blankets, my radio with the shiny antenna and knobs.

But then I saw it: there, pushed in a dusty corner, lay the book of fairy tales. I ran my hand over the greasy cover, a firebird flying over a frozen kingdom, above glittering spires that soared for ever above golden, onion-shaped domes.

I held the book to my chest and looked one last time around my mother's kitchen. A broken plate rested in the sink. How long had it been since I had eaten from a plate, a bowl, or drunk from a cup?

I walked to the corner in the bedroom and knelt. I touched my finger to the red stain the pig-faced woman had not been able to scrub away. The stain was larger, much larger than I remembered.

A cold sweat battled a heat that swept through me. I vomited on the floor.

I passed the woman in the stairwell as I walked down one flight, then two. She muttered something I could not understand.

I stood at the top of the low hill. One raindrop, then many, pelted my face. I slid my book under my jumper. I pointed the toes of my Famous Basketball Player shoes down the hill and followed them back to the train station and The City and Leningradsky Station.

Chapter 12

RAIN

It rained for days. Some days the rain was cold and thin; other days it drowned out the sounds from the street above the train station. The rain kept us below ground, away from begging and stealing and food and drink.

The first day, we slept on our beds of newspaper and cardboard. Even Rudy slept when he was not playing some trick on Yula or Viktor. I watched for red coats, chestnut hair and dogs.

The second day, Tanya refused to steal a woman's purse and Rudy beat her. Yula left with a man in a grey suit. When she returned later, she had clean hair, a bag of food and beer, and bruises on her neck.

On the third night, I read to everyone from my book of fairy tales. True, I could not read all of the words, but I heard my mother's voice reading the stories to me well enough. The only sound as I read the story of the Little

Match Girl was the clack of the trains and the scrape of Pasha's cough. Rudy cleaned his fingernails with the tip of a pen knife.

'She was just like us.' Tanya sighed, wiping away a tear when I closed the book. 'No one cared, even then.'

'Someone did, though,' said Pasha. 'There was that light that lifted her up and took her away.'

'It was God,' Yula said. 'It was God who took her away.'

'Or angels,' said Tanya. 'It could have been one of God's angels come to take her away.'

Viktor snorted. 'Where were the angels, where was God when she was starving and freezing? Where were they when she was turned out on the street?'

Everyone looked at the floor.

'I'll tell you where the angels are,' he said, snatching my book from my hands. 'They're in here with all the other fairy tales. That's all they are: fairy tales!'

I jumped at his outstretched arm. 'Give me back my book,' I cried.

He held the book higher. 'Jump, little mouse,' he sneered.

I jumped and I jumped as high as my Famous Basketball Player shoes would take me.

'Look, he's a circus mouse,' Viktor said. 'A stupid, little circus mouse!'

Tanya leapt to her feet. 'Give Mishka back his book, Viktor, or I swear to God—'

'Swear to God all you want, Tanya,' Viktor said. His face was twisted in a way I had never seen. 'It won't make any difference.' His face glistened in the light of an oncoming train.

'God's not here,' he went on. 'God is just a stupid, stupid fairy tale.' And with that, he flung the book high. It soared above our heads and our outstretched hands. It flew through the air, the pages lifting like lovely white wings. The book was an angel, a firebird. It hung for an instant in the shining white light of the train and then fell beneath its wheels.

Tanya punched and kicked Viktor. 'See what you've done!' And because Yula does what Tanya does, she took off her shoe and smacked Viktor in the face. Pasha retreated to his bag of glue.

After the train pulled away, I crawled over to the edge of the platform. There, in a heap, lay the remains of my book.

I started to scramble down to the dirt when a hand grabbed the collar of my jumper and pulled me back.

'No,' Rudy said. 'Are you too stupid to see? A train's coming.' And indeed there was.

Rudy leapt down to the dirt. His boots sent up little puffs of dust. The eye of the train grew larger and larger.

As if he had all the time in the world, Rudy picked through the remains of the book. He examined pages as if he were shopping for vegetables on a summer afternoon. He squinted at the pages through the smoke of his cigarette.

The light of the train grew brighter and brighter. The whistle screamed.

'Rudy! Get out of there!' Tanya cried. Viktor's eyes were as big as the train's headlight. My heart thundered down the tracks with it.

Rudy stuffed a handful of pages in his coat pocket. The train was now in the station entrance. The whistle shrieked again. The brakes screamed.

Rudy flicked his cigarette at the rushing light. And with all the grace and disdain of a put-upon cat, he leapt to the platform. He dusted off the knees of his black trousers. Without a word, he pulled out the pages from my book of magnificent tales and handed them to me.

'Screw the rain,' he said. He took Tanya's hand and they disappeared into the crowd.

Chapter 13

The rain stopped. The days grew cold. I shivered in my jumper and hatless head and mittenless hands. The people in the streets rushed from one place to another to escape the cold. They did not want to stop long enough to reach in their pockets.

The cold and our empty pockets infuriated Rudy. 'Why do I waste my time with you worthless pack of dolts,' he said. 'You're useless. Useless!'

He spat at my feet. 'You particularly. You think just because you're little and you're younger than the rest, you don't have to pull your share? You think you're too good to steal.'

'Come on, Rudy,' Tanya said, touching his shoulder. 'Mish doesn't eat much.'

Rudy slapped her hand away. 'And you,' he roared. 'You think you're too good to go with men, do you?' He shook

Tanya until her teeth rattled. 'It's time, Tanya. Just you wait and see.'

Pasha coughed and coughed. Rudy whirled on him. 'Stop it! Stop coughing!'

Pasha wiped his nose with the back of his hand. His hand came away streaked with red.

On warm days, Pasha and I begged in the parks and squares in hope that the sun would bring the lunch eaters outside. But not so many came out anymore, and if they did, they were reluctant to part with their money.

'Soon we will leave the train station,' Pasha said.

I watched a brown and black dog approach a woman and her small child sitting on a bench.

'Why would we leave?' I asked.

'When winter comes, the police make us leave the station.'

The dog wagged his tail and grinned up at the woman and child.

'They say too many bomzhi and vagrants stay in the train stations in the winter to keep warm.'

The child laughed and clapped her hands. The mother ignored the dog.

'But we aren't tramps,' I said. 'We are children.'

'Bomzhi, vagrants, street children – it's all the same to the militsiya. We're cockroaches, all of us. We have to be driven out.'

The dog laid his head in the mother's lap and gazed up at her, his whole body wagging back and forth. I held my breath.

'We have places we go in the winter to keep warm,' Pasha said. The woman smiled and petted the dog's head. I laughed and clapped my hands. 'What kind of places?' I imagined the police taking us to places with blankets and hot soup and coats. 'Underground,' he said. 'Next to the steam pipes, where it's warm as toast.' The woman broke off part of a sandwich. She handed it to the child, who fed it to the dog.

The dog took the chunk of bread and meat gently from the child's small hands, and then licked her fingers clean.

I rubbed my finger over and over the black button in my pocket.

Pasha punched me in the arm in a not-mean way. 'It's not so bad, Mish. It's warm and mostly dry. People feel sorrier for us and give us food. Sometimes the church people come to the square and feed us soup and bread. Sometimes they even bring cast-off clothes and shoes.'

'Is it dark down there?'

Pasha shrugged. 'Sure, but we have plenty of candles and stuff. It's fun! A lot more fun than my old home in the countryside. All we had to eat was the stuff we fed the cows and the goats. Here it is much better.'

'What about your mother?' I asked. 'She must be looking for you.'

Pasha flicked the side of his neck with his finger. 'She was a drunk. So was my father. As long as they had vodka and each other to yell at, they didn't care about me or my brothers and sisters. The last time my father beat me, I stuck him in the belly with a knife and left.'

I sucked in my breath. 'You stabbed him?'

Pasha nodded.

As much as I hated him, I could not imagine sticking the bad man in the stomach with a knife.

A man with brown boots and shiny buckles dropped a coin at each of our feet. 'Thank you, sir,' I called to the legs and boots walking away.

Pasha flipped his coin in the air and caught it in his teeth. I laughed and clapped. 'Do it again,' I demanded. And he did.

The brown and black dog rose from the feet of the little girl. He shook himself and then trotted across the park as if he had an important appointment to keep.

The days grew colder and there were more coats to watch. But I did not watch the coats so much anymore. I watched the dogs. They were everywhere – curled up in doorways, sleeping on heat grates, riding the trains, crossing the streets one way and then the other. They begged, they stole. Sometimes they found a kind person and sometimes they were cursed and spat upon. They were just like us, only they were not like us at all. I watched the dogs steal from the sausage cart or from the lunch bags left on the ground. I watched them beg from women and children and old men. I watched them tip over rubbish bins behind butcher shops and grocery shops. And always, always, they shared. The small ones ate, the sick ones ate, the old ones ate. That is how it was with the dogs.

On a hard day, a bitter cold day, I sat huddled next to a steam grate in the pavement. The cold made my eyes stream tears. I told myself they were not tears for my mother. They were not tears for the weeks it had been since I had slept in a bed and taken a bath. Perhaps it had been months or only days. I didn't know or care anymore. The tears were only for the cold. I bowed my head and rested it on my knees.

Something warm pressed against me. Warm breath stroked my cheek. I lifted my head. There beside me stood a large brown and black dog.

The dog sniffed my hair and ran his warm, wet nose across my cheek and ear. I held my breath. Did the dog think I was something to eat?

Satisfied, the dog curled up at my feet next to the steam vent with a sigh and closed his eyes.

We sat like that together, the dog and I. People rushed past us and around us and stepped over us. A woman in a blue coat stopped and handed me two coins. A man in a black coat and white collar gave me his sausage sandwich and hurried away. The dog wagged his tail hopefully. I broke the sandwich in half and shared.

Coins dropped at my feet and in my hand. One coin, two coins. The dog and I trotted across the street to the potato man's cart. The coins jingled in my pocket.

'Please, could I have two potatoes?' I said, holding out coins. The potato man fished two plump, hot potatoes from the metal pan. He handed them to me in a piece of newspaper. I handed him the coins. He studied me for a minute. One eye looked me up and down while the other eye wandered off to a more interesting scene far to the side.

He grunted and fished out another potato. 'For your dog,' he said.

I laughed. I could not believe my good luck! Three potatoes! I heard my mother say, *Remember your manners, Mishka.*

'Spasibo, sir,' I said. 'Thank you very much.'

Two hot potatoes to warm my hands and another in my pocket. Two hot potatoes to fill my belly.

The dog and I trotted back to the steam grate. I started to stuff one of the potatoes in my mouth. The dog let out a low *woof.* He wagged his tail.

'Please forgive me,' I said. I broke the potato in half. He took it gently from my fingers and swallowed it in one gulp.

And still, I had two warm potatoes. I smiled at the dog. I reached out and touched his shoulder. 'You've brought me luck today,' I said. He licked my fingers. I laughed. 'I'm going to call you Lucky.'

Lucky stretched and sniffed the air. He looked at me and then trotted off.

'Wait!' I cried. I dashed off after him, the potatoes bouncing in my jumper pocket.

He looked over his shoulder and slowed to a walk. I ran up beside him. My breath came in frosty puffs. I had not run in a long time. We children mostly sat and lay with our hands outstretched.

'Where are we going, Lucky?' I rested my hand on his shoulder.

I followed him to the corner of two busy streets. Lucky sat down and looked up and down the street. A child on the other side of the street dressed in rags and too-big shoes darted in and out of traffic. Tyres screeched and horns blared. I had seen Pasha and Yula play this game of chicken before with the cars.

'That girl is stupid,' I said to Lucky. 'My mother said to always wait for the light to turn green.' Lucky looked up at me and wagged his tail in agreement.

We crossed the street when the light turned green. We trotted past empty buildings with their windows either smashed or boarded up. We trotted past big, shiny buildings with fake women in the windows wrapped in warm fur coats.

We trotted past other dogs sleeping in patches of warm sunlight. Sometimes they opened their eyes and barked a greeting. Sometimes they slept on.

We passed other children begging and sleeping on newspapers or sitting in doorways drinking from bottles. Lucky swerved around two older boys fighting on the pavement. One tried to grab my arm. 'Hey, you,' he snarled.

Lucky whirled and growled, showing the boy long white teeth. The boy backed away.

Finally, we stopped outside a tumbledown shop at the end of a long alley. It may have once been a bakery, or a barber's, or a grocery store. Now, it was nothing but bricks and weeds.

Except, it was where Lucky was going.

He looked at me. Then he went round to the side of the building. He let out a low bark. And then he disappeared through the weeds and through bricks.

I gasped. How could that be? Was he a ghost?

Then I heard one bark, then another bark. I walked closer to where Lucky had disappeared. I heard a high whimper and a soft mewling.

I pushed aside the weeds and laughed.

Lucky was not a ghost dog. He had not walked through the brick wall. There, covered up by the weeds and rubble, was a small opening in the wall. An opening just big enough for a dog or a boy to squeeze through.

'Lucky,' I called into the dark opening. He answered with a bark.

Two shining brown eyes and a black nose appeared in the opening.

Woof, Lucky said, and then wheeled away into the dark.

I looked up the alleyway. The two fighting boys walked past, still arguing. Fat, white snowflakes drifted lazily down onto my head. I peered into the dark place where Lucky had gone.

I could walk back up the alley and across the street and past the other dirty, sleeping, fighting, begging children and back down to the train station where Pasha would be in his own dream place with a brown paper bag on his lap and Viktor with his rat face and Tanya with her sad eyes and Yula with her cigarettes and men in dark suits.

I dropped to my knees, wriggled through the opening that was just big enough for a dog or a small boy, and slipped into the pocket of darkness and onto the dirt floor.

Chapter 14

THE PACK

Slowly, slowly my eyes adjusted to the dark. The weeds outside the building let tiny bits of light in through the small opening.

The light caught an ear here, a pair of eyes there, and there. And over there.

I froze.

Lucky nudged my hand with his wet nose. Woof!

I heard small yips and whimpering from one corner. Lucky tugged on my sleeve.

I followed him through the dark over to the corner. And in that corner, resting on top of a pile of rags and newspapers and dirty blankets, lay a mother dog with her puppies.

'Oh!' I cried. 'Look at the puppies!' I reached out a hand to touch them. The mother dog growled. Lucky licked the side of her face and nuzzled the puppies with his nose.

'Is that why you brought me here?' I asked him. 'To see the puppies?'

Lucky pawed at my pocket – the pocket that still held two potatoes.

I took out one potato and broke off a piece. I handed it to Lucky. The mother dog whimpered. Lucky dropped the potato chunk in front of her. She snapped it up in one breath. Lucky looked at me as if to say, *Go on, then, give her some more.*

I broke off another chunk of potato and stretched my hand out to her. I broke off another piece and another. She licked the last of the potato from my fingers. Then she settled her puppies against her belly and let them eat.

I sat back on my heels and smiled. 'You're a good little mother,' I said. 'And you, Lucky, are a good father.'

I turned to look for Lucky, to tell him what a good father he was to provide for his family.

I froze.

Dogs surrounded me. Brown dogs, black and white dogs, a small scruffy dog with a badly torn ear. A brown dog with a silver face and soft eyes limped from the corner. Lucky pressed close to me and wagged his tail.

'Hello,' I said to the dogs. 'Are you hungry too?'

The dog with the torn ear yipped and did a little dance.

I laughed. I broke off a piece of potato and tossed it to him. And then I fed the others. After all the potato was gone, the dogs pressed close, sniffing my clothes, my ears, my hair. The mother dog rose from her sleeping puppies and washed my face with her tongue. I rolled in the dirt, laughing. 'No, stop! That tickles! That's slobbery!' She licked me all the more. A black dog with patches of white on his legs and back lowered his chest, his hind end stuck in the air. He cocked his head to one side and wagged his tail.

I rolled to my hands and knees, dropped my chest and stuck my bottom up in the air. 'Woof!' I said. I wagged my bum from side to side. The black dog with the patches slapped one paw on the ground. I slapped my hand and laughed. The old dog watched us with the pleasure of a grandmother.

The weeds rustled at the hole in the wall. In the weak light, I could see something pushing its way through the opening in the bricks. All the dogs stood to attention. I stood too and moved closer to Lucky.

Something dropped lightly to the dirt floor. I squinted into the weak light. That something was a dog.

The dogs pinned back their ears and whimpered their greetings. The little mother dog and the dog with the ripped ear crouched before this dog and licked his chin and the side of his face. That was when I noticed the dog had something in his mouth: a long, thick sausage.

The dog dropped the sausage in the dirt. He seemed to barely notice as the dogs tore pieces of the meat. His eyes were fixed on me.

I pressed closer to Lucky. All of a sudden, I felt like a little mouse in the wolf's den.

The dog stalked over to me. Lucky stepped back.

'No!' I whispered. But before I could hide behind Lucky, the new dog, the leader dog, circled my legs. He sniffed the backs of my legs and my filthy trousers and my jumper and my pocket that once held two warm potatoes. He pushed his nose into the palm of my hand and read it like a gypsy. He sat in front of me and studied my face.

'I'm Mishka Ivan Andreovich,' I whispered. 'I am five years old and I won't hurt you.'

The dog trotted over to the pile of puppies. He sniffed each one from the tips of their little noses to the ends of their tails. When he was satisfied I had not harmed them, he trotted back over to the opening. Without a backwards glance, he leapt through and slipped out like smoke.

The one I now called Patches jumped up and out. The little mouse-coloured dog with the ripped ear followed as best as his short legs would manage.

Lucky dropped a last chunk of sausage at the paws of Little Mother. Then he too scrabbled through the opening.

'Hey!' I called. 'Don't leave me!'

Lucky stuck his head into the cellar. Woof!

I knelt and touched each of the three puppies gently. 'Goodbye, Little Mother,' I said. 'I'll bring more food for you tomorrow. I promise.'

I wriggled through the opening. It was almost dark. Snow blanketed the alley. And at the end of that alley stood the pack, waiting for me.

I ran with the dogs across the streets, past the gangs of older children drinking, laughing, fighting, and not scaring me one bit. I was with the pack and we ran together.

Finally, we reached the heat vent where I had met Lucky earlier that day. The dogs stood around me panting and grinning.

I touched the top of each of their heads. 'Thank you for bringing me home safely,' I said. 'We'll get more food tomorrow, just wait and see.'

I skipped down the steps to the underground. Wait until I told Pasha and Tanya about the dogs and the puppies! Maybe if they were nice, I'd take them to meet them. Maybe we could all live together in the cellar and not have to go live in the dark with the hot water pipes. We could feed the puppies until they grew fat and strong. We would be a family with the dogs.

I skidded to a stop in front of the big statue of a man riding a horse. I leapt up and touched the horse's nose. I bowed before the man. 'Evening, sir.'

'Well, well, well,' a voice said. I gasped. Did the bronze man speak?

Rudy stepped out from behind the statue. He held a bottle in one hand and the other one stretched out. 'The little mouse returns.'

I smiled up at Rudy. 'I had the best day,' I said. 'I met this dog and—'

Rudy snapped his fingers. 'Turn over the money.'

My stomach dropped. Money.

I dug into my pockets. I felt two round, smooth things. I dropped the coins in Rudy's hand.

'That's all?' he said.

I nodded.

'You were gone all day and half the night, and this is all you have to show for it?' My heart hammered in my chest. I nodded again. 'Yes, Rudy. I used the other money to buy food.'

Rudy cuffed me on the side of my head. 'How many

times have I told you! You don't use money to buy food. You steal food!'

'But my mother said—'

Rudy hit me again, this time knocking me to the floor. 'I don't give a damn what your mother said.' He jerked me up off the floor and shook and shook me. 'Your mother isn't here, Mishka. You listen to *me*, now. You do what I say. Do you understand?'

Rudy shook me so hard, I thought my teeth would fly out onto the floor. 'Because if you don't start listening to me—'

A large woman in a big coat and brown head scarf rushed over to us. She swung her handbag at Rudy. 'Leave that little boy alone!' she commanded.

She beat Rudy all about the shoulders and head with her bag. 'You're nothing but a bully,' she scolded. Rudy threw his arms and hands over his head. 'Ow!' he cried. 'Leave me alone, you crazy old woman!'

I ran as fast as fast could be through the sea of legs and arms and coats to my place under the long bench over the heat vent.

Chapter 15

SWEEP

I got up earlier than the rest in the mornings now. I'd slip from beneath my bench just as the first train arrived. The rest slept huddled together for warmth, newspapers for blankets, cardboard for mattresses, and hips and bellies and legs for pillows.

And every morning, Lucky waited for me at the same spot we had met that first day. Some days he was by himself and other days Patches or Rip, the dog with the torn ear, waited with him. But never Little Mother and never the smoke-coloured dog, although I did see him watching us. He watched as we warmed ourselves on the grates and in patches of sunlight. He watched as I asked the people hurrying from the cold to the tall glass buildings, 'Please, can you spare some change so we can eat?'

He watched, his coat black and silver as smoke, as I bought sausages and bread and bones from the butcher shop. I was careful to save coins for Rudy. Then we raced to the alleyway and through the opening in the wall and into the dark warm of the cellar and ate like kings and queens. We'd wrestle there on the dirt floor and play in the small confines of the cellar. And then we curled up together and slept.

Sometimes when I woke, the smoke-coloured dog was there, watching. I would say goodbye to Little Mother and the puppies and to Grandmother, the old dog who watched over the puppies. 'More food tomorrow,' I promised.

And every day, Lucky and the others would race with me through the streets and across the square to the heat grate across from Leningradsky Station. Just at the edge of the streetlight shadows watched the smoke-coloured dog.

And every night, I gave Rudy the coins I had and he said it was not enough. No matter how much I gave him, it was not enough.

'Kopeks!' he spat. 'All you bring me are stupid kopeks?' and he'd throw them to the floor.

'Whatever I give the dogs, it is always enough,' I complained to Pasha one night as the trains galloped by. 'They never yell at me or hit me or tell me I'm stupid.' I rubbed my ear, sore from another Rudy beating.

Pasha shrugged. 'This is the way it is, Mish. It is the life we have.' And that was true, until the sweep.

Tweeeet! Tweeeeet!

I jerked my head up from my sleeping place, banging my head on the bottom of the bench.

Whistles, voices, legs running this way and that. My heart sank. I must have slept past the first train.

I started to scuttle out from under my bench when I heard a scream. And then a voice. 'OK, all you *bomzhi*, you sewer rats. Get up!'

More screams and thumps. Tanya's voice crying, 'Rudy! Rudy!' I squirmed back under the bench and made myself as small as possible.

Tall black boots so shiny I could see my face in them marched past my bench. The heels rang out like gunshots on the marble floors. 'Grab that kid,' a voice called above me. I squeezed my eyes shut and rubbed the black button over and over.

Tweeeet! Tweeeeet! 'Clean the rubbish out,' commanded the voice attached to the tall black boots standing just centimetres away. Someone – perhaps Viktor, perhaps Pasha – cried, 'Leave us alone! We're not hurting anybody!'

Smack! A head hit the ground. I saw Viktor's hat fly across the dirty floor and off the platform.

I rubbed the button hard. It jumped from my fingers and clattered through the heat vents.

'No!' I cried. I jammed my fingers into the vents.

'What's that under there?'

A hand grabbed my foot and pulled. 'No!' I screamed, jamming my fingers further into the vents and kicking as hard as I could.

A grunt. A curse. The hand pulled hard. Off came one Famous Basketball Player shoe.

The hand grabbed my leg and yanked. I screamed in pain as the heat vent cut into my fingers. 'Mother! Mother!' I cried.

A cruel laugh. A laugh that sounded like him when he told me I was no bigger than a cockroach. 'I've got a live one under here.'

The tall black boots and big hands were attached to a man in a policeman's uniform. But this could not be a policeman. My mother had always said policemen helped you when you were lost. And hadn't I been lost for such a long time?

I opened my mouth to tell the policeman this when he spat in my face. 'What a filthy little beggar.' He threw me over his shoulder like a sack of potatoes. 'It's to the orphanage for you.'

'No!' I screamed. 'Put me down! Put me down!' I pounded on his back with my fists, which only made him laugh. On the floor I saw Viktor holding his bloody head and Yula kicking a policeman. His baton cracked against her shoulder.

The policeman carrying me turned and my world span. He started up the stairs.

And then something slammed into him. A whirling, kicking, punching, screaming devil. The policeman threw me from his shoulder. The side of my head cracked against the stone step. Everything went grey then black then grey again. I felt myself slipping, slipping...

Until I heard a voice cry, 'Run, Mishka! Run!'

Pasha! Pasha on the steps all in a tangle with the shiny black boots that kicked him over and over and over, screaming, 'Run, Mishka! Run!'

I scrambled to my feet and ran, stumbling and falling, up the stairs to the world above where the sun was just rising. I ran as fast as I could with just one Famous Basketball Player shoe. I ran until I could no longer hear the whistles and the shouts and the screams.

I ran and ran down the street and through the busy

intersection and across the square. I was a small boy – a boy of five – running with just one shoe and a broken face and bloody fingers. I ran through an army of legs rushing this way and that, crying. And no one – not a single person – saw me.

Finally, I came to the long alley I knew so well. They would just be waking, the dogs would. The puppies would be crying for Little Mother's milk. Patches and Lucky would stretch and lick each other's faces, wag their tails. Rip would uncurl himself from Grandmother. Perhaps Smoke would be there.

I stumbled to the back of the building and pushed aside the weeds. They would be happy to see me. Here with the pack, I would be safe from the tall black boots and the cruel hands.

'Lucky,' I called through the opening in the bricks. 'It's me.' I dropped into the pocket of darkness.

No warm nose pressed into my palm and searched my pockets for food. Nothing stirred. I heard a whimper. I thought, *The puppies.* And then I realised: the whimper had come from me.

There was nothing else in the cellar but the dark and the sound of my heartbeat.

The pack was gone.

Chapter 16

THE DARK

I do not know how long I lay there in the dark. Just as in the train station it was always daytime, in the cellar it was always night.

I curled up in the mound of blankets and rags Little Mother had used as a nest for her puppies and closed my eyes. I remember the cold. I remember the pain. I remember getting up once to vomit in the corner.

But it did not matter anymore. There was no button to reunite with the red coat because there was no mother. There would never be a red coat because there would never be a mother. There was only the red, sticky smear on the floor.

And without my mother, there would never again be Mishka.

Chapter 17

SMOKE

Something warm stroked my cheek, over and over.

I had been dreaming of angels, of warm, feathered wings – wings that would scoop me up and carry me away just like the Little Match Girl.

I stretched my arms out to be carried away in a blanket of feathers. Instead, my hands met thick, soft fur.

I opened my eyes and squinted into the weak light coming through the opening in the wall. A pair of yellow-amber eyes stared down at me. My fingers were buried in a smoke-coloured ruff.

'Smoke,' I breathed.

He licked my cheek and my ear again, then lay down next to me with a sigh. Before I could ask him about the rest of the pack, I fell asleep.

A warm, wet something pushed into my face. I pushed it

away. It pushed at my face again, harder. I rolled away from the thing. 'Leave me alone,' I whispered and closed my eyes.

Woof!

I drew my knees up to my chin and buried my face in my arms. 'Go away and leave me alone.'

A snort. Then something tugged on the back of my jumper.

'I mean it!' I said, over my shoulder. 'Go away!'

Another snort, and then I was being pulled across the dirt from my bed of rags in the dark and into the block of sunlight in the middle of the cellar floor.

'Hey,' I croaked. I squinted in the sunlight. The squinting made my face hurt. I sat up and put my hand to the side of my face. It felt big as a melon.

Smoke stood before me with a fat sausage in his mouth. He dropped it and stepped back.

'I don't want it,' I said, and looked away.

The dog picked up the sausage and dropped it in my lap.

I looked at Smoke. He looked at me with solemn eyes. 'OK, OK,' I said. I brushed the dirt from the sausage and broke off a piece. 'Just a bite to please you, then leave me alone.' I chewed the sausage on the side of my face that did not hurt. I had never, ever tasted anything so good. I closed my eyes and savoured the rich taste. I ate one more bite, then another and another, until the sausage was gone.

'Thank you, Smoke,' I said, opening my eyes. But the dog was gone.

I heard a drip drip coming from somewhere in the back of the cellar. I licked my lips. How long had it been since I had had a drink of water?

I followed the sound, feeling my way through the dark. I stumbled over boxes and through cobwebs, but finally I found the source of the sound: water dripped from an overhead pipe. I cupped my hands beneath the drip. Drips from a leaky pipe do not fill even small hands very quickly. By the time my throat was no longer dry I was exhausted. I made my way back to the patch of sunlight in the middle of the floor and slept.

In this way, time passed. I slept. Smoke woke me with food. I drank from the dripping pipe. I slept some more. The days grew colder; what little light there was in the cellar did not stay.

Sometimes I wondered about Tanya and Pasha and even Viktor. Had they escaped the beatings? Were they taken away in the vans with the flashing lights? Had Rudy come and saved them?

And I wondered even more about the rest of the pack – Lucky, Little Mother, Patches, Rip, Grandmother and, of course, the puppies. Had Smoke abandoned them? Why had they left the cellar and where were they now? I turned these questions over and over in my mind like I used to turn the button between my fingers. My fingers ached for that button.

One day I lay in the patch of sunlight, waiting for the dog to bring food. My stomach growled and grumbled. My fingers and ears burned with cold.

Something blotted out the sunlight. I sat up and said, 'Where have you been, Smoke? I'm hungry and cold.'

I waited for him to slip inside and drop something at my feet.

But this time he didn't. He stood at the opening and peered in.

I waved my hand. 'Come down here,' I said.

He barked and backed away.

'Smoke!' I called.

He barked again, further away this time.

I crossed to the wall and called out, 'Smoke! Come back here!'

Two barks, high and commanding.

I leaned my head against my hands already gripping the edge of the opening. If I left, where would I go? How would I live?

I heard Smoke's voice again.

With one backwards look at the cellar, I pulled myself up and through the opening in the brick wall and into the world again.

Chapter 18

THE WORLD

The world had turned white and cold during my time in the cellar. Snow covered the rubbish and weeds in the alley. The sun hurt my eyes.

My toes – one set living in only a sock, the other living in one Famous Basketball Player shoe – pointed their way down the alley. I followed. I went the only way I knew to go: back to Leningradsky Station.

I watched for faces I might know and for a smoke-coloured dog as I clumped my way through the frozen streets. I saw the faces of children going to school and the faces of children sleeping in doorways and in cardboard boxes. But I did not see the faces of Pasha or Tanya or Yula.

I stood at the top of the stairs leading down and down into the belly of Leningradsky Station. I clung to the cold metal of the handrail. My heart hammered so hard I thought it would burst through my chest.

Someone pushed me from behind. 'Move it, kid.' I stumbled down two steps, then four, five, and then I was swept down in the current of legs and bags and carrying cases until I was at the long, gleaming cavern of the station. There stood the statue of the man on the horse. There were the sparkling glass lights that made it always daytime in the station.

I stopped before my bench over the heat vent, the place I had slept night after night after night since coming to The City, and the place where I'd lost that one piece of my mother: the shiny black button. Tears stung my eyes. 'You are a stupid, stupid little boy,' I muttered.

Something fluttered beneath the bench. I dropped to my hands and knees and crawled under. Pages from my book of fairy tales were just where I'd left them. I smiled as I gathered them to me. There was the firebird soaring high above the shining city. There, on the other page, was the evil witch, Baba Yaga, with her house on chicken legs. The eyes of the Little Match Girl stared up at me, asking – what was she asking? I brought the page close to my face and whispered, 'What?'

'So the little mouse is back.'

A chill ran through me. I knew that voice. I knew this time it belonged not to a giant rat but to a rat-faced boy.

I tucked my pages under my jumper and crawled out from under the bench.

Viktor sneered at me through the smoke of his cigarette. His face was many colours of black and purple and green and yellow, all fading. His head had been shaved.

'What are you looking at?' he said.

I pointed. 'Your hair,' I said. 'It's gone.'

He ran his hand over his nearly bald head. 'Yeah, well, that's what they do to you at the police station. It's better. The lice are gone.'

I thought it looked sad and painful. I touched the pages beneath my jumper. 'Where are the others?' I asked.

Viktor tossed his cigarette to the floor. 'I found Rudy, Tanya and Yula at Kurskaya Station.'

'Pasha too?'

Viktor spat on the floor. 'Who cares where he is.'

He pointed at my one shoe and my one foot with just a sock and laughed. 'You, on the other hand, look pathetic.'

'What's "pathetic"?' I asked.

'It means lots of people will feel sorry for you and you'll bring us plenty of money.'

Trains pulled in and out of the station. People poured into the trains and people poured out of the trains. They hurried around us and past us and through us without looking. Nothing had changed.

'Money for new shoes?' I asked.

Viktor studied my feet – one with shoe, one without shoe – his hands on his hips. 'I think you'll do even better without any shoes.' Before I could puzzle out what he'd meant, he knocked me to the ground and wrenched my one Famous Basketball Player shoe from my foot.

'No!' I cried. 'Give it back!'

He held the once-white shoe above my head. 'Jump for it, little circus mouse,' he said as he laughed.

I did. I jumped and I jumped. Without Famous Basketball Player shoes, I could not jump very high. 'Give me my shoe,' I sobbed.

I kicked Viktor's shin. He shoved me to the floor. He kicked my side. 'I'll teach you, you little runt.'

He swung his leg back. I curled into a ball. Even before it came, I could feel the toe of his pointed black boot in my side. I knew how it would feel when it came, so I waited.

But it didn't come. Instead, Viktor screamed in pain. 'Get off me!'

A whirling fury of silver and grey and black flew all over Viktor. It grabbed first his arm and then his leg. It grabbed his coat and shook it and shook it.

'No!' Viktor screamed.

'Smoke!' I cried.

The dog dropped Viktor's arm.

A train screeched to a halt. People poured out.

Smoke shook himself and trotted towards the train.

Viktor scrambled to his feet. The sleeve of his coat hung in shreds. He grabbed for me. 'Come on,' he said.

I jumped away.

Smoke barked. He stood at the door of the train. He barked again.

Viktor made another lunge for me. 'You come with me, Mishka! Now!'

Mishka? There was no button; there was no mother.

There was no Mishka.

I ran as fast as I have ever run down that long platform. The train whistle blew. The tracks whirred. The white tip of Smoke's tail disappeared into the last train car.

'Smoke! Wait for me!'

I dived through the train doors just as they closed. I lay in a panting heap on the floor as the train rattled its way out of Leningradsky Station.

A wet nose nudged my face. I rose and followed Smoke to the back of the train. We sat together, a small boy and a smoke-coloured dog, and watched the world click by on the other side of the windows.

Chapter 19

THE GLASS HOUSE

And so it was, I threw in my lot with the dogs.

The day Smoke led me from Leningradsky Station, he took me further into The City. All this time, I'd thought I was already living deep in The City, with its tall glass buildings and everything made of steel and bricks and concrete.

When at last we pulled into a train station and the voice that was not a voice announced, 'Last stop,' Smoke stood. With barely a glance at me, he left the train car and set out. I trotted as fast as my socks would carry me, trying to keep him in sight.

'Wait,' I called as I raced up the stairs and out of the station. Smoke paused at the top of the stairs just long enough for me to catch up, then he was off again.

I ran alongside him. My feet quickly became wet and cold through the socks. I barely noticed my new surroundings. All I knew was we ran and ran, up one narrow street and down another, past old buildings and long, black cars so shiny I could see Smoke and myself running on the side of the car. I waved. The car slid past.

Finally, we came to a small wooden shed. I bent over, breathing hard, my hands on my knees.

Woof!

I straightened and looked around. The shed lived in a small forest of trees and overgrown brambles. The door to the shed sagged to one side. The window lay in many pieces on the ground.

I followed Smoke behind the shed. We climbed over a crumbling brick wall and pushed our way through vines and bushes.

I gasped. It stood before me, shining in the sun. A house made of glass!

And out of the Glass House tumbled two little puppies followed by Lucky, Rip and Grandmother.

'Lucky!' I cried. I threw my arms around the neck of the big brown and black dog. I buried my cold face in his warm fur.

Grandmother licked my fingers and Rip barked and danced and twirled on his hind legs. I laughed. I dropped to my knees and scooped the puppies into my arms.

They kissed and kissed my face with their little pink tongues. We rolled in the snow, Rip barking and dancing, the puppies nipping and tugging on my clothes. Lucky sat with Grandmother and wagged his tail.

Finally, I sat up and shook the snow from my hair. 'Where is the other puppy?' I asked. 'Where is Little Mother? Where is Patches?'

And where was Smoke?

I followed his tracks into the Glass House, past wooden tables and rows of empty flowerpots. There, under a table, lay Little Mother in a nest of empty sacks. Smoke stood beside her, his amber eyes filled with worry. She was much thinner than I remembered. Her big brown eyes were filled with sorrow and with questions.

I knelt down next to her. Pressed into the fur of her belly was the third puppy. It did not move. Little Mother whimpered and nosed the still puppy. I touched the little body with my finger. It was cold and stiff.

'Oh, Little Mother,' I sighed. I stroked her side. There was nothing between her fur and her bones.

Smoke whined. He looked from me to the puppy and back again.

'Is this why you brought me here?' I asked him. I shook my head. 'There is nothing I can do for him now,'

I said to Smoke and Little Mother. 'The puppy is dead. I cannot help.'

Woof, said Smoke.

'I am just a boy,' I said to Smoke. 'A small, pathetic boy.'

I picked the puppy up and held it to my chest. So soft, so silent. All the dogs watched as I wrapped the tiny body in a page from my fairy-tale book. I folded his body in the wings of the bright angel that came for the Little Match Girl.

The dogs trailed solemnly behind as I carried the paper-wrapped body out into the fading light. I dug a hole with a rusted spade. Even the puppies were silent as I laid the body in the dirt. I covered the puppy and sat back. 'The angels have him now,' I said to the dogs. 'He has gone to a place that is warm and where there is more food than he can ever eat. Everyone is kind there,' I said to the dogs and the first stars. 'He will be filled with love.'

The dogs and I sat that way on the cold ground beside the little grave. We watched the stars come out one by one. Finally, Little Mother took her two remaining puppies back into the Glass House. I followed behind. I lay down beside her. Grandmother lay on the other side. We watched as the puppies pushed against their mother's belly crying for milk. I ran my hand over her belly. Her nipples were dry.

'I am just a boy,' I said to Little Mother. 'A small, pathetic boy with no mother.'

I curled myself closer to her and the puppies. Rip and Grandmother pressed in close to me.

'But tomorrow,' I promised her, 'tomorrow I will get food so you can make food for your babies.'

Chapter 20

WINTER

Where we now lived in The City long black cars purred up and down the streets with beautiful ladies and fine gentlemen inside. They stepped out of the long black cars wrapped in fur coats and fur hats and fur gloves and paraded inside the finest restaurants. The first time I tried to beg money from the beautiful ladies, the doorman chased me away. 'Get away, you filthy little beggar boy,' he growled. 'Get away or I'll call the militsiya.'

I watched the long black car waiting by the curb, Smoke and Lucky by my side. 'The beautiful ladies and their gentlemen are so rich they don't even have to open a door for themselves. Surely they can give a shoeless, pathetic boy a ruble.' I tucked my feet under my bottom. My stomach pressed into my spine. I could not remember the last time I had eaten.

I leaned into the warmth of Lucky and watched the

sun on the golden domes and crosses rising in the sky. Surely any minute a firebird would swoop across the towers and – Woof!

Smoke watched the entrance of the restaurant. The beautiful women and fine gentlemen swept through the door held open by the doorman in his white gloves. A gentleman in a long grey coat handed the doorman a ruble.

Smoke whined. I thought about the two puppies and Little Mother. I leapt to my feet and raced across the wide square, the red bricks bruising my feet.

I skidded to a stop in front of the man with the long grey coat just as they reached the car.

'Pozhalsta, please,' I said, panting. 'I am just a small, pathetic boy with no shoes. Could you please spare a ruble?'

The doorman rushed over, waving his arms. 'Go away, you filthy little beggar! Leave these good people alone!'

I dodged the white gloves of the doorman. 'Pozhalsta,' I said, looking from the gentleman in the grey coat to one of the beautiful women.

'Leave the boy alone,' the woman snapped. She nodded to the gentleman in the grey coat. 'For God's sake, Renni, give the poor creature some money for shoes.'

'You mustn't, madame,' the doorman said. 'It will only encourage more begging.'

97

'Shut up, you idiot,' she said. Then, 'Renni, the money.'

With a sigh, the man named Renni opened his wallet and pulled out some money.

'More,' the woman commanded.

The man shook his head and handed over a fistful of notes.

'Spasibo, sir,' I said, using my best manners. I bowed to the beautiful lady. 'Spasibo, madam.' They slid into the long black car and drove away. I watched them go, my hand full of rubles and my heart filled with joy.

The doorman cuffed me on the side of the head. 'Hand it over,' he said. He held his fine white glove under my nose and the back of my jumper with the other hand.

'It's mine!' I cried. I squirmed under his hand. 'Let me go!'

He shook me harder.

A low growl came from behind the doorman and then another. Smoke and Lucky stepped beside me. They pulled their lips back. Their long teeth gleamed in the winter sun. Smoke crouched as if to spring.

'What the hell is this?' the doorman said, his eyes darting like rats from Smoke to Lucky. Lucky growled louder and stepped closer to the doorman.

The doorman dropped his hands.

I sprinted as fast as I could away from the angry door-man and his white gloves.

'Don't you ever come back here again,' the doorman called as we ran and ran and ran.

Finally, we stopped on the other side of the great city square. My feet and my head and my stomach hurt, but I did not care. I held more money in my hand than I had ever seen in my life.

'Look,' I said to Smoke and Lucky. 'We can eat like kings! We can eat like kings and queens for the rest of the winter! I can buy shoes!' I tossed the rubles up in the air and let them fall about me like snow. I laughed and laughed. Lucky yipped and nipped my sleeve. I chased him around the stone benches and statues. We rolled in the rubles. 'I am a small, pathetic boy,' I said, laughing. Lucky squirmed on his back in the snow, waving his legs in the air.

Smoke let out a low, gruff bark.

I sat up and gathered the rubles off the ground. 'OK, OK,' I said.

I soon discovered there were no carts with men who sold potatoes and sausages and sandwiches in the great town square with the red bricks and gold domes. A few stalls lined the low brick wall just outside the train-station doors. There I could buy only bread. The other stalls sold cigarettes and magazines and cheap wooden dolls. I went to the bread stall and bought thick black bread.

I had to visit the shops for anything else, and they were very expensive. One shop had strings of cooked sausages hanging in the window and jars of pickled eggs and bins of potatoes and cabbages. But I had no way to cook potatoes and cabbages.

I counted on my fingers: Little Mother, Smoke, Lucky, Rip and Grandmother. And me.

'How much for six sausages?' I asked the man behind the counter.

'Twenty-five rubles,' he said.

I counted my money. My heart sank. 'I don't have enough for six sausages,' I said.

He took my money. He wrapped five sausages and two pickled eggs in brown paper.

All my money was gone. There would be no new shoes today.

That afternoon, it was black bread and pickled eggs for me and sausages for the dogs. Lucky and Smoke had left me as soon as the Glass House was within sight. I gave two sausages to Little Mother and one each to Rip and Grandmother. I put the remaining sausage away for Lucky and Smoke.

I broke off pieces of black bread and fed it to the dogs.

'I thought I had all the money in the world today.' I sighed.

Grandmother licked my fingers in thanks. Then she curled up with a groan.

'But the food in shops costs so very much. We need more food and I need shoes.' A cold wind blew against the Glass House. A gap between the ground and the bottom of the Glass House welcomed the cold. Little Mother and Grandmother shivered.

'Soon it will be much colder than this,' I said. I remembered my mother stuffing old newspapers and rags around our leaky window in the bedroom.

'Let's see what we can find,' I said to Rip.

We found nothing but wet, crumpled newspapers and an old towel in the Glass House. The towel I stuffed in the gap, but it was not enough.

'Let's check that shed.'

Rip followed me through the brambles and over the crumbling brick wall. The shed brooded in the weak afternoon light. It looked dark and like the kind of place a troll or an evil witch might live. I licked my lips. 'I don't know if we should go in there, Rip.'

But Rip was already pushing his way through the

sagging door, his stub of a tail wagging. He poked his head back out and looked at me as if to say, 'Come on, what are you waiting for?'

The shed was filled with all kinds of things – buckets and shovels and empty sacks that had once held rich-smelling dirt. A wheelbarrow leaned against one corner. And inside the wheelbarrow the most wonderful sight: a pair of leather gloves! They were much too big for my small hands, and something had chewed away most of the fingertips on the gloves. But still, they were gloves.

'If only I would find shoes,' I said as Rip poked his nose beneath a wooden crate. His tail wagged with great excitement.

Above a long wooden shelf running the length of the shed was a cupboard.

'Do you think there could be food in that cupboard?' I asked. Rip dug furiously beneath the wooden crate.

'If I can get up on the shelf, I can reach the cupboard,' I said. But I was too small a boy to pull myself up onto the shelf. The cupboard and what might be in the cupboard called to me.

I grabbed a bucket and turned it over. I climbed onto the bucket and up on the shelf. I laughed. 'Look at me up here,' I called to Rip, waving my hands. Rip barked.

I stood on tiptoe and pulled open the cupboard door. I peered inside.

'No food,' I called down to Rip in disappointment. But then, something even better: matches. Matches and lighter fluid and a long, sharp knife. A package of cigarettes and a bottle of vodka crouched in a dusty corner. These I left behind. But the matches, knife and lighter fluid I threw down to the wheelbarrow. I reached my hand into the back of the cupboard to see if there was anything I'd missed. I had. I had missed three long candles and a dented, rusted cup.

I climbed back down with my new treasures and loaded everything into the wheelbarrow with all the sacks I could find.

Suddenly, Rip barked and yipped and lunged at something running across the shed floor. I jumped behind the wheelbarrow. Rip crashed this way and that. Finally, he grabbed the something up in his mouth and shook it, hard. Then he dropped it to the floor. I inched out from behind the wheelbarrow. A rat – a large rat – lay dead on the dirt floor. Rip looked up at me, eyes shining, tail wagging.

I smiled. 'You are a fine hunter, Rip,' I said.

So we returned to the Glass House, me with my wheelbarrow full of treasure and Rip with his bloody rat.

As I stuffed sacks into every crack I could find, Rip shared his rat with Little Mother. I shuddered at the sound of snapping bones and the crunch and smack as they ate. But I laughed as the two puppies played tug of war with the rat's long, naked tail.

Later, Smoke and Lucky returned with more food. Smoke dropped a meaty bone on the dirt floor, Lucky a raw potato. Little Mother and the puppies gnawed the bone, the puppies muttering and growling to themselves. Rip crunched the potato. Grandmother looked on with milky, hopeful eyes.

'Grandmother,' I said, stroking the top of her silvered head, 'you must eat too.' I snatched the raw potato away from Rip, who had, after all, shared a rat with Little Mother.

I offered the potato to Grandmother. She took it gently in her mouth, rolled it about and then dropped it. She pinned her ears back in apology and wagged the tip of her tail.

Why had she not eaten the potato? I carefully lifted her lips. I looked and looked for the long white teeth I had seen in Lucky and Smoke's mouth. The teeth of the dog. The teeth of the wolf. But Grandmother had no teeth, or very few. And the few she had were broken or worn to nothing more than nubs.

I pulled her to me and hugged her. She rested her head against mine. 'Don't worry, Grandmother,' I said. 'I will take care of you.' With my new knife I cut the one sausage into tiny pieces and cut what was left of the black bread up as well. I mixed it all together in an empty flower-pot with a bit of water until it formed a gruel.

'My Babushka Ina would fix soft food for me when I was too sick to chew,' I said to her. 'She would mix honey with mine to make it sweet. If I had honey, I would do that.'

I set the pot of gruel down for Grandmother. Rip and Lucky pushed her aside.

'No!' I said.

Lucky and Rip looked from me to the pot of food. They inched forward. I stepped between Grandmother and the pot of food and the two hungry dogs. 'No,' I said in a low growl.

I locked eyes with these two dogs who were my friends and who could tear me to pieces.

'No,' I said again and took one step towards them.

A look passed between Rip and Lucky. It was brief as a shooting star and full of questions.

Finally, they lay down and licked their paws as if nothing had happened, nothing at all.

Chapter 21

THE HAT

The days grew short and very cold. When the sun was shining, the Glass House was warm as springtime. The puppies played and wrestled. Grandmother watched over them while Little Mother and Rip went out to hunt rats. But at night, the Glass House turned into a house of ice.

I begged and bought what I could. Perhaps I would have got more money if I had begged with one of the puppies. But I knew it would break Little Mother's heart if I took one of her children away.

Lucky proved to be my good-luck charm again – Lucky and my shoeless feet. It had become so cold that I wrapped them in sacks I cut with my knife and tied with string from my ragged jumper. Still, by the end of the day, my feet were wet and frozen.

As the sun faded in the grey afternoon, I hobbled to the bread shop and the butcher shop and the everything-in-it shop. Some days, I had enough to buy bread and sausages and even a pickled egg or two. Sometimes, I did not. On those days, I would swallow my shame and take the long stairs down into the belly of the train station and dig through the trash bins for discarded food.

'There are no children or grown-up beggars in that train station,' I said to Lucky and Smoke as I nibbled at what was left of the roasted pork shashlyk. I pulled a piece of black meat from the wooden skewer and tossed it to Smoke.

'Perhaps they are living underground like Pasha and the rest,' I said, pulling the last piece of meat from the skewer and handing it to Lucky. I licked the grease from my fingers and pulled on the gloves I had found in the wooden shed. I shivered. I was still so very hungry. And tired.

Back above ground, Lucky and I lay down in a weak patch of sun on top of a heat grate. Smoke drifted off to where, we never knew.

Lucky sighed as I rested my head on his sun-warmed belly. I reached up and touched his face. 'I'll get some money in a few minutes, Lucky.' I closed my eyes. 'I just need to rest for a minute.'

When I awoke, my head still resting on Lucky's side, the day had turned lead grey. Fat snowflakes drifted down.

And in my hand that had laid outstretched as I slept, winked coins and rubles growing wet in the snow.

Lucky and I hurried to the wooden stalls for our bread.

The woman who sold the bread huddled deep in her coat. As always, a cigarette hung from her lip. And as always, she took my money and handed me the loaf of black bread without speaking. But as Lucky and I turned to leave she said, 'Wait.' She dug through a plastic bag, muttering to herself. She pulled something from the bag. 'Here,' she said.

I gasped. It was the most beautiful thing I had ever seen. It was a hat. I ran my fingers over and over the rows of knitted wool – brown and black and dirty white – thick and rough. I showed it to Lucky. 'See, it's just like you. It is my Lucky hat.'

Lucky sniffed the hat and sneezed.

'Don't just stand there and pet it like a dog,' the bread woman said. 'Put it on.'

Carefully, I pulled the beautiful hat on my head. It came down over my forehead, covered my ears and eyes, and rested finally on the tip of my nose.

The bread woman grunted. She folded the brim of the hat up to my eyebrows. She nodded. 'Better.'

Oh, the delicious warmth of it! My head was warm and my ears warm for the first time in weeks. I wiggled my toes in my socks and sack shoes. They were warm too.

I smiled at the bread woman and wrapped my arms around myself. 'Spasibo,' I said. 'It is the best hat ever. There could never be a better hat.'

The bread woman stacked her unsold bread in a box. She folded up the top of the box and then unfolded it. She pulled a loaf of bread from the box. 'Here,' she said. 'Take it.'

'But I have only enough money left to buy sausages,' I said.

'It is too old to sell,' she said, shoving the loaf of bread across the table. 'It's not worth the trouble to carry home.'

My heart soared like the firebird. Two loaves of bread and enough money left for sausages!

I raced back to the Glass House with Lucky. We leapt over the brick wall and ran to our home.

'Tonight we will eat like kings and queens,' I said as we burst in the door. And we did. Two pots of gruel for Grandmother rather than one, extra slices of bread and sausage for me and for the dogs.

I lit the candles I had found in the shed and placed them in pots. Their light danced and flickered on the glass around us and above us. A fine layer of snow and ice coated the top of the Glass House. The light from the candles shone through it like blankets of delicate lace.

'The lace of the Snow Queen,' I said to the dogs all piled and sprawled around me. 'Do you know the story of the Snow Queen? She was a beautiful but evil queen. She stole children who became lost and kept them in her Winter Lands for ever,' I explained. 'It was my favourite story for my mother to read to me in the winter.'

Lucky thumped his tail. Rip rolled on his back, paws waving in the air. Grandmother yawned.

I burrowed in the nest of dogs and stared up at the glass and ice and lace ceiling. 'Let me see if I can remember... Once upon a time,' I began, 'in the land of ice and snow, there lived a queen. She was so beautiful and delicate, yet she was of ice, of dazzling, silver ice. And her eyes were like twin stars and filled with endless winter.'

The next morning our little forest and our Glass House were blanketed in snow. The dogs chased each other and wrestled in the clean whiteness of it. Even Grandmother left the Glass House and rolled with great delight, her eyes closed and her mouth smiling. Little Mother did too.

A whimper and a yip came from a mound of snow.

One little head popped up, then another.

'Oh, puppies,' I laughed. 'The snow is too deep! We'll never find you.'

I put the puppies in the wheelbarrow and pushed them through the snow. Lucky and Rip chased along beside. We ran and laughed until the wheelbarrow turned over and we all went sprawling in the wet snow. Lucky and Rip licked the snow from my face.

'Thank you for the bath,' I said.

A bath. Once a week I had taken a bath. My mother would scrub my ears and my neck and my feet so hard I thought surely my skin would come off. 'Now you are my clean Mishka. You are no longer a smelly little bear.'

I took off my hat and placed it in the wheelbarrow. I scrubbed my face and my hair and my neck as hard as I could with snow. The sun was warm and the snow was cold. I took off my jumper and my trousers and put them in the wheelbarrow too. I yelled and whooped as I scrubbed my body with the snow. The dogs pranced and rolled.

Lucky grabbed my hat from the wheelbarrow and raced to the shed.

'Come back here,' I cried. Just as I caught up to him, off he'd dash again, waving my hat in the air. Rip grabbed the hat from Lucky and dashed past me. Even Little Mother joined in the keep-away game. I laughed and laughed, chasing the dogs in our little forest. And for just that time, we did not feel the cold and the hunger. We were a boy and his dogs playing with a hat in the snow.

Chapter 22

DOG BOY

Snow fell every day now. Sometimes it fell thin and stingy as the woman at the fancy bakery. Other times it fell in generous white curtains. On those days, I stayed in the Glass House with the dogs – all but Smoke – and we slept the day away.

But still, there were days of brief sun. I followed Lucky past the shed and over the crumbling brick wall, up and down alleys to the great square and the shops and the wooden stalls huddled together by the train station. Now that Grandmother and Little Mother were stronger, Rip tagged along too. And always, always, just out of sight was Smoke – a whiff here, a smudge of silver and black there.

We wandered further from the great square with its gold-roofed buildings and marching soldiers with their white gloves and tall black boots. The restaurant doormen with their white gloves had chased me away from the long black cars and the beautiful ladies.

I found a book shop with an old woman and a cat. The old woman gave me kopeks and the dogs milk. The cat had eyes like Rudy: grey and cold. My eyes longed to find the words they knew in the books; my hands itched to feel the weight of the book and the smooth cover. But the woman would not allow me to touch the books. Instead, she helped me sound out words from old newspapers. 'Food,' 'men,' 'dogs,' 'guns,' 'cold.'

I found a shop where a man with a huge moustache painted the faces of saints on wood.

'Can you make a firebird?' I asked him. 'Can you make the face of the Snow Queen or the Little Match Girl?' I asked as I ran my hand over the rough face of Saint Bernadette.

The man blew out a long sigh. His moustache fluttered above his lip. 'No, boy. People will not pay for such things. They want the saints, always the saints.' He hammered two pieces of wood together. 'They think they will bring them good health and fortune.' He hammered harder. 'Where were the saints when I lost my son in the war?'

'I don't know,' I said. 'Maybe they were sleeping.'

He sighed again and handed me a coin. 'Maybe you're right. Even God and the saints must sleep, I suppose. But who,' he asked, stroking Rip's head, 'looks after us when God and the saints sleep?'

'Dogs,' I said.

I also found a school near the book shop and the shop with the wooden saints. In the late morning when the sun shone just so, Rip and Lucky and sometimes Smoke followed me to the school yard.

'Watch,' I'd say. The bell rang and the children burst from the mud-coloured building and swarmed like bees over the playground. Through the wire fence we watched the boys throw snowballs.

'I don't like that tall boy in the blue scarf,' I said to the dogs. 'He put a rock in the middle of his snowball.' The boy in the blue scarf hurled his snowball at a small boy off by himself holding a book. The snowball smacked the little boy in the side of his head. He cried in pain, dropping his book in the snow.

'See, I told you he was mean,' I said. Lucky and Rip barked in agreement. 'He is a bad, bad boy.'

The small boy ran towards the school building, holding the side of his head.

'Hey! Hey!' I called through the chain-link fence. 'You forgot your book!'

'Who are you?'

I turned. A girl studied me through the fence.

Before I could answer, she pointed and asked, 'Are these your dogs?'

'Yes,' I said.

Lucky pushed his big black nose through the wire and wagged his tail. The girl reached through with her small hands and scratched under his chin. Rip stood up on his back legs and yipped and twirled.

'That one too?' she asked, pointing to the patch of sun on the pavement where Smoke slept. I hesitated. Smoke did not belong to anyone. I nodded. 'Sort of.'

'You're lucky,' she said. 'My mother and father won't let me have a dog. They say they take too much care and I am too lazy to look after one.'

'The dogs look after me,' I said. 'We look after one another.'

She looked at my soggy, bag-covered feet. 'Why don't you have shoes?'

I shrugged. 'I had shoes once. Famous Basketball Player shoes. I could run faster than anybody in those shoes.'

'Where are they?'

'One was lost. One was stolen,' I said.

The snow swirled around us. Birds fluffed their feathers against the cold. Snow fell on the white fur hat of the girl. She stared at my feet.

The bell rang. The girl turned to go. 'Goodbye,' she said. 'I hope your mother gets you some new shoes.'

'My mother is gone too,' I said. 'Like my shoes.'

'I'm sorry about your mother and your shoes,' the girl said.

'Anya! Come in now!' a big woman called in an angry voice.

'I have to go,' the girl said, and she dashed across the school yard.

Anya. Wasn't that my mother's name?

'Wait!' I called.

The girl stopped. I rubbed my eyes. She was not my mother. She was a schoolgirl named Anya with a white fur hat.

'The book,' I said. 'The boy dropped his book.'

She picked the book up out of the snow and wiped it. She waved and ran to the woman waiting on the edge of the playground.

Winter closed down like an iron fist. The City was encased in a cold so sharp, so bitter it hurt to breathe. Worse, my shoes made of socks and sacks froze. They stood up all by themselves in the morning like little brown trolls.

Finally, on the fifth day, the cold broke. The dogs and I awoke that morning to the sound of birds and the steady drip drip of ice melting off the roof of the Glass House.

The dogs shook the cold from their coats and stretched. The puppies unwound themselves from the warmth of Grandmother's fur. They stumbled over to Little Mother's belly and rooted about for milk. There was no milk to be had. All of us were starving. We'd only had what food Lucky and Smoke brought to the Glass House.

I wrapped my feet in the wet boots of old sock and sack. I scrubbed my face with snow. 'I'll get us food,' I said to Little Mother and Grandmother, and set off with Lucky and Rip and Smoke.

Later in the morning, after visiting the book-shop woman and the man with the giant moustache, I stopped to watch the children playing at the school. I had barely arrived when the girl with the white fur hat stomped over to the fence.

'Where have you been?' she asked, her fists planted on her hips. 'I've waited for you every day,' she said with a scowl.

I rubbed my raw feet. 'It's been too cold,' I said. 'We were trying to stay warm in our house.'

She squinted her blue eyes. 'Where do you live? I thought you said you have no mother.'

I pointed back toward the onion-shaped gold domes. 'We live in the Glass House over that way.'

She shook her head, her brown curls bouncing underneath her hat. 'You talk like a crazy person. No one lives in a glass house.'

'We do,' I said. 'The dogs and I.'

'What is your name, anyway?' she demanded.

What was I to say? I had always been my mother's Mishka. But there was no Mishka because there was no mother.

She waved away the words rising from my throat. 'It doesn't matter. I call you Sobachonok, Dog Boy. To me, you are Dog Boy.'

I nodded. 'Dog Boy,' I repeated.

The teacher in the big coat on the other side of the playground blew a whistle.

'Oh, I almost forgot.' Anya pulled a bag from beneath her coat. She squinted up into the sunlight and swung her arm, her hand clutching the bag, around and around in a big circle.

'One! Two! Three!' and the bag sailed high and higher over the fence. Rip barked and danced on his back legs. Lucky crouched in fear. And Smoke, my beautiful Smoke, tipped his head and caught it with ease. He dropped the bag at my feet and lay back down in the sun.

'Open it,' Anya said. 'It's for you.'

I opened the bag and pulled out boots. Glorious grey boots with rubber on the outside and cloth on the inside.

I clutched the boots to my chest. 'How could these be for me?' I asked. 'Did you steal them?'

Anya laughed a small, tinkling laugh. 'No, silly. They belonged to my little brother. He's outgrown them. Mummy threw them in the dustbin, but I thought they'd be better off with you.'

I turned my face away and pretended to carefully inspect the boots.

She planted her fists on her hips again. 'Are you crying?' she demanded. 'Because if you are, you have to give them back.'

I shook my head and scrubbed my face. 'It's just the cold,' I sniffed.

The bell rang. The children scattered like birds.

'I have to go, Sobachonok,' she said. 'I got in trouble with my teacher last time.' And with that, she ran across the school yard. When she was almost to the big woman in the grey coat, she turned and called, 'See you later, Dog Boy!'

I pressed my hands to the wire fence. 'See you later, Anya,' I whispered.

Chapter 23

FIRE AND ICE

The last time I saw Anya on the other side of the fence, the sky was heavy with snow and she was filled with light.

'Three weeks!' she crowed. 'We have three weeks off from school!'

'You won't be here?' I asked. I did not understand this. Seeing Anya every day had become as much a part of my life as begging and searching bins for food.

'No, silly,' she said. 'It's Christmas! We always get three weeks off at Christmas and the New Year. Don't you know that?'

I scratched at something crawling in my hair. My head had been crawly since the bread woman gave me the hat. 'I'm not sure what month it is,' I admitted.

'How can that be?' she asked. 'Everyone knows when Christmas and New Year are.'

I scuffed the toe of my wonderful boot in the snow

and shrugged.

Anya said, 'Mummy says my little brother will get a new coat for Christmas, Sobachonok. I will bring you his old one. And I think Papa is taking us all to St Petersburg to see Grandmother and Grandfather and all the aunts and uncles and cousins.' She clapped her hands and twirled like Rip did when he was excited. 'Oh, we will eat and eat until we can't eat anymore.'

The smile dropped from her face. 'What will you do, Sobachonok? Where will you go for the holiday?'

I buried my cold hands in Lucky's fur. He licked my face. 'Oh, we have many, many places to go. We will be very busy, the dogs and I.'

The teacher blew her whistle. Rip barked and wagged his tail. Smoke stood and stretched. Lucky pressed his head against the wire fence for the rub he knew was coming from Anya's small hands.

A cold blast of wind blew open her coat. I shivered in my jumper. Finally she said, 'I must go, Dog Boy.'

I lifted my hand. 'See you later, Anya.'

'I'll see you back here in three weeks,' she said. 'Right here, like always.'

'Like always,' I said.

*

123

For days and days and days, it snowed. Snow upon snow upon snow.

It snowed for so long, I forgot when the snow started. I forgot colours other than white and grey. It snowed so long and so hard the crumbling brick wall disappeared. Even in the night, I had to push the door to the Glass House open and shut, back and forth so we would not be trapped. After days and nights, the snow was too deep for the dogs – except for Lucky and Smoke.

When the sun was at its strongest, I waded with Lucky and Smoke through the drifts of snow to the great plaza in search of food. Gone now were the stalls selling black bread and sausages. The book shop was closed for the holiday. The man with the big black moustache was closed too.

I dug through the rubbish bins in the train station. How wonderful it was to be warm, I thought, as I ate the last of a discarded sandwich. How wonderful to be in a place where it was always light.

'Leningradsky was not so bad,' I said to Lucky as I checked the last bin in the station. 'I don't know why Smoke brought us here,' I complained over the growl of my stomach. 'People are stingy, the food in the shops is expensive.' I forgot about the wonders of the Glass House and Anya.

I sat on the marble floor. 'How am I going to keep us fed?' I asked the painted faces of the people on the wall marching towards something shining and wonderful. These painted people were healthy and had new clothes, and the children held their mother's and father's hands. They all looked with eyes like steel at something up ahead, something grand.

A pair of tall brown boots stopped in front of me. Brown boots with fur the colour of Rip puffing from the tops. A red coat brushed the tops of the boots. A red coat with black buttons. I counted the black buttons, *one, two, three, four*. The last button pressed against the throat of a woman, a woman with hair the colour of dried blood. Had my mother's hair been that colour? Or had it been dark as a raven's wing? Or perhaps yellow like a lemon.

I shook my head. 'I cannot remember,' I said to the woman's red coat. 'But I do remember the red coat. She loved her red coat.' Lucky pressed in close to my side and leaned against me.

I put my arm round his shoulders. 'She–she lost one of the black buttons and I found it, but then I lost it again.'

'I am so sorry,' the woman said.

I blinked up at her. 'You see me?' I asked.

The woman nodded and wiped her face. She reached

into the leather bag that hung from her shoulder.

She handed me a fistful of coloured paper – rubles of every amount. My mouth dropped open.

'There is a place you must go, child. They are the Sisters of Mercy. They will feed you there, give you some clothes. You will find them on Petrovsky Boulevard.'

I frowned. 'Is it an orphanage?' I asked.

She shook her head. 'It is not an orphanage,' she said, 'but you must go there.'

I felt Lucky stiffen beside me. A low growl rumbled in his chest. Two policemen in long grey coats and tall black boots walked towards us, swinging their batons lazily from their hands.

The woman raised one white-gloved hand and waved to the policemen. 'Officers!' she called. 'Over here.'

I scrambled to my feet. The side of my face throbbed at the memory of the crack of my head against the stone steps.

I may not have been able to run as fast in boots as in my Famous Basketball Player shoes, but I could still run faster than any policeman. As Lucky and I flew up the long stairs rising up and up into the almost-dark day, I remembered my manners. 'Thank you!' I called over my shoulder to the woman in the red coat.

Lucky and I ran and ran, my boots slipping and sliding in the snow and ice. First we went to the butcher's shop. I pulled the cloth bag that had carried my boots over the school-yard fence out of the front of my trousers. 'Six sausages and two of your meatiest bones,' I said. 'Please.'

Lucky licked his lips.

Then we went to the shop that had everything. I bought a fat loaf of bread, a can of sardines, a bottle of pickled vegetables.

I counted the last of my money. I looked across the street at the fancy bakery. The white cakes trimmed in swirls of red stood like queens in the bakery window. Even through the glass and across the street I could smell the hot cross buns, the sugared cookies, the braided fruit bread and the frosted sticky buns. I remembered the skinny woman chasing me away from the bakery with her broom when she caught me going through her rubbish. 'Get out of here, you filthy little beggar,' she had said, whacking the backs of my legs with her broom.

As was his habit, Smoke appeared out of thin air. He sniffed the cloth bag. He nudged my side.

'You're right,' I said.

I marched across the street; my eyes fixed like steel, my shoulders thrown back with purpose just like the painted people on the train station wall. Lucky and Smoke marched like good soldiers by my side.

I pushed through the front door. A bell tinkled. I almost wept from the warmth and the smell.

The stingy woman looked up from behind the glass case. 'Get out of here, you filthy little tramp,' she snapped. 'I won't have you stinking up my place and offending my customers.'

I marched right up to the tall glass case and pointed at the frosted sticky buns resting, glowing in the case. 'How much?' I asked.

The woman shook her head. 'Get out, boy.'

I handed her the last of my money. She unfolded it like it was covered in rat poo. She looked at me and looked at the paper money smiling from the counter.

She sighed and snatched a paper sack from under the counter. She slid open the doors to the glass house where the sticky buns lived. 'God only knows who you stole the money from,' she muttered.

Anger burned my face. 'I do not steal,' I said. 'I *never* steal.'

She eyed me again and dropped one and then two buns in the bag. She flung the bag across the counter. I grabbed it just before it slid to the floor.

'Now get out,' she said.

I bolted out the door and skittered onto the pavement. I danced and laughed in the swirling, wheeling, blowing snow. 'Two buns!' I cried. 'Two hot sticky buns for the pathetic little boy,' I sang. I raced Lucky and Smoke all the way home through the snow, the bag of food and the bag of precious buns bouncing against my legs.

After the snow stopped, a bone-cracking cold encased The City. The remaining sausages from our shopping spree froze on the wooden shelf along with the last of the bread. The jar of water I kept on a window ledge froze solid.

On the third night of the crushing cold, the dogs – all the dogs, including Smoke – and I piled together for warmth. Still, I shook and shivered, rattling the old newspapers I had stuffed in my trousers and under my jumper for extra warmth.

'It must be New Year by now,' I said. 'We don't have a *yelka* tree to light, so I have lit all our candles.'

I snuggled down deeper into Lucky's side. Rip lay across my legs. 'My mother and Babushka Ina used to make the most wonderful *kutya* on Christmas day,' I said. One of the puppies whimpered in her sleep.

'My mother would stir and stir the big pot on the

stove. And at just the right time, Babushka Ina would say, 'Mishka, I need your help.' I stroked the top of Grandmother's head. 'I was always a big help,' I assured the dogs.

'It was my job to help my grandmother add just the right amount of fruit and honey to the kutya. She said she had old taste buds and needed my young ones to tell exactly the perfect amount to add.'

Grandmother thumped her tail in her dream.

The world in the Glass House glowed gold in the candlelight. It waved and folded and danced in the cold. My eyelids slid halfway down, as I remembered the warmth in my mother's kitchen and the golden strings of honey swirling in the pot of kutya. I could not see my mother's face anymore. I was not sure of the colour of her hair or eyes. But I remembered her hands, her beautiful white hands on the handle of the wooden spoon, stirring and stirring the pot.

Something woke me. Barking and growling. Teeth pulled on my jumper, hard. I curled into a ball. It was so warm. I just wanted to sleep.

A high, frantic, piercing bark. A howl of utter despair right beside my ear. Sharp, hurting teeth on my hands and my legs.

I sat upright. 'Leave me—'

My words were cut by flames. Flames danced and licked all around me. The Glass House was no longer a Glass House. It was now a house of smoke and fire.

Smoke.

I staggered to my feet. The dogs crowded and cowered around me, whimpering, their eyes huge with fear.

Smoke was at the far end of the Glass House hurling his body violently against the wooden door. I ran to him and threw my weight against the door too. It barely budged.

'It's the snow on the other side,' I said, coughing. I pushed with all my strength. Smoke and Lucky scratched frantically at the frozen dirt. Rip dug beneath the door until the snow was streaked with blood. Little Mother, the puppies shivering beside her, looked up at me with those eyes, the eyes of the Little Match Girl.

I beat my fists on my legs. 'I am just a pathetic, motherless boy,' I wailed. One of the tables crawled with flames. The wooden ribs joining the glass panes together smoked and sizzled. One rib fell away, crashing to the ground. Glass shattered.

'Mother,' I whimpered. I looked around the Glass House.

And then my eyes came to rest on the wheelbarrow.

I ran to the end where we slept and ate and nested together. I grabbed the handles of the wheelbarrow. Flames licked at my back.

I dug the toes of my boots into the frozen earth. 'One, two . . .' and I shot down the length of the Glass House and rammed the wheelbarrow against the door. A sliver of night shone through the tiny bit the door opened. But it was not enough. None of us could squeeze through.

The house grew hotter. Smoke stung my eyes and burned my chest. The sacks fed the flames.

I ran with the wheelbarrow back down to the other end of the Glass House. A spark came to rest on my cheek. I smelled burning hair.

Once again, I dug my toes into the earth – softer now from the heat – and prayed. I prayed to my mother wherever she was and I prayed to Babushka Ina and the saints with their wooden faces and I prayed to God and the angels and hoped they were not asleep on this cold and fiery night.

The table we slept under collapsed in a heap of sparks. I pushed off and ran as fast as any boy who is five years old without Famous Basketball Player shoes has ever run. I hit the wooden door so hard I flew over the handle-bars of the wheelbarrow, crashed against the door, and landed on my back in the snow. I looked up with wonder at the star-filled sky. Sparks spiraled and floated like tiny red and orange eyes above us, looking down in wonder. 'The angels are not sleeping this night,' I said to the eyes. 'They are watching us.'

A cold, wet nose pressed into my cheek. A tongue licked the other side of my face. Teeth pulled on my arm.

I sat up and counted: Smoke, Lucky, Rip, Grandmother, Little Mother and the two puppies. I felt underneath my jumper. The pages from my book of fairy tales were right where I'd put them.

We sat together in the snow and watched our home burn bright, like a firebird in the night sky.

'Well, Smoke,' I said to the dog sitting beside me. 'Where do we go now? Our house is gone. The bread woman and the man with the sausages is gone, and so is Anya.'

For the first time since I had met him, Smoke's eyes were sorrowful and his ears were pinned against his sleek silver head in apology.

I pulled from my memory the place the woman in the train station gave me. I said the words aloud to the light of the fire: 'Sisters of Mercy.'

I stroked the top of Smoke's head and cradled the puppies in my lap.

'I'll take care of us.'

Chapter 24

VADIM

And so it was, the dogs and I left The City centre and the great square and Anya on a bitter January morning. We rode the train past one stop, then another. The dogs followed me past the sleeping children on the floor and on the benches. I looked for the faces of Pasha, Tanya and Yula. I did not see them. I saw only dirty faces troubled in sleep, hands outstretched and begging.

I shifted the heavy weight of the puppies in my cloth sack as we went up and up and up the gleaming moving stairs. 'Sisters of Mercy,' I whispered.

I touched the sleeve of a man sweeping the street. 'Please, sir, can you tell me where Petrovsky Boulevard is?'

He squinted at my face and shrugged before turning away.

'Petrovsky Boulevard,' I said to the dogs. 'We must find Petrovsky Boulevard.'

I tried to stop the people coming and going from the train station. 'Excuse me, sir,' 'Pardon me, madam,' but they all pushed past me. Finally, an old woman in a grey head scarf stopped long enough to wave her hand and snap, 'Ten minutes that way,' before she disappeared below ground.

So off the dogs and I went, the puppies whimpering in their bag. We trotted past heaps of snow-covered rubbish in the gutters and grown-up *bomzhi* sleeping in doorways. We wound our way round sleeping dogs and empty bottles on the pavement. 'This is not as nice a place as the great square,' I said as we waited for Grandmother to catch up.

Finally, we found the street named Petrovsky and a low, grey building with the faded words *sisters of mercy* on a sign in front. Peeling painted wings spread across the door.

No light shone from the two small windows. I pushed on the door. It did not open. 'Perhaps they are sleeping,' I said to Lucky. I knocked on the wings. The door rested in silence. I pounded on it with my fists. Still, it did not open.

I slid down to my knees and leaned my head against the door. '*Pozhalsta* – please,' I said to the outstretched wings.

'They're not there today. It's Christmas.'

On the pavement stood a bundle of rags with a boy inside.

'Today is Christmas?'

'Of course, stupid. It's the seventh of January .' The boy cocked his head to one side. 'Don't you even know what day it is?'

I shook my head. I had not known what day it was for a long, long time.

'Will they be back tomorrow?' I asked.

The boy shrugged and picked at a scab on his face. 'Who knows? Maybe yes, maybe no.'

Every bone in my body ached under the weight of disappointment. I could not remember the last time I'd eaten or got food for the dogs. I could not remember the last time I'd been warm.

'What's that in your bag?' the boy in rags asked.

I hugged the puppies closer to me. 'Nothing,' I said. 'Just stuff.'

The female puppy poked her head out of the top of the bag and whimpered.

'Puppies!' the boy cried. He hurried over to the doorway where I sat with the puppies in my lap. 'Can I see?'

Little Mother and Grandmother closed around me, eyeing the boy warily. The boy reached out to touch the puppy's head. Little Mother growled.

'This is Little Mother,' I said. 'She doesn't know you well enough to let you touch her puppies.'

The boy pulled his hand back and nodded. 'She's a good mother to protect her babies.'

The puppies squirmed and mewled with hunger. 'How many are there?' asked the boy.

'Two,' I said. 'There were three but one died.'

The boy nodded again. 'My friend Janina died too.'

I reached into the bag and stroked the puppies, feeling their ribs against my fingers. 'They're hungry,' I said. 'I need to find food for us.'

The boy jammed his thumb against his chest. 'I'm the best there is at getting food,' he said. 'Come on.'

And so the dogs and I followed this skinny bundle of rags away from the Sisters of Mercy. By the middle of the day, we'd collected enough food from the rubbish bins behind the shops to feed us all.

The boy stretched his legs across the heat grate. 'I'm Vadim,' he said. 'Who are you?'

I stroked Grandmother's head resting on my leg. 'Sobachonok,' I said.

Vadim laughed. 'Your mother named you "Dog Boy"?'

I shrugged. 'Not my mother,' I said.

Vadim took a deep breath. He closed his eyes and let

loose the loudest, longest belch I had ever heard. I laughed.

'Try it,' he said. 'Take a really deep breath and swallow lots of air.'

I closed my eyes and did just like he said.

'Now, let it rip.' And I did.

We laughed and laughed as people hurried by.

'I am King of the Burps!' Vadim cried.

'No, I am King of the Burps!' said I.

Vadim socked me in the arm. I socked him back. I had seen boys play like this on the playground at Anya's school.

'You stink,' Vadim said, grinning.

'I am the King of Stink,' I said.

'We are the Kings of Burps and Stink,' we crowed together.

The sky turned the colour of dirty sheets. Snow began to fall.

'Let's go,' Vadim said. And because the Sisters of Mercy were celebrating Christmas, and the dogs and I had nowhere else to go, we followed the boy deep underground to the huge steam pipes in the belly of The City.

Children filled this world beneath The City – children all sizes and ages. Some were from The City, but many had ridden trains from far away.

'In my village, all we had to eat was chicken feed,' a boy perched atop one of the pipes bragged.

'In my village, all we had to eat was dust,' said a girl in a pink shirt with a big, grinning mouse on the front.

'Oh yeah, well in my village all we ever ate was snow,' said a tall, dark-eyed boy breathing in and out, in and out of a brown sack. He reminded me of Pasha.

Two small boys wrestled each other amid the rubbish on the ground. Another boy ran a tiny toy car along a pipe. Someone passed a bottle to me. Without thinking, I drank.

'Agh,' I cried and spat the foul liquid in the dirt. Everyone laughed.

'He's a street baby,' someone said.

'I am not a baby,' I said. 'I am five years old, but in the spring, I will be six.'

'Not that kind of baby,' Vadim said. 'Street baby. That means you're new to the streets.'

'No, I'm not,' I said. To me, it seemed I had lived this way a very long time.

'How long?' a tall boy with no hair tossed out. 'How long have you been on the streets?'

I shrugged. 'There was no snow when he brought me to The City. The days were still warm sometimes and it was light all day. I would have gone to school soon.'

'Pah,' said the tall boy, lighting a cigarette. 'Only months. I've been here years.'

'Me too,' a girl chimed in.

'I've been here two years,' said another boy.

A very small boy – smaller than me – curled into a pile of dirty blankets and cried.

Candles flickered on top of the pipes, throwing shadows against the walls. The play-wrestling between the two boys turned into a fight.

'Why did you have to hit me in the head like that?' one screamed.

'I didn't mean to,' the other said.

'I hate you!' the hurt one cried.

I crept into a far corner with Little Mother, the puppies, Grandmother and Rip. Smoke and Lucky would not follow us beneath the earth. Little Mother watched the children nervously as she fed her hungry puppies.

The candlelight made the children look big and wild, their eyes and faces hollow.

'We'll go back to the Sisters of Mercy tomorrow,' I promised the dogs. 'At least for now, we're warm and we're not as hungry.'

*

Vadim stole. He stole from shops, he stole from passers-by, and he stole from other beggars and bums. He stole to feed himself and us, yes, but he also stole because he could.

'You have to steal,' Vadim said to me on a day the cold held us in a vice.

'I can't steal,' I said.

'I'll teach you to steal,' Vadim said. 'I am the King of Thieves in all of Russia!' And just to prove his point, he slipped behind a woman waiting for the bus, and eased something from the bag at her feet.

He tossed a book to me. 'Here,' he said. 'It's yours now.'

I thumbed through the small paperback book. There were no pictures and far too many words I could not read. It was of no use to me.

I made myself small as a mouse and crept over to the woman. Just as I slipped the book back into her bag, the bus rattled to a stop. The woman bent to pick up her bag – her bag with her book and my hand still clutching the book.

Her eyes widened.

I froze.

'Thief!' she cried. 'Dirty little thief!' Her great arm swung in an arc high over her head. Her black, shiny hand-

141

bag hovered in the air above my head. I cowered on the pavement, waiting for the sky to fall.

A hand grabbed the back of my neck and yanked me to my feet. 'Run!' Vadim commanded.

Chapter 25

SISTER OF MERCY

And we did. We ran and ran and ran, slipping and sliding on the ice-rutted sidewalks. Rip and Lucky ran behind us. We ran until our feet could run no more. We collapsed in a laughing, panting pile of boys and dogs.

'You are a crazy boy,' Vadim said, laughing. 'She could have killed you with that purse.'

My eyes streamed from the cold and the laughing and the words 'dirty thief'. I wiped at my eyes. 'She would have knocked my head off,' I said. 'If you hadn't saved me.'

'And your head would have rolled down the street, saying, "Oh, help me! I seem to have lost something!"'

A door creaked open. A voice called, 'Boys! You, boys, there. What—?'

Vadim was up and running before the voice finished.

As for me, something held me. I clutched Lucky's neck and squinted at the person standing next to a door with faded, outstretched angel wings.

'Are you a Sister of Mercy?' I asked.

'I am,' she said. 'I am the only one left. And you look like you're in need of some mercy.'

I shuffled my boots in the snow and held tighter to Lucky.

'Well, come on in, boy. I don't have all day.'

The inside of the House of the Sisters of Mercy was dark and cold and clenched. The dogs pressed close to my legs and whimpered.

The Sister grabbed me, her fingers digging in like claws. She turned me this way and that and felt my arms, my legs. 'There's nothing to him,' she muttered to herself. 'Nothing at all.' Then, 'How old are you, child?'

'I am five years old,' I said.

'Lord help us,' she said, 'they get younger and younger.' She sighed. 'I suppose there's no use asking if you have parents and where they are.'

I shook my head.

'I didn't think so. There never is.' She coughed. The cough rattled like rusty chains. '*Chto delat?* What should be done?' she said to herself.

'Well, first things first,' she said, and dragged me by the arm to the back of the House of the Sisters of Mercy.

A large metal bath squatted in the corner. 'Take everything off,' she said as she turned the taps.

A bath. I could barely remember the last time I'd had a bath.

I stripped off my jumper, my shirt and my trousers. The old newspapers I'd used to keep the cold out dropped like leaves to the floor. The pages from the book of fairy tales fluttered to the floor too. I pulled off the glorious boots Anya had given me and pulled out the wet newspapers stuffed in the toes.

The woman turned from the steaming bath. She snatched the hat from my head. 'Give me that lice nest,' she said, and threw it into the bin. Then she looked me over from my toes up to my bare head. 'A filthy little bag of bones,' she said. She pointed to the bath. 'In.' She handed me a brush and a hard bar of soap. 'Scrub,' she said.

I scrubbed.

'Pah, not like that.' She snatched the brush and soap from my hands and scrubbed. She scrubbed like she was trying to remove my skin, my muscles, my bones and all the dirt from the streets of The City.

'Ow!' I cried. The dogs whimpered from the doorway.

'Hold still, child,' she said. The water turned black. The Sister poked and prodded in my ears. 'There's enough dirt in there to grow potatoes,' she grumbled. When she turned to grab the soap bar that had slipped from her hand, I poked a finger in my ear. Potatoes?

Then she attacked my hair and my head. 'Just like I thought,' she snapped. 'Lice.' She poured a bottle of foul-smelling something all over my head and scrubbed it into my hair with her claws.

'Ow!' I cried again. Lucky growled from the doorway.

'Stop being a baby,' she said.

Finally, she grabbed a threadbare towel. 'Out,' she commanded.

I stood wet, shivering and naked in the freezing room on the cold cement floor.

'Dry off,' she said. 'I'll find some clothes for you, although Lord knows if I have anything small enough.'

Rip and Lucky inched over and sniffed my legs and hands. 'It is me,' I said to them, scratching their heads. Lucky's brown eyes were doubtful; Rip licked the water dripping down my legs. I laughed and scooted away from him. Rip snatched the corner of the towel and pulled, shaking his shaggy head back and forth. We played tug of war, with Rip pulling and me sliding across the wet, cold floor and Lucky barking.

'Here now, what's this nonsense?' the Sister snapped.

I froze. Rip dropped the corner of the towel. Lucky cowered under the woman's steel-grey eyes. 'I didn't just break my back over that bathtub to have you get all filthy again from those flea-bitten mongrels.'

'I'm sorry,' I whispered.

'Here.' The Sister thrust an armful of clothes at me. 'They're too big, but it's the best I could do.'

The clothes were indeed too big, but they were clean and all the holes were patched. 'Spasibo, Sister,' I said.

'You're welcome,' she said. 'And I have a proper hat, coat and gloves for you. I'm afraid, though,' she said with a wheezy sigh, 'I have no shoes that will fit you.'

'That's OK,' I said. 'Anya gave me those boots. They are glorious boots for a pathetic little boy.'

The woman frowned. 'Who's Anya? I thought you said you have no family.'

'My friend,' I said. 'Anya is my friend. And she gave me the boots.'

The Sister pulled a pair of shiny scissors from her big apron pocket. She pointed them at a stool. 'Sit.'

I sat.

She ran a comb none too gently through my hair. 'What a mess,' she muttered. I felt the cold metal of the scissors press against my neck. Snip snip. Hair fell around

147

my shoulders and onto the floor like ashes. Comb comb, snip snip.

Finally she stopped. She tilted her head to one side. 'Well, at least you don't look like a walking bundle of sticks and rags now.'

I ran my hand over the stubble and sores and bumps of my head.

She tilted her head to the other side and laughed. 'Actually, boy, you look a bit like a plucked chicken, but I don't suppose they'll care.'

I hopped off the stool and ran my hand over Rip's wiry fur. 'No, the dogs don't care,' I said. 'Put your boots on and let's find you a coat and hat before they come,' she said.

A coat. Oh, the luxury of a coat! 'You don't have to give me a hat,' I said. 'I have a hat.'

'Pah,' the Sister said, coughing. 'What you *had* was a vermin-infested rat's nest.'

The Sister pawed through a box of clothes. 'Too big,' she'd say. Or, 'I wouldn't give this to a *bomzhi*.'

My stomach rumbled. 'Do you have any food?' I asked.

She stood and rubbed the small of her back. 'Perhaps a biscuit or two.' She shuffled over to a tin on a shelf. She handed it to me. 'My old fingers can't open this lid.'

I pried open the tin lid. Inside, resting on a napkin, lay two dusty biscuits. I popped one in my mouth and divided the other between Rip and Lucky.

'What are you doing?' the Sister said, snatching the tin from my hands. 'Giving perfectly good food to dogs?'

The stale biscuit stuck in my throat. 'Sorry,' I said. 'They are hungry too.'

She threw a coat and hat to me. 'Try those on,' she said.

The coat came well below my knees and the sleeves flapped at the end of my arms like useless wings. But still, it was a coat and it was wonderful in its coatness. I stuffed the pages from my fairy-tale book into the big pockets.

I smiled up at the Sister. She sighed and coughed. 'It's the best I can do.'

I heard a sharp bark outside, beyond the door – Smoke's bark. My heart leapt. I hadn't seen Smoke for two days. Lucky yipped and pawed at the door. Rip danced in frantic circles.

'I have to go,' I said.

'Wait,' the Sister commanded. 'They'll be here any minute.'

'But they *are* here,' I said. 'Smoke is waiting for us.'

I threw open the door with the faded feather wings. On the other side stood the raised Fist of God. The Fist was attached to a long grey coat and an even greyer woman. 'What took you so long?' the Sister snapped.

Chapter 26

BETRAYAL

'Is this the boy to be taken?' Water-coloured eyes raked over me from behind glasses as thick as river ice.

The Sister clamped her hand on my shoulder. Fingers too old to pry open a tin lid dug into my skin through the new shirt, jumper and coat. 'Yes,' she said. 'He says he has no family. From the looks of him, he's been on the streets a long time.'

I squirmed under the iron grip of the Sister. 'What do you mean, taken?'

The Sister ignored me. She and the Grey Woman, the woman with the Fist of God, passed words back and forth over my head: 'homeless,' 'filthy,' 'wild.'

I squirmed and passed questions up to them: 'Why?' 'Where?' But once again, I had become invisible.

The Sister shoved me into the folds of the greasy grey coat. 'The orphanage is the best place for him.'

Orphanage! The word shot through my heart and down to my legs. It gathered like a great coil in my stomach and sprung loose with the word, 'No!'

I wrenched away from the Grey Woman and the Sister and stumbled headlong into the street.

'Grab him!' the Grey Woman barked. Hands I had not seen reached down and pulled me to my feet. I screamed and kicked and cried, 'No! No!'

The hands clutched and pinned and, finally, slapped me to the ground. A million stars exploded in front of my eyes. 'Don't hurt him!' the Sister called from the doorway. 'He's not a criminal.'

The Fist of God wrenched me to my feet and shook me. 'He needs to learn.'

I howled in pain.

Something sailed through the air, over my shoulder. Teeth clamped down on the Fist of God. The Grey Woman shrieked. Smoke knocked her to the ground. Lucky and Rip growled and snapped at the man with the hands I had not seen.

'Get this mad dog off me!' the Gray Woman cried.

'Smoke,' I called. 'Let's go!'

With a final snap and snarl, Smoke and Rip and Lucky ran with me down Petrovsky Boulevard, away from the Sister of Mercy and the Fist of God, the long arms of my coat sleeves flapping like wings.

We ran until we could no longer hear their words – *Get him! Come back!* – chasing us down the street.

We skidded to a stop near the entrance to the world beneath the earth. Here we would be safe and warm and away from the Sister of Mercy and the Fist of God and the word 'orphanage'.

Perhaps Vadim had found food to share.

'Just let me get a little bit to eat and then we'll get Vadim to help us find some more food,' I said to the dogs as we turned the street corner. 'I know the puppies are—' I stopped dead in my tracks. Running towards us, eyes huge with fright and desperation, were Little Mother and Grandmother. Little Mother jumped against my legs, nearly knocking me to the ground, crying piteously; Grandmother panted and moaned.

'What?' I asked. 'What is it? Where are the puppies?'

Little Mother tugged at the bottom of my too-big coat, pulling me towards the opening that led to the underground.

I scrambled behind her into the dark underworld. Candlelight flickered off the grimy walls and the network of pipes. Little Mother led me over to the corner where she and the puppies stayed with Grandmother. The nest of rags and newspapers was empty.

'They have to be here,' I said. I looked behind every crate, under blankets and rugs, beneath piles of rubbish the children had piled against the walls. Nothing. No puppies.

I shook the boy breathing in and out of a brown paper bag. 'Where are the puppies?' His sunken eyes swam to my face and then slid away.

I scrambled over to a boy and girl sleeping beneath a rug. 'Where are the puppies?' I said, pulling at the rug. Empty brown bottles rolled from beneath it.

The girl opened her eyes. She blinked slowly. 'What d'you want?'

'The puppies,' I said, pointing to the corner. 'The puppies are gone. Where are they?'

The girl yawned. 'Oh, that. Vadim took them.'

'He what?'

'You heard me. He took them.' She pulled the rug up to her ears.

I yanked the rug down. 'Why? Where did he take them?'

The girl slapped my hand away. 'He took them because, as everybody knows, you can make more money begging with puppies than alone. As for where, I have no idea.'

She rolled over against the boy. I buried my head in my hands. 'No,' I moaned. Little Mother licked my fingers.

'Vadim said he might try to sell the puppies,' the girl said from beneath the rug.

My head snapped up. 'What?'

'Sure,' she said, her voice slipping away into dreams. 'They would bring good money.'

I ran.

The dogs and I ran up and down streets, darting in and out of traffic, and across the still, frozen squares. We checked the doorways and heat grates I knew Vadim favoured. We ran and ran until the snot and tears were frozen parts of my face; we ran until Grandmother could run no more.

I slumped against a crumbling brick building. The light was already fading from the day. The dogs formed a half-moon around me, waiting for answers.

I beat my fists against my head. 'Stupid, stupid, pathetic little boy. How could I have been so stupid!' Grandmother leaned against my leg and sighed.

I looked into the eyes of the dogs and finally locked my gaze with Smoke. 'Where?' I said. 'Where would Vadim take them?'

I swam in the warm amber of Smoke's eyes, the flecks of gold and the flecks of night. His eyes said he believed

I was not a stupid, pathetic little boy. I was Sobachonok, Dog Boy. Those same eyes that commanded me to follow him onto the train and to the home of the pack. The eyes that led me away from the train station and—

'That's it!' I cried, springing to my feet. 'Come on!'

I ran as fast as I have ever run to the train station. I raced down the stairs two at a time, skidding on the marble floor, Rip, Little Mother and Grandmother streaming behind me, and Smoke and Lucky ahead weaving in and out of the coats and legs and boots and arms and bags and eyes that did not see us.

Smoke stopped. Lucky skidded into Smoke. Smoke cocked his head to one side. I stopped and tried my best to hear above the crowds coming and going and the sigh and whistle and hum of the trains.

And then I heard it – a young boy's voice further down the long hallway calling, 'Puppies! Puppies for sale!'

I ran and pushed my way through the crowds until we found Vadim. There he was, sitting at the feet of a statue, the puppies sleeping in his lap. Little Mother yelped with joy and began sniffing her puppies all over.

'What do you think you're doing?' I screamed.

Vadim shrugged and scratched at a sore by his mouth. 'I just thought I'd get a little more money… And, besides, they'd be better off in someone's home than starving on the streets with you.'

I snatched the puppies from his lap. They whimpered in my arms.

'They need to be with their mother,' I snapped. 'They need her.'

Vadim sprang to his feet. He pushed his face close to mine and growled, 'What good do mothers do, Dog Boy? Tell me that.' His face was red and pitted with pain. 'Do you see our mothers here?' he demanded. 'Do you see anyone here taking care of us?'

I wrapped the puppies under my coat. 'I thought you were my friend.'

'We can't afford to have friends out here on the streets, you stupid little kid,' he said. 'We can only look after ourselves.' He shoved me backwards. Smoke and Lucky stepped towards him and growled.

Vadim threw up his hands. 'You're crazy,' he said. 'You with these dogs.'

He pushed through the crowds of people, away from us. Then he stopped and shouted, 'You'll never make it, Sobachonok. The winter will get you, or the gangs, or the militsiya, but you won't make it.'

And then he was gone, lost amid a forest of legs.

I slumped to the floor and took the puppies from my coat. The dogs hovered around us, sniffing and nuzzling and licking.

I leaned my head back against the cold wall. The lights dripping like ice shone above us, each grand cluster marching in a straight line down the long hallway of the train station. I closed my eyes against the brightness.

Chapter 27

THE COLD

Where could I go now? Our Glass House was burned to the ground. I could not go back with the children beneath The City, I could not go back to the Sister of Mercy. I could not trust any of them.

'What do we do?' I asked Smoke. Smoke sighed and laid his head across his paws. All of us were huddled in a far corner of the train station. We had gone above ground earlier to buy food. The world above was cold, so very cold. The air cracked inside my lungs every time I breathed in. We saw few other children and even fewer dogs. The small, lifeless bodies of frozen birds littered the pavements. Before I could stop them, Rip and Lucky snapped up the birds and swallowed them whole.

'Perhaps we can stay here in the train station,' I said. 'Just for a while. Surely the police wouldn't force us out into this cold.'

And so we stayed for a time. We left the station only to buy food. Even Smoke, who normally went his own way, stayed close and slept. The cold marble floor was hard on Grandmother's old bones. She limped and had trouble getting up from her sleep. So during the day, I gave her my coat to sleep on. It was not so cold in the train station during the day, and besides, I was a young boy and she was an old babushka.

There were other people who came to the station for money. No children, but grown bomzhi. One old man came dressed every day in a tired suit and a big fur shapka on his head. Pinned to his skinny chest were grand ribbons and medals. In his hand he clutched a small tin.

'Did you get those ribbons for running the fastest?' I asked.

Clink! A hand dropped a coin in the tin held by the man of the ribbons and medals.

The old man glared down at me and did not answer.

'I have never been given a ribbon or a medal, but I can run very fast,' I bragged.

Another hand stuffed a folded ruble in the tin. 'Spasibo, sir,' said the man of the ribbons and medals.

'My mother taught me to always say thank you too,' I said, nodding. 'Do you still have a mother?' I asked the man.

Still, he would not look at me, he would not answer.

I stroked Lucky's ears. 'I had a mother,' I said. 'I have not seen her in a long time – since the leaves were just beginning to fall. I am starting to forget her.'

The old man of the ribbons and medals glanced down at me. He rubbed a dirty finger behind his glasses. 'Chto delat? What is to be done?' he said with a sigh.

He took the folded ruble from the tin and handed it to me. Then, without a word, he walked down the long hallway, up the stairs, and to the world beyond.

Days passed but the bitter cold did not. It was so cold, the great river that wound this way and that through The City froze solid. It was too cold to snow, I heard people in the shops say. 'I did not think such a thing was possible,' I said to Little Mother as she nursed her growing puppies. The cold was endless, like winter in the Snow Queen's eyes.

I began dreading my trips above ground for all the frozen bodies now lying in gutters and next to the heat grates: not just birds now but cats and dogs and puppies. One day I saw a crowd gathered around a spot on the pavement. I pushed my head through the forest of legs. There, curled next to a doorway on a piece of cardboard, was a small girl. She could have been just taking a nap, resting after playing in the snow at the park. But her face was grey and her lips were blue and her eyes with the dark half-moons beneath stared at nothing. A great sadness swept over me. The Snow Queen had stolen her away in sleep. Where was God, where were the angels and the saints when this girl lost her way?

A siren wailed in the distance. Rip, Lucky and Smoke threw back their heads and howled a sad, sad song of goodbye to the frozen girl.

I thought of Vadim's words: 'You'll never make it, Sobachonok. The winter will get you, or the gangs, or the militsiya, but you won't make it.'

Chapter 28

THE GANGS

One morning, I awoke to a beautiful sound filling the train station. It was not the hiss and whirr of the train track, or the whistle of an approaching train. It was not the whoosh of the train doors opening and closing or the click click of boot heels on the marble floors. This sound brought to mind summer and painted wooden horses going up and down and round and round in a circle, and the circuses I had seen on TV. This sound soared and swooped and dipped like swallows.

I jumped to my feet and clapped my hands. 'Do you hear it?' I asked the dogs. 'Music!' Lucky yawned and wagged his tail. The dogs and I followed the sound.

The maker of the music was a man with a long white beard. Against his chest he held a box with yellowed piano keys and shiny buttons. One hand swept across the keys while the other hand pushed the buttons. All the while, his arms squeezed the box in and out. It breathed, the box did, in great sighing, singing gulps like a dragon without fire.

'What is it?' I asked the man.

He turned his face in my direction but looked past me. 'It is an accordion,' he said to the air beside me.

'I think the accordion is the most beautiful sound on earth,' I declared. The man smiled and nodded and played.

I sat at the feet of this man and listened. I rocked and smiled and sometimes even danced. The dogs yipped. Lucky tried to sing along.

And always the clink clink of money in his tin.

At the end of the day, the Man of the Accordion folded his stool and put the money from the tin into a small leather bag.

'Where are you, boy?' he asked, his milk-coloured eyes passing over me.

I laughed. 'Why, I am right here.'

He gave me a handful of rubles. 'You brought me luck today.'

'Thank you very much!' I had not seen so much money in a long time.

The Man of the Accordion unfolded a long white cane with a red tip. 'You're most welcome, young man.'

He slung his accordion over his shoulder and tap tapped his way down the long hallway to the stairs.

Again he was there the next day, and the day after, and the day after that. And always, I sat with him and listened to his music.

'Good morning,' I would say to him as he unfolded his stool and folded his long white cane.

'Good morning to you too, my young friend,' he would say, smiling in the general direction of my face.

Halfway through his day of playing, he would hand me a wad of rubles and say, 'We need food and drink if we are to play and dance the rest of the day. Do you think someone is selling pirogi today?'

Up the stairs the dogs and I would dash in search of pirogi. I liked my pie filled with cheese. The old Man of the Accordion preferred his stuffed with potatoes. After the second day, he gave me an extra coin and said, 'The dogs need lunch too.'

The days passed now with music and dancing and hot pirogi. I did not feel bad taking some of the old man's money at the end of every day. He said I brought him luck. 'Who can resist an old blind man and a young boy with dogs?' he said, as I walked him up the stairs to the world above.

That night, the wind was sharp as a knife, but it had warmed up enough to snow. 'Ah,' said the old man. 'Perhaps that killing cold has finally broken.'

I nodded.

His hand gripped my shoulder. 'But what about you, my young friend? Where do you go at night?'

'Go?'

'Do you have a home?'

'This is my home,' I said. 'Mine and the dogs.'

He sighed like his accordion. 'I have heard of children like you – *bezprizorniki* – the neglected ones. It is Russia's dark shame.'

I shrugged. 'We are warm, the dogs and I, and not as hungry thanks to you.'

The old man shook his head, his long white beard waggling. 'You must be careful, my friend. It is not safe for a young boy like you. There are gangs of teenagers just looking for someone weaker to prey upon.' He shook his head again. 'Very bad, these boys. They are like wolves.'

I had seen these gangs of boys the old man talked about. They wore chains and leather and their hair rose in impossible ways. From time to time, they would approach me, flinging hard, nasty words in my face. If I had spoken those words, my mother would have slapped me. But I was not afraid of these gangs: the dogs never let them get close.

I touched the old man's hand. 'Don't worry. The dogs watch over me.'

Two days later, I once again searched for the best pirogi for me and the Man of the Accordion, and meat for the dogs. The day was unaccountably mild. The brutal fist of winter had opened. The wind blew warm, soft air from the sea; the frozen branches of the sleeping birch and fir trees relaxed and dripped. Shop owners stood outside in the sun and talked.

I will admit, we were gone longer than we should have been. Even the dogs turned their faces up to the sun. 'We should bring Grandmother and Little Mother and the puppies up here to enjoy the warmth and the fresh air,' I said to Smoke and Lucky.

Reluctantly, I took the steps down and down into the train station. Lucky and Smoke refused to leave their sunny spot on the pavement. 'I'll be back with the others soon,' I called to them.

I had not gone far down the long hallway when I heard a sound that turned my blood to ice: the frantic barking of Grandmother and Little Mother. I dropped the package of food and sprinted down the hallway.

The barking of the dogs mixed with cries of 'Leave me alone! Leave me alone!'

The sight that greeted me was this: the Man of the Accordion surrounded by four skinny, leather-clad things – like a gang of crows – with chains and impossible hair. At the feet of the old man were a growling, snarling, shivering Grandmother and Little Mother trying their best to protect him and the puppies.

The gang shoved the old man off his stool. The tin with the coins and the rubles clinked to the floor. One of the boys swooped in and scooped up the money.

'No!' cried the old man. 'How can you steal from an old blind man?'

'Get the accordion,' the tallest of the Crow Boys commanded.

Grandmother stood over the old man, growling and snapping at the boys.

A boot-clad foot flew out and kicked Grandmother in the side, sending her skidding across the floor.

The sight unfroze me. 'No!' I screamed.

I flew at the Crow Boys with all my might. I whirled and spat and kicked and punched. 'Leave them alone!' I cried.

One of the boys punched me in the face. A warm,

coppery taste filled my mouth. I spat out a tooth.

'Don't hurt them,' the old man pleaded.

The gang turned their attention back to the old man and his accordion. The tallest of the Crows smacked the old man in the face and grabbed the strap of the beautiful accordion. 'Give it to me,' the boy snarled.

I rushed at the boy and slammed into the back of his knees. He folded in half. A hand grabbed the back of my coat and flung me aside like rubbish. I grabbed a long, pencil-thin leg and bit as hard as I could. Little Mother bit the other leg.

'Get off me!' the voice above the legs cried. He flung first Little Mother, then me against the wall. Little Mother let out a pitiful scream. I tried to rise, I tried to call to her, but I could not breathe. It was as if, like the old man's accordion, all the air had been squeezed out of me.

And then I heard two things: the faraway tweet tweet! of a policeman's whistle, and the roar of angry dogs. Then I heard the frantic cries of the Crows. 'Help!' 'What the—?' 'Get them off me!'

I pushed myself up on one elbow. Smoke and Lucky tore and lunged at the boys. Blood speckled and smeared the floor. Even though they were only two dogs, they fought like twenty.

I crawled over to Little Mother and Grandmother, who cowered over the puppies.

The *tweet tweet* of the militsiya's whistle grew closer.

A crowd had formed around the boys and the Man of the Accordion.

Someone helped the old man up from the floor. Blood streaked his white beard. 'They saved me,' the old man said, trembling. 'The boy and the dogs.' Even though they could not see, his milky eyes searched for me anyway.

The policeman trotted up to the crowd and blew his whistle one last time. 'What's going on here?' he barked. His tall black boots shone like black mirrors.

I wanted to take the old man's hand and tell him I was OK and that the dogs had protected his beautiful music and us. But I was no longer a stupid little boy. I knew the policeman would not help me. The police meant the orphanage or worse. The policeman would take me away from the only family I had.

Quietly, while the crowd helped the old man, and while the policeman gathered up the Crow Boys, the dogs and I slipped into a bathroom and hid.

I checked the dogs over for wounds. Grandmother was very sore on her side and would limp the rest of her life. Little Mother had a lump the size of a small potato on the side of her head. The puppies licked and licked her ear and her face.

I slumped against the cold tile wall and cried myself to sleep.

When I woke, I washed the blood from my face and hair. I poked my tongue in the empty space where my tooth had been. When I was a little boy living with my mother, I would have saved the tooth under my pillow for the tooth fairy. But I was no longer a little boy. I did not believe in fairies.

It was unusually quiet on the train platforms. I had no idea if it was day or night or had become day again. I walked back over to the place where the old man with the snow-white beard had played his accordion. He was not there, but the bloodstains were.

I knew then, he would not be back.

Rip sniffed behind a trash bin near the bloodstains. He looked at me, wagged his little tail, and yipped his come-and-see yip.

'What is it now, Rip?' I asked, kneeling beside him. And then I saw it: a small white tooth glowed like a pearl in the train-station light. My baby tooth.

I picked up the tooth. 'I should throw it away,' I said to Rip. 'It is only a stupid baby tooth.'

Instead, I dropped it in my pocket and ran my thumb over its bumpy hardness.

A train eased to a stop. Smoke looked up at me. I looked at Smoke.

The train doors slid open. I lifted the puppies into my arms. 'Let's go,' I said.

Chapter 29

THE TRAINS

And so in this way, and for the rest of that long winter, the trains became our home. And because the trains were our home, so The City was our home.

The trains were warm and the trains were mostly safe. We learned we were most invisible when we rode them late at night and early in the mornings. The people who rode the trains at those ghost hours mostly slept or were too drunk to care about a small, dirty boy and his seven dogs.

We learned the best stops to find food. At this stop, the rubbish bins in the station were rarely emptied. At that stop, the butcher put out meat scraps and bones in the alley for the dogs. A kind grocer at a stop on the west side of The City saved old bread and expired tins of fish for me.

And once a month, in the tumbledown buildings near the rail tracks, the Christian Ladies came with food and clothes and, sometimes, doctors. Homeless children crept and ran and swaggered from every direction for a bowl of kasha or shchi – made with only cabbage and a thin broth – and hunks of bread.

The Christian Ladies set up in the empty peasant market. 'Come, children,' they would call. And come they did.

They pushed and shoved and elbowed their way to the pots of porridge and soup and the loaves of bread. The dogs and I watched. When the crowd thinned and the children were busy eating, I took my turn. I held out a bowl and said, 'Please,' and when I returned my bowl, I said, 'Thank you.'

The Christian Lady would smile and take my bowl. 'What a good boy you are, so polite.'

I smiled.

'What's your name?' the Christian Lady would ask.

And always I would reply, 'My name is Dog Boy.'

One time as I sat with the dogs atop a heap of concrete and bricks eating a piece of bread, I thought I spotted the dark hair and loose legs of Pasha.

I leapt to my feet and scrambled to the ground. 'Pasha!' I cried, pulling on the arm of the dark-haired boy waiting for a bowl of soup.

The boy turned his head and looked down at me.

The eyes were dark like Pasha's and tilted up at the corners, like Pasha's.

'It's me,' I said, plucking at his sleeve. 'Remember? Leningradsky Station?'

But although the eyes may have been Pasha's, what lived behind them was not. Because the place behind the eyes was dead. Behind the eyes lived only a ghost.

My first winter with the pack passed in this way. The trains rocked me to sleep, and the trains showed me the world. And always, the dogs loved and protected me.

I no longer looked for a red coat. I knew I would never see her again.

Now when I read the stories from the few torn pages of my book of fairy tales, I heard only my voice – the voice of Sobachonok – not the sound of my mother's voice. The dogs lay close to me as I read to them of witches and snow queens and the magic firebird. Grandmother's white head rested on my knee, Rip sprawled half on and half off my lap, and Little Mother, Lucky and the puppies lay close by. Smoke dozed always a little apart from the rest, watchful, even in sleep, for trouble.

On through the night, and the months, and the winter we travelled with the train, until one day it was spring.

Chapter 30

SPRING

The hand of The City opened.

Once again, shopkeepers stood outside their shop-fronts talking and smoking. Once again the wooden stalls outside the train stations filled with people selling everything: food, drink, newspapers, books, cheap wooden dolls nesting one inside the other, shiny metal replicas of St Basil's church, boxes of cigarettes.

The people coming and going in the train stations and on the pavements slowed long enough to drop coins in this boy's outstretched hand. And when I said, 'Spasibo,' they sometimes smiled.

Once again, workers in office buildings took their lunch to the squares and the parks. They turned their faces to the sun and closed their eyes.

This brought a new trick from Lucky. He stole. The first time I saw him do this was on a warm day. The trees in the small square were tipped with the youngest of green. The snow was all but gone, leaving behind many interesting things in the small piles of rubbish. I was searching with great interest through one of these piles when the corner of my eye caught sight of Lucky. He crept on his belly up behind a man with his paste-white face turned to the glorious sun and his eyes closed in contentment. At his feet a brown bag of lunch waited to be eaten.

Slowly, slowly Lucky crept towards the bag. I held my breath as he stretched his neck as far as it would go. He snatched the bag with great tenderness. Slowly, quietly backwards he crept with the bag while the man continued to worship the sun. When Lucky and the bag were clear of the man, he trotted over to us, head and bag held high, tail wagging. He dropped the bag at my feet.

'Lucky,' I scolded. 'We do not steal.' I said this even as I unfolded the top of the bag.

We moved out of sight of the man – still enjoying the sun – and I divided up the contents of the bag. I scratched Lucky's ear. 'I'm not mad at you. Your mother didn't tell you it's wrong to steal.'

I gasped. There, at the bottom of the bag, glowing like the sun setting in the winter sky, was an orange.

I held the orange under my nose and drank in the

wonderful smell of its orangeness. 'Oh, he must be a very rich man,' I said to the dogs. They sniffed the orange and turned back to their bread. I smiled. The orange would be just for me. I had eaten an orange only once or twice in my life. This one, I would make last for many days.

I was no longer content to ride the trains, and neither were the dogs. Smoke disappeared for longer and longer periods of time, as he had before. Grandmother spent long hours on the sun-warmed pavements, sleeping. Little Mother did her best to keep track of the puppies, whose long legs carried them further than she liked. Lucky and Rip made new friends of all the dogs on the streets after the long winter.

And like the dogs who lived on the streets, with each passing day, more and more homeless children emerged from wherever they had been during that winter. They emerged pale and thin and hungry for whatever they had not had.

As the days grew longer, packs of older children roamed the streets looking for those made weak by the long winter. I watched a pack of younger children steal the shoes and coat and hat from another child sleeping in a doorway. I watched a snarling pack of older boys torment a drunken man cowering in a bus shelter. It was not enough for them to steal what little money he had and to steal his bottle of vodka; they also taunted him.

'You crazy pig!' they cried. One boy knocked the drunkard in the head with a stick. 'You stupid fool,' another boy sneered. He kicked the drunken man in the bottom as he tried to stumble away from the pack of boys. The man fell to his knees. The boys descended on him like vultures.

Grandmother and Rip pressed against my knees and whimpered. We turned and walked away from the cruel, cruel laughter of the boys. I rubbed my thumb over and over the edges of the tooth in my pocket.

'I don't know why humans act the way they do,' I said that night to the dogs. We were all curled together in the warmth of the cellar beneath an abandoned, crumbling church. Little Mother had found this place and brought us here.

'Sometimes they are cold and heartless like the Snow Queen. Sometimes they are full of ugliness and hunger like Baba Yaga.'

Little Mother scrubbed my hand with her tongue, one paw pinning the hand to the ground. I pulled a small insect from my hair, no bigger than a grain of rice. I crushed it between my fingers. 'Too many are like the Little Match Girl – lonely and starving.'

Lucky rolled onto his back, waiting for a scratch. 'Ah, Lucky, my thief,' I said with a smile. 'Why should I scratch your belly when you steal?'

He had a new trick to steal food. He picked one particular person from the crowd leaving the food stalls with their lunch packet. He followed them a short distance across the stone square. Then he would let out a loud woof. The lunch packet would fall to the ground from the startled person and, before they even knew what had happened, Lucky snatched up the food and ran. Sometimes he shared with us, and sometimes he did not.

Mostly he shared. I scratched his belly.

The rains of spring came and with them, hunger. People no longer ate their lunch in the squares and parks. The rain and wind pushed the people too quickly down the pavements to stop and give a small begging boy a few coins so he could eat. I retreated to the stations, where it was always daytime and dry, and the people coming and going to and from the trains were not in such a hurry to go out in the world. Coins clinked in my hand, and bread and sausages filled our bellies.

But, of course, soon rain also drove the children from the streets and the doorways and their homes of cardboard to the world below. They begged, they stole, they fought and they formed their own packs for protection against the gangs of older boys and against the militsiya.

And as always, the dogs and I watched from the shadows and from the corners and from behind gleaming statues of brave men.

It was on one of these rain-filled days in the Kitay-Gorod underground station that I heard a familiar voice as I rooted through an overflowing bin. 'That little cockroach is barely big enough to do his work.'

I turned round and looked into the silver-grey eyes of Rudy. There he stood, squinting at me through a cloud of smoke, cigarette dangling from his lip. He still wore the tattered policeman's jacket and the skinny black trousers. His face looked thinner. A dark bruise sprawled the length of his jaw.

The smallest finger of warmth touched his ice-cold eyes. 'Well, look who we have here. It's the little circus mouse.'

I wiped my hands on my trousers. 'Hi, Rudy.'

He looked me up and down as he walked around me in a slow circle. 'What dead bum did you steal those clothes from?'

'I got them from the Christian Ladies,' I said.

'Ah,' he said, flicking his cigarette onto the floor and crushing it beneath the heel of his boot. 'God bless the Christian Ladies. They fill your belly and steal your soul.'

'Where's Tanya?' I asked, looking past him. Rarely was there a Rudy without a Tanya.

He ran a dirty hand through his hair. 'Gone. She is gone.'

A chill ran through me. I had heard those words before.

'Is she dead?' I asked, rubbing the tooth in my pocket. Yes, there had been a scream, there had been a sticky, red spot on the floor that no amount of scrubbing could—

'She might as well be,' Rudy said, his voice heavy and soft. 'They took her away to an orphanage somewhere outside the city.'

Rudy stared at the pictures made of tiny square tiles on the walls. 'I tried to find her, you know. I asked around, even took a bus to a place I heard about north of the city, but…'

'Perhaps she will come back, now that it is spring,' I said. 'And she'll have new clothes and she'll have had good food to eat, and—'

A slap to my face sent me stumbling backwards against the rubbish bin.

'Stupid kid,' Rudy growled. 'Don't you know anything?' He grabbed me by my coat and shook me.

'The orphanages are surrounded by fences that will cut you to pieces if you try to get in or out. They work you like a dog and beat you and feed you next to nothing. The orphanages eat you alive.'

I gasped. 'Like Baba Yaga.'

Rudy raised his hand. I backed away to avoid another slap.

But instead, he ran his hand over his bruised face. 'Yeah, kid, like Baba Yaga.'

It made me sad to think of kind Tanya trapped in the witch's house surrounded by a fence made of bones and grinning skulls.

Rudy put his face back together in a cold, hard mask. 'Anyway, she is gone and you should be too.'

'Why?' I asked.

'You need to get far away, kid. You need to get out of the train stations.'

'Why?'

He grabbed me again and shook me. 'Because I said so, that's why. Isn't that enough?'

I shook my head.

He pushed his face close to mine. His breath was like fire and smoke. 'Listen to me,' he hissed. 'The gangs are taking over the streets and the stations. They will crush little cockroaches like you beneath their boots. Do you understand?'

I tried to swallow beneath his clenched fist. 'But the dogs will protect me.'

Rudy glanced at old Grandmother sleeping in the corner, the puppies curled against her belly. 'I will only tell you this once: Get. Out. If I see you again, I won't know you.'

Rudy and I stared at each other for a long moment. 'What about Pasha and Yula?' I whispered.

'Yula is dead,' Rudy said. 'And Pasha is a ghost.'

'But—'

A high whistle echoed from the station entrance. A voice called out, 'Hey, Rudy!'

Rudy's head jerked up, his face went white then red. Three tall boys draped in chains and black, their hair spiked like iron teeth, sauntered towards us. Crow Boys.

Rudy shoved me hard to the floor. 'I told you, get out of our train station, you little cockroach!'

The boys in black were getting closer. I could hear them laughing and spitting.

Rudy grabbed my hand and jerked me to my feet, pressing something into the palm of my hand. In a low voice he hissed, 'Run.' Then he yelled, 'You and those stupid dogs get the hell out of here.'

I woke the puppies and Grandmother and ran as fast as I could down the long hallway, with Grandmother panting at my heels. As we raced up the stairs, I heard laughter and a voice calling, 'Run, cockroach, run!'

We ran all the way to the small park with the duck pond where Little Mother and Rip liked to hunt. They raced over to greet us. Little Mother sniffed the puppies from nose to tail; Rip yipped and licked my face as I stood panting, my heart banging in my chest. Rip nudged the fingers of my closed fist. I opened my hand, the hand Rudy had pressed something into. A wad of damp rubles unfolded in my palm.

Poor Grandmother limped to my side and lay down with a groan. Her back legs quivered.

'We'll rest here,' I said to the dogs, 'and wait for Lucky and Smoke. I'll get us some food thanks to Rudy. Then we'll go back to the church cellar. We'll be safe there.'

Chapter 31

BURIED ALIVE

Days of rain passed in the damp dark, below the broken-down church Little Mother had found for us the week before. Grandmother coughed and shivered. The puppies cried and squabbled. They pestered Little Mother endlessly to nurse, even though they were too big for that now. The rain and the damp dark made her forget she was their mother, because she snapped and snarled and, finally, stalked out into the rain. When the puppies tried to follow, she rounded on them viciously. They ran back to me, their tails tucked between trembling legs.

'She'll be back,' I said as I stroked them. But would she?

Then one day, when I didn't think any of us could bear the rain and the dark any longer, the sun came out. We woke to wide bars of light striping the muddy floor. We woke to the sound of birds rather than rain.

Someone woofed at the entrance of our den. Lucky bounded down the heaps of rubble, wagging his tail.

Woof!

What could we do but follow him up into the sun?

We squinted against the first strong light in many days. The air smelled alive and green.

Rip and Lucky dashed back and forth, chasing each other through the shimmering puddles. Little Mother wagged her tail for the first time in weeks and allowed the puppies to nip her delicate feet. Grandmother found a sunny dry spot and stretched long in the warmth. Even the ever-serious Smoke joined in a game of catch. We ran, the dogs and I, in widening circles through the bare bones of the crumbling church. We ran and ran through the weeded land rambling next to the old building. Bits of coloured glass glittered in the sun. 'You can't catch me!' I called to Lucky. 'You can't catch me now!'

Suddenly, the toe of my boot caught on something. I rose into the air. My arms and legs span like pinwheels. I landed with a thud on my back.

Rip and Lucky rushed to my side and licked my face and hands. 'I'm OK,' I said, sitting up. Smoke pawed at something beneath the wet weeds and leaves.

I crawled over to him. 'What are you looking for?'

Smoke pawed a mat of leaves and sticks aside. A tiny grey face stared up at us.

'Oh!' Smoke and I jumped back. Then we inched forward to get a better look.

I touched the face. It was hard and cold. I brushed the rest of the mat away. A stone slab slumped into the wet ground. The still face stared out from the middle of the slab. I traced the words carved into the stone with my finger. 'I can't read most of this,' I said to Smoke and Lucky and Rip, who were gathered at my side, staring and sniffing at the discovery.

I touched one word. '"Loved",' it says.' I touched another word. 'This one says "death".' I ran a finger along a trail beneath the stone face. 'These are dates. I think they are 1932 and 1975.' Heaviness settled in my stomach. Babushka Ina. She too had a stone slab with her dates on it. It had cost every ruble my mother had.

I stood and looked around. Stone markers of all sizes surrounded us. Some were only humps beneath the mouldering leaves; others rose above the matted earth, furred by moss and lichen.

'This is a cemetery,' I said to the dogs. 'It's a place where dead people live.'

We wandered through the rows of markers. On the

top of one slept a stone lamb, its head resting on tiny white hooves, its eyes closed and peaceful. On another, crossed swords were carved into stone. I pointed to one word. 'Brave.' I pointed to another. 'War.' A cloud passed across the sun. I shivered in my damp clothes. 'This place makes me sad,' I said. 'Let's go back.'

We did not return to the cemetery again.

A rumble and a crash woke us a few days later. The earth shook like a great beast, waking. Dirt and wood and bricks shook loose. The floor of the church above rained down upon us.

The dogs and I scrambled away from our sleeping corner just as a wooden beam crashed to the ground. 'What is happening?' I cried. 'Is the world ending?'

A terrible shriek. I looked behind me and gasped. Grandmother lay trapped beneath the fallen beam!

I ran to her side. Blood trickled from her mouth. Her faded eyes searched mine. I stroked her silvered head. 'Don't worry, my babushka. I'll get you out.' She tried to thump her tail, but it would not lift.

Something screeched above us like the voice of a dragon. The earth moaned and shook again. Dirt and rubble fell upon us. Great iron teeth and claws ripped through the dirt roof above us. I threw my body across Grandmother's head and shoulders.

Smoke barked a sharp command. He stood at the pile of rubble leading to our door above. The opening was smaller, had become filled with crumbling bricks and dirt. Little Mother pushed her puppies out ahead of her, and then squirmed behind them. Rip frantically dug his way after her. Lucky must already be out, I realised.

Smoke barked again, this time frantic.

'I can't leave her!' I cried.

He raced to me and tugged on my sleeve.

I pushed him away. 'No!'

He grabbed my arm and pulled hard, ripping the sleeve of my shirt. I tumbled away from Grandmother. The earth shuddered. A fine curtain of dust fell across Grandmother. I crouched beside her head and wiped the dirt from her eyes.

Her eyes did not search my face. Her eyes did not smile as they had so many times.

Her eyes were empty.

I shook her and shook her and shook her. 'Wake up, Babushka, wake up!' Blood rushed from her mouth and pooled beneath it. Still, her eyes looked at nothing.

'*Please,*' I whispered. I pressed my head to hers.

Smoke sniffed Grandmother's face and whimpered. He licked the side of her mouth.

Something roared and clawed at the entry to the cellar.

Smoke raced to the other side, barking and digging frantically. The passageway up and out of the broken church was buried.

He looked at me and barked. The look and the bark said, 'We must live!' I took off my coat and draped it across Grandmother's head and shoulders.

I joined Smoke and we dug together, trying our best to get out, until my fingers were bloody. 'It's no use,' I said to Smoke. 'I can't get us out.'

Smoke's eyes told me he believed I could. Then I remembered the bucket I had used to bring water to our den.

I grabbed the bucket and dug with all my might. Smoke dug next to me. Finally, the earth gave way beneath his paws and my bucket, and we pushed into the light.

I coughed and sputtered and flopped onto my back, gasping for air. Something rumbled towards me. Smoke barked in angry fury.

I sat up and rubbed the dirt out of my eyes. A huge digging machine on wheels like army tanks bore down upon me. I had seen these machines before in our village when they tore down the old factory. I could just make out a man sitting atop the machine.

Smoke and Lucky barked and lunged at the machine. Rip darted this way and that just out of reach of the rolling ribbon of wheels.

'No!' I screamed.

I rolled to the side and scrambled to my feet. The man barely glanced at me. I was nothing but a cockroach scuttling beneath him.

I grabbed a fistful of rocks and flung them at the man and the machine. 'You killed her! You killed her!'

Rip and Smoke and Lucky ran to the far edge of the weedy lot and barked. With all my strength, I flung a large rock at the man. 'I hate you!' I said, tears making dirty tracks down my face. 'I loved her and you killed her!'

The rock flew through the air like an arrow, straight and true. It smashed squarely into the side of the man's face.

'Hey!' he cried. His cigarette fell from his mouth. For the first time he saw me. Blood trickled down the side of his face.

I looked up at him, empty-handed. 'I loved her,' I sobbed. 'I loved her and you killed her.'

Then I ran to join the other dogs. With one last look at the place holding the body of Grandmother, we raced out of sight.

Chapter 32

RUBBISH MOUNTAIN

For days the dogs and I ran. We ran away from The City and the people and the machines and the body of Grandmother. We ran past squat apartment buildings, one after another, all looking the same. We ran past falling-down warehouses, skirting broken glass and bottles and skinny, wary dogs and men with hard black eyes.

We stopped long enough to dig food out of the bins. There was no use begging here; no one had anything to spare.

One day, from the far side of a weedy, glass-sparkled lot, the cries of screeching birds drew us. The wind carried a smell both rotten and sweet. We followed our noses to the source of the smell. There, rising before us like a living, breathing, stinking hulk, towered a mountain of rubbish.

Humans of all sizes crawled over the mountain pulling out scraps of this and bundles of that – ragged clothes, broken pots and pans, twisted heaps of metal. A small girl in rags and no shoes squealed with delight as she pulled a naked, armless doll from the mound. A woman with her head wrapped in rags dragged pieces of wood over to a tumbledown hut on the edge of the woods on the far side of the Rubbish Mountain. A pack of children played king of the mountain on top of a pile of tyres.

Two men argued over a rusty wagon. 'It is mine!' said a man with a striped hat.

'No, I saw it first!' said a man with one arm.

The man with the hat hit the one-armed man over the head with a bottle.

We made our way around Rubbish Mountain just inside the edge of trees. Even the puppies kept silent as we passed. Here and there, people huddled around small, smoky fires. I did not understand this. It was warm and the sun was high. Still, they stood and sat by the flames, passing bottles and laughing. Skinny, skulking dogs hovered at the edges. Their tails said they were scared and hungry.

The wind shifted, blowing the smoke through the trees to where we watched. Rip sneezed.

The talk stopped at the nearest fire. Heads turned in our direction. The dogs of Rubbish Mountain growled. 'Who's that?' someone demanded.

Slowly I left the cover of the trees and stepped into the light. The dogs – my dogs – pressed close to my legs. I rested a hand on Smoke's back. A low growl rumbled up through his chest and to my hand.

'What's your name, boy? Who do you belong to?'

'I belong to them,' I said.

'Who?'

I rested my other hand on Lucky's head. 'The dogs,' I said.

'Ha,' said a woman with no teeth. 'Who heard of a child belonging to a pack of dogs?'

'You come over here with us,' a man in a long coat said, waving me over to the fire with a bottle. 'We'll look after you.'

'And bring those young dogs with you,' another man said, licking his lips like a wolf.

The low, skulking dogs, stay-by-the-fire dogs, inched forward and growled.

My heart thundered in my chest and told my legs to run. But my legs would not run.

The toothless woman grinned and cackled. 'Come over here, little boy. Come to Granny.'

My brain told me to run but I was frozen like a statue. Perhaps the toothless woman was a witch and had cast a spell on me. I closed my eyes and rubbed the baby tooth in my pocket.

Just then, a high tweet! tweet! pierced the air. Cries of 'Militsiya! Run!' crisscrossed Rubbish Mountain. Birds and dogs and people scattered.

The spell broke. My legs came to life. The dogs and I ran as far and as fast as we could away from Rubbish Mountain.

We ran as if on fire, faster than we had ever run before. We left Rubbish Mountain behind, we left the tribe of Rubbish Mountain behind. We ran until our feet no longer skimmed and skittered over asphalt and broken glass. We ran until our feet fell upon green grass, and a gentle trail led us into the woods.

Chapter 33

THE WOODS

Into the woods, the trail led us deeper and deeper. Never had I heard such quiet. The only sounds were my footsteps and the snuffling of the dogs. Everything was to be sniffed; everything was to be peed upon.

I had never imagined the world could hold so many trees. In my village, the only tree was the *yelka* tree in the town square at Christmas time. In The City, the trees grew confined in corrals of brick and iron, as if they might walk away on their own and wreak havoc in The City. Here, the trees grew and soared and sighed and sang where they wanted.

And birds! Oh, the birds and their sweet music!

For the rest of that day and the next, we followed the trails. They led us across small meadows dotted with bright yellow flowers, past clear streams, and through places where the trees hugged so close together the sun barely reached the forest floor. We drank from the streams and rolled in the grass. We napped to the drone of bees and the press of warm sun. My heart ached when I thought how much Grandmother would have loved sleeping in sun-warmed grass.

That second day, Smoke dropped a dead rabbit at my feet. It was large and brown and soft as soft could be.

'Thank you, Smoke,' I said as I stroked the still-warm body of the rabbit. 'But I can't eat this.' I pushed the rabbit back to Smoke. Smoke looked at me with puzzled eyes. He picked up the rabbit and threw it at my feet.

'No,' I said.

Smoke sat and looked at me for a long time. He took in my short, stubby fingers without claws. He studied my small, useless nose and equally useless teeth.

Smoke snorted. He picked up the rabbit and carried it to Little Mother and the puppies, who were watching from beneath a flowering bush. Smoke and Lucky and Rip trotted off along the trail; when they returned they carried another rabbit and two squirrels. My stomach rumbled. I watched miserably as they ate.

The third day was cool and overcast. Clouds spat rain. Once again, I watched in misery as the dogs ate mice for their meals. Even the puppies were more successful than I.

I crawled beneath the umbrella of an evergreen's wide branches. I stuck my thumb in my mouth, then pulled it out. 'I am not a little baby,' I said to the rain and the dogs beyond the branches. 'I got us away from the evil witch who eats children and puppies.' I reached underneath my jumper and ragged shirt for the pages of my fairy-tale book. 'Yes, just like that witch who tried to lure those children into her oven.'

The pages weren't there. I frowned and dug down in the front of my trousers. No pages there.

And then my heart fell away down to my toes. 'My coat,' I whispered. 'The pages were in the pocket of my coat.' Which was covering the body of Grandmother.

'No!' I cried as I flung myself from beneath the tree. 'How could I have forgotten? What will we do without the stories?'

I beat the bushes furiously with a stick. I knocked off the showy heads of flowers. 'Stupid, stupid boy,' I said as I beat and smashed. 'You are useless and pathetic.' I watched the puppies play tug-of-war with a squirrel tail. 'Even the puppies are smarter than you,' I said.

Little Mother watched me with worry-filled eyes. She was torn between wanting to comfort me and fear of my anger and the swinging stick. Rip nipped at my leg. I swung my stick and brought it down hard on the little dog's shoulders. Rip yelped in pain. His eyes were huge with fear. He rolled over onto his back, exposing his throat and belly. He wet himself. The forest grew utterly silent, except for Rip's whimpers. The dogs all backed away from me as if I were a stranger.

I dropped my stick and ran into the forest.

I curled up under a bush and rocked myself back and forth. 'Everything is wrong. Everything is lost! Grandmother, the fairy tales ... and look what you've done now, you stupid boy,' I sobbed. 'You worthless cockroach.' I buried my face against my arm and bit down. Hard. I bit my own arm until I drew blood. 'You hurt Rip,' I said over and over as I continued to bite.

Something warm and wet and rough stroked the side of my face. I lifted my head and looked into the smiling, worried eyes of Lucky. Just behind him stood Smoke.

'I'm sorry,' I said.

Lucky sniffed my arm.

'I am nothing but a stupid, pathetic boy.'

Gently, Lucky licked the blood from my arm.

Finally, Smoke nudged my side. He pushed at my legs and knees. When I didn't obey his command, he pulled on my sleeve.

I crawled from beneath the bush. 'What do I do?'
I asked the dogs.

Smoke barked twice. Lucky wagged his tail. *Let us show
you*, his eyes said.

Chapter 34

HUNTING

They led me along narrow trails crisscrossed with animal tracks. They led me across one meadow and then another. They led me across a stream, past a pond. The narrow trail grew wider, and then met a gravel path. The gravel path curved this way and that. It crossed a stone bridge littered with leaves and empty acorn shells. Something big startled at our passing and bounded away into the forest.

We loped along the gravel path for a long time. My legs trembled from hunger. I stopped. The wind blew and rain pattered the puddles in the road. 'I can't,' I sobbed. 'I can't go any more.'

Lucky leaned into my legs and licked my hands. Smoke barked up ahead. There was no sympathy in his bark, only a command.

Finally, the gravel path stopped. A black-topped road crossed in front of us. A road that hissed with rain and cars.

I swayed on my feet and shivered.

When the road was clear of cars, the dogs dashed across. What could I do but follow?

We trotted along footpaths. Here there were signs of people: aluminum cans, glass and plastic bottles tossed to the side of the path; empty sweet wrappers and tufts of tissues. The trees thinned and then opened. I gasped.

A huge wheel higher than a house loomed above us. Wooden seats dangled from the giant wheel. They swayed in the wind. The wheel was still, but it didn't fool me.

I clapped my hands. 'It's a Ferris wheel! You brought me to a Ferris wheel!' I had seen them on television before.

The dogs glanced up at the wheel with little interest. They trotted across the puddle-strewn square, noses held high in the wind. Reluctantly, I followed.

We passed a large pond. Ducks and geese huddled on the shore. We skirted a wooden stage and a scattering of tables and chairs. Sodden plastic bags hugged the chair and table legs.

The dogs led me to rows of empty wooden stalls and stopped. They sniffed and I sniffed. Food! I followed my nose behind the wooden stalls and a narrow, stinking shed to a large metal bin. Delicious smells met my nose. My stomach groaned and burned. Lucky and Smoke looked from the bin to me with pride.

'Oh, thank you,' I said.

But the bin was tall and the metal slick. I jumped and jumped but still could not reach the lip of the bin to pull myself up. Viktor's voice mocked me. *Jump, little circus mouse!*

Then I remembered: tables and chairs! I dashed back to the stage and grabbed a chair. I dragged it to the bin. I clambered up, pulled myself into the bin and landed in a gloriously stinking pile of rubbish. I stuffed bread into my mouth, and pieces of half-eaten chicken. I ate and ate until my poor shrunken belly could hold no more. And still, there was so much food.

I climbed back out of the bin and rescued two plastic bags. Lucky and Smoke watched with shining eyes as I filled the bags with cast-off food. With this, I could eat for days. This human park, this bin, would be my hunting ground.

The sun was setting as we crossed the last meadow to the place where we'd left the others. Rip yipped a happy greeting. He raced in circles around us, licking Lucky's mouth and face and my hands. Little Mother and the puppies crawled from under a shelter she had dug in the deep well beneath a sprawling evergreen. They sniffed and sniffed me all over. The puppies pulled at my sleeve. I laughed and pushed them away. 'I am not something to eat, even though I smell like it,' I said.

I picked up Rip and kissed the top of his head. 'I am sorry I hit you,' I whispered in his torn ear. 'Sometimes I am not the best boy.' I took a piece of meat from my pocket that I had saved just for Rip, and fed it to him.

One of the puppies – the boy puppy – grabbed the bottom of one of the plastic bags and tugged. Food spilled out of the bottom onto the wet ground.

The dogs leapt upon the food. My food.

'No!' I roared. 'It's mine!'

The dogs slunk away on their bellies. I stood over my food, Rip still in my arms, and growled. I flashed my teeth.

They looked at me with round, piteous eyes. All but Smoke. He sat a metre away and regarded me with cool, amber eyes.

I tied the bottom of the torn bag. I took off my tattered jumper and tied the arms in such a way as to create a cradle.

I stepped away from the food on the ground. 'OK then, eat,' I said. All but Smoke ate in grateful gulps.

Smoke watched with great curiosity as I climbed the

wide branches of the evergreen and stashed the cradle of food.

That night we all curled close together in the well beneath the bottom of the evergreen tree. It was dry here, despite the rain. The generous skirt of bottom branches provided a thick, lacy green roof. The puppies played with pine cones while Rip and Lucky slept against my legs. Little Mother washed and washed my face and ears and neck. I fell asleep to the rasp of her tongue, the tickle of her whiskers and her warm, smelly, wonderful breath on my face.

And just outside, in the glow of the rising moon, Smoke watched over us all. His pack. My family.

The days grew steadily warmer and longer. The puppies grew in leaps and bounds, the dogs shed their winter coats, and I shed most of my clothes.

The dogs hunted together and alone. There was plenty in the forest for them to eat: rabbits, mice, squirrels and the occasional bird. Their coats grew shiny and sleek. The shadow of ribs and angle of hipbones fell away.

I quickly learned the rhythms of the park with the Ferris wheel. If I went there just after sunrise, workers were mowing and cleaning, setting up the chairs and tables and emptying rubbish bins. Every few days a big truck came and emptied the metal bin I hunted in. If I came late at night after the park closed, shadow-people crept into the park. They argued over things they took from their coat pockets. Gangs of Crow Boys came too with their chains and knives.

So I came in the time before sunrise, just before black gave way to grey. The dogs and I watched from the edge of the woods for shadow-people and for Crow Boys. We knew after the winter that no good could come from people.

I searched the smaller bins as well as the big metal bin. The big metal bin was for food; the smaller ones were for treasures: elastic bands, a bandana, a plastic rain cap, a broken kite and the greatest treasure of all, a knife. Often I found matches or lighters. But after the Glass House, I was afraid of fire.

In the early part of that summer, the dogs discovered the eggs ducks had laid by the big pond. I gathered up eggs for myself to eat. I loved their wonderful slippingness as they slid warm and rich down my throat, like a small, fat yellow sun.

Chapter 35

HOUSE OF BONES

Now that we were all stronger and the puppies had grown long legs, we explored the forest. Further and further we went into the wildest parts, the Border Lands. Here the trails were not made by humans. There were no bottles or metal bins left to the side of the trails. There were no wide trails or straight trails. These trails, such as they were, were barely wide enough for my small boy feet placed toe to heel, one in front of the other. These trails wound in and out, back and forth in secret ways known only to the animals that had made them.

We followed these trails, Smoke always in the lead, me behind and the rest of the dogs close. Smoke talked to me with his ears and tail. I watched which direction his ears swiveled. Were they thrown forward or were they relaxed? If he raised his tail high, something exciting was ahead – perhaps a deer to chase or a fox. We had seen many deer in this far border of the forest and tracks in the damp earth of something much larger. But even the small dappled deer were too big and too fast for the dogs to kill, except in their dreams at night. Once they had tried, but all they managed to catch in the end were empty stomachs.

One grey day thick with mist, the dogs and I came upon something altogether wonderful and mysterious and frightening deep in the Border Land of the forest.

The puppies found it. The pack and I had stopped to drink from a stream and investigate a large hole dug into a small hillside. I heard the puppies' yips and their growls of curiosity and argument on the other side of a huddle of boulders. We paid them little mind. They were puppies, after all, always going on about something.

Her head and tail held high, Girl Puppy trotted towards us with something big in her mouth. We all sat on our haunches and watched her until she dropped the big something in front of me.

It was a long, curved bone. The bone still had bits of meat and tattered hide attached. I held it to my nose and sniffed. It smelled of damp earth and wet leaves and a sweet rot.

'Show me,' I said to Girl Puppy.

We followed her across the stream, behind the huddle of boulders and into a stand of silver trees. There, Boy Puppy chewed with great satisfaction and concentration on a large hoof. The dogs and I gathered round for a better look.

'It was a big animal,' I said, surveying the length of the skeleton. 'And maybe not dead for long.' The dogs looked from me to the skeleton and nodded. Some of the bones were scattered from the body, but most were where they should be. Rags of hide and leathered meat draped some of the bones; others were picked clean, some crushed.

While the dogs gnawed and chewed on this mystery, I searched around the skeleton for clues as to what it was and how it died. There, hidden under a pile of leaves, was the biggest leg I had ever seen. The long, elegant leg ended in a massive black hoof. The hoof was smeared with dried blood. At the other end was a bony knob. I stood the leg up on its pointy hoof. The knob reached just above my waist.

I swung the leg bone this way and that. I swung it in a high arc like the golfers I had seen on the television once. I swung it like a hockey stick I'd seen the boys on my street use. The weight of it sang. The weight of it, the way it fitted just so in the palm of my hand, said yes, I am yours.

That night, we lay in the little meadow beside our den

beneath the tree and watched the stars come out one by one. The puppies lay in an exhausted sleep from our adventure; the older dogs chewed contentedly on prized bones they had brought back from the skeleton. I ran my hand along the leg bone as I stared up at the darkening sky. I thought about the blood on the hoof. 'What could have killed something that big?' I wondered aloud. 'What is out there in the Border Lands?' And even though the evening was warm, I shivered.

We returned to the skeleton the next day and the day after. The mystery of its story drew me. Who had done this? Who had done this to something so big?

The first day, I asked the dogs, 'Do you think it was a horse?' And, 'Could it have been the biggest deer in all of Russia?' The dogs didn't care what it had been. They only cared what it was now: a wondrous, stinking hill of bone and hide and stringy muscles.

I crawled inside the house the ribcage made, and curled on my side, fitting just so. The elegant bones arched over and around me. The dogs peered through the bars of bone in puzzlement and concern. Little Mother pawed at the ground and whimpered. Rip pushed his nose through the ribs and licked my face.

I laughed. Lucky wagged his tail and dropped to his elbows in an invitation to play.

Smoke watched. His eyes locked on mine. And then a voice that was not really a voice spoke inside my mind. It said, This is not right.

I gasped. 'Smoke, was that you?'

He lifted his silver eyebrows.

I laughed and clapped my hands. 'You talked to me!'

A low grumble rattled in his chest. Come. It is not right.

I shivered at the feel of his voice curling like smoke inside my mind.

I crawled out from the House of Bones and chased through the forest with the dogs.

It was the next day that I found the head of the animal. Again, we had returned. And again, the puppies found the answer. It had been dragged far from the rest of the body and half buried. I dug and pulled and tugged the skull until it finally broke free of the earth.

It was not a horse. The head of the animal was as big as a horse's, but antlers spread wide above the crown of the head like bony, featherless wings. The antlers were stained and smeared with the colour of rust. Blood.

The dogs gathered round this discovery, drinking in

its smell. I sniffed it too, trying to read its story.

'I have never heard of a deer as big as a horse, but a horse does not have antlers.'

Lucky clamped his teeth around a branch of antler and pulled.

'No!' I barked. I growled in his face and showed my teeth and shook my leg-bone club. 'It's *mine*.' The dogs backed away, their eyes downcast.

I placed the skull in my lap. It was heavy despite the emptiness of its eyes. I allowed Smoke to sniff the stains on the antlers.

'It fought whatever killed it,' I said to Smoke. 'It was very brave.' Smoke shifted uneasily. He cast a worried look – a look I'd never seen before – around the forest. He trotted over to the trail we had made that led back to our meadow and our tree. He barked a command.

The dogs all stopped what they were doing. They looked at Smoke and then at me.

I looked at Smoke. He said, We must go. Now.

Thunder rumbled in the distance. The dogs whined.

'It's just a little thunder,' I grumbled. Smoke barked again.

'OK, OK,' I said. 'But I'm bringing this.'

I grabbed the skull by the antlers and dragged it all

the way back to our home beneath the tree. I lifted it atop the stump of a long-dead tree, out of reach of the puppies. The empty eyes gazed out into the wild and windy night with its secret.

Chapter 36

INTRUDERS

The next time we returned to the House of Bones, Smoke would not cross the stream. And if Smoke would not go, neither would Little Mother. She watched miserably as I stormed across the creek with her puppies splashing close behind.

We scampered up the grassy hill. At the top of the rise, Lucky and Rip sniffed the air. Rip whined uncertainly. Lucky shifted nervously next to me.

'Come on,' I said, and trotted along the faint trail our feet had worn. The puppies galloped ahead, into the grove of silver trees.

I heard a bark, a yelp and then a scream of terror.

The puppies! I ran for the trees. This was the sight that greeted me: the House of Bones swarmed with dogs. One of the dogs had Boy Puppy pinned to the ground with its teeth clamped around his throat. Two other dogs towered over the cowering Girl Puppy. A fourth dog – the largest by far and black as night – stood atop the House of Bones. Its eyes narrowed with hate; its lips pulled back in a vicious snarl. It crouched, preparing to spring.

'No!' I screamed. I ran towards the dog holding Boy Puppy by the throat, my club held high.

The dog lifted his muzzle from the puppy's throat. His muzzle was smeared with blood. The dog snarled and lunged.

Lucky knocked me to the side and fell onto the attacking dog in a fury. Rip raced to Girl Puppy, barking like a much bigger dog than he really was. The dogs were not fooled. They set upon Rip.

I leapt to my feet and grabbed my club. A cry that was neither boy nor dog tore from my throat. I threw myself upon the two dogs ravaging Rip. I brought my club down as hard as I could. I felt it *crack!* against the skull of one of the attackers. The dog yelped and retreated. The other dog leapt for my arm. I swung the club like a baseball bat and *crack!* the dog fell to the ground in a heap.

Lucky stood over Boy Puppy and snapped at the dog who'd had the puppy by the throat. I realised for the first time that the wild dog was bigger than Lucky. Blood trickled from Lucky's ear.

'Leave him alone!' I shouted, swinging my club.

Another high-pitched scream. My heart slid to my stomach at what I saw: the big black dog, the one that had crouched atop the House of Bones, now held Girl Puppy by the scruff of her neck. Black Dog shook Girl Puppy, hard. The puppy screamed in terror. Black Dog's eyes dared us to move, to breathe.

And then it was as if a fury was released from the forest. Something – a brown blur – roared into the silver trees and hurled itself upon Black Dog. The two tumbled backwards in a black and brown snarling, gnashing twist of bone and blood and fur. I screamed and swung my club high. Black Dog leapt aside to dodge my club.

The other dog, the one who had set upon Black Dog like a hellhound, whose eyes were of a crazed demon, was Little Mother. She positioned herself over Girl Puppy's body. I had never seen such hate, such rage in her face.

Something snarled behind me. Teeth sank into my leg. I whirled round just in time to see Smoke knock the wild dog at my leg to the ground. First he savaged that dog, then he attacked Black Dog. Black Dog twisted away and retreated to the edge of the woods. He barked once. The other three in the pack followed.

As quickly as it had happened, the fight was over.

My legs quivered, and then gave way altogether. I sank to the dirt. I surveyed the battleground.

Little Mother had her puppies next to her. She explored them with worried grunts and sighs. Lucky sniffed Rip, who was pulling himself up off the ground. I crawled over to Rip and gathered him in my arms. He growled at the eyes still watching us from the forest.

'You are so brave,' I said to the little mouse-coloured dog. Why had I never noticed how small he was?

Twin growls rumbled from the chests of Smoke and Lucky. Black Dog stepped into the light. I stood as tall as I could and held Rip to my chest. Little Mother snarled. The puppies, grown brave now, growled from behind her.

Black Dog stalked over to the House of Bones. He looked at us in utter contempt. Then he raised his leg on the bones and urinated, all the while staring directly into Smoke's eyes. One by one, the other wild dogs did the same. The message was clear: This was their kill, their territory. We were the intruders.

We made our way back to our meadow. I checked the dogs over for wounds. Despite the blood and the screams, none of us were too worse for wear. The puppies each had torn ears. Lucky had a shallow slash on his shoulder.

Although I could find no wound, Rip limped for the rest of the summer.

We washed ourselves in the stream. I watched as Lucky and Smoke methodically marked the trees at the far side of our meadow with their urine. This was our territory.

That night in our den beneath the great evergreen tree, we licked the cuts and bruises and fear from one another.

Days passed, perhaps weeks. We still explored the far borders of the park, but never again did we visit the House of Bones. I kept my knife and my club with me. From time to time, I caught a glimpse of something from the corner of an eye and the hair rose on the back of my neck. Something watched as we passed. The fur bristled on the back of each dog's neck and spine. A smell dark as old blood filled the air. The puppies pressed close to Little Mother. Smoke stood guard as we passed. I had no doubt from the smell it was Black Dog watching us.

One early morning we made our way back to our meadow from the Ferris wheel park, my bags filled with food. I was so tired, so sleepy. We were not far from home.

The dogs froze. I almost fell over Lucky. I was about to growl at him when I spotted what had caught their attention: in a misty clearing stood the most beautiful creature

I had ever seen. It was as tall as a horse. The legs were long and delicate; the head proud and fine. And atop that head rose spreading antlers. I blinked. Was I dreaming on my feet? Could this be our House of Bones come to life?

The wind shifted. The creature turned its head towards us and searched the air for our scent. Smoke tensed beside me, his eyes locked on the animal. Lucky crouched. The puppies quivered in anticipation.

I growled at the dogs. They looked from the animal to me in confusion.

Why? Smoke asked.

Leave it, I replied. We are not like Them.

The creature tossed its head and stamped one black, shiny hoof. Then as if in a dream, it bounded into the forest with a grace so old, so wild, my heart ached.

I ran in its wake. I knew I could not catch up to it.

That night, the moon rose full and bright. 'This is the second full moon since we've been here, I think,' I said to the dogs. Rip looked from me to the moon and barked and wagged his tail. Lucky lay on his back, belly bathed in moonlight; Little Mother and Smoke lay side by side while the puppies play-fought over a rabbit leg. We were always together now ever since our battle with the Others at the

House of Bones. Even Smoke. We hunted together, we slept together, we played together and we fought together.

I watched the puppies in the moonlight. 'They're no longer puppies,' I said to Rip. And it was true. Both were bigger than Rip now. Boy Puppy stood shoulder to shoulder with Little Mother, who herself was not that much smaller than Smoke.

I stood and clapped my hands. The dogs gathered around me.

'It is time to name the puppies,' I said. Lucky wagged his tail and panted in agreement.

I studied Boy Puppy. He had Smoke's amber eyes and grey colouring. He had Little Mother's bushy tail and delicate feet. A white star of fur graced his chest. He was swift and silent.

I stroked his chest. 'Star. I will call you Star.'

He wiggled and licked the side of my mouth.

His sister watched us. She glowed pale in the moonlight. She was not brown and black like her mother, nor was she silver and grey like Smoke. She was pale, pale yellow like the moon, and watchful as the moon.

I kissed the top of her head. 'You are Moon.' She licked my hands.

'You could not be other than Moon.'

Chapter 37

THE BIGGEST PIG
IN ALL OF RUSSIA

And so the summer passed, and before we knew it, the leaves changed from green to gold and red, and the days grew shorter. The light turned buttery. Many mornings, frost pricked my bare feet. I was glad my hair had grown long enough to cover my ears and neck.

The winds came and the leaves fell to the ground. The dogs had a harder time hunting with the crunch of leaves beneath their paws. Even Moon and Star had to learn to walk on ghost feet.

One afternoon I sat in the autumn sunlight and watched the last of the birch leaves in our meadow fall to the ground. A cold wind lifted my hair. An aching sadness I had not felt since we had lost Grandmother washed over me. Tears stung my eyes and spilled down my cheeks.

Moon nudged my face with her cold, wet nose and licked my cheeks. I buried my face in the deep fur across her shoulders. 'It must be a year,' I said. She looked at me with her mother's worried eyes.

'The leaves were falling off the trees and it was just beginning to turn cold when I lost my mother, and when he left me in The City alone.'

I leaned my head against Moon's shoulder. A year since I'd slept on a bed and eaten from a bowl. A year since I had heard my mother's voice. 'I no longer remember her voice,' I said.

I knew the playful yip of Star, the deep grumble of Lucky, the beautiful voice of Little Mother when we all howled at the moon. I no longer remembered the colour of my mother's eyes. Were they blue as the sky or did they flash black like Rip's?

I stood and shook off the weight of my sadness. I grabbed my bone club. The bone was smooth and cool where my hand had worn away the stiff hair.

'It has been a year,' I said to the dogs as they stretched in the sunlight. 'And that means I am no longer five. I am now six.' I swung my club this way and that. 'I am no longer a little boy holding on to his mother. I am no longer a little cockroach hiding in the dark.' I swung the club high in the air and brought it down with a *crack* on the skull of a rabbit. 'If *he* came to our apartment door now, I would kill him.'

The morning was encased in cold and frost. I climbed the tree of our home and retrieved my trousers, jumper, socks, and boots. I pulled on the trousers and smiled. They were no longer too long. The jumper sleeves no longer covered my scarred hands; my toes pushed painfully against the ends of the boots. I left the boots and socks and trotted across the meadow with the dogs.

We sniffed our way along faint trails on the far side of the vast forest we'd rarely travelled. This part of the forest made me uneasy for reasons I could not say. Perhaps it was the thickness of the trees and the lack of sunlight. Perhaps it was the way the mist seemed to never leave this part of the woods. But hunting was getting scarce and the dogs needed to eat. With the cold days, fewer people came to the Ferris-wheel park. It was harder for me to find enough for all of us to eat.

We crept through the wet, darkened wood. 'At least last night's rain keeps the leaves from being so noisy,' I whispered to Moon. Still, a feeling of dread slowed my steps.

Up ahead I heard the snapping of sticks and a grunt and snort. We froze. Smoke, in the lead as always, raised his head and sniffed. His ears followed the sound of feet shuffling in the leaves. Smoke looked back at me, his eyes puzzled. It was not something we had smelled before. The hair rose on the back of my neck and along my arms.

There was another grunt, closer this time. Red eyes peered through the mist. Something white flashed like a sword.

I crouched to turn. Let's leave, I said to Smoke.

Just then, Star shot forward into the swirling mist.

'No!' I cried.

Star snarled and growled. I heard the snapping of teeth. A cry of panic. Star burst through the mist and the trees running towards us, his eyes wide with fear and his tail tucked between his legs.

Thundering behind Star was the Biggest Pig in All of Russia.

'Run!' I shouted.

The pig was fast and agile. Long white tusks curved up from its snout like twin crescent moons.

The pig hooked Star with a tusk and threw him aside. Little Mother leapt upon the beast, sinking teeth into the back of its neck. The pig tossed her to the ground. Just as it was about to stab her with its tusks, Lucky and Smoke rushed to it. Lucky grabbed the pig by one ear while Smoke grabbed a back leg.

The pig squealed in fury and pain. It shook Lucky off as if he were no more than a bothersome flea. It swung its massive neck and scraped Smoke off with a rake of its tusks. Smoke yelped in pain and rolled to the side. The pig lowered its head, its tusks aimed at Smoke's belly. The pig pawed the ground.

'No!' I roared. The beast swung its head. The red pig eyes gleamed with hate. I raised my club and brought it crashing down on the pig's shoulders. Crack!

The beast staggered under the blow. Smoke leapt to his feet. I glanced at him. Blood streamed from his side.

The pig charged and slammed into my leg. A tusk tore through my trousers and sank into flesh. I screamed in pain and fell backwards. The pig prepared to charge again. First Moon, then Smoke and Lucky set upon the huge pig. Blood and fur and snarls and yelps filled the air. I pulled myself to my feet and raised my club. Smoke glanced up from his hold on the back of the pig's neck.

Now, he said.

The dogs froze. The pig's red eyes locked on mine. I brought the club down with such force on the pig's head that the club broke in two. The legs of the beast buckled. For just a blink, the red eyes gleamed again with hate, then dulled to nothingness. My knees gave way. I sank to the wet, blood-spattered leaves. I gulped the air with ragged breaths. The dogs sniffed the great pig. Lucky licked at the blood on its torn ear. Little Mother pawed its side. It did not move.

I watched and shivered as the dogs tore into the pig.

I am six years old now, I thought. *And I killed it.*

My stomach heaved, and I vomited in the grass.

For two days and two nights, the sickle-shaped gash from the pig's tusk festered. My leg burned and pulsed. I grew hot, then cold, then hot again. I slipped in and out of feverish dreams – dreams of being chased by big black things with glowing ember eyes. Sometimes the thing was a giant wolf with wings, sometimes Baba Yaga chased me. Sometimes *he* chased me.

I'd wake with a cry and always, the dogs surrounded me: Moon and Star were pressed into my side, Rip and Lucky lying at my feet, Little Mother busy licking Smoke's side over and over.

Once, I dreamed of my mother's hands. She smoothed the damp hair from my fevered face. She washed my face over and over with a wet rag. 'There, Mishka,' she said. 'My brave boy.'

'Mother,' I said, opening my eyes. I expected to see her face, the face I no longer remembered, hovering over me. But it was not my mother washing my face. Instead, Little Mother hovered over me, washing and washing my face with her rough wet tongue.

Smoke stood next to her, gazing into my eyes.

Brave Malchik, he said. My brave boy.

PART TWO

Chapter 38

MALCHIK

Winter came early that year. Winter came and people left the Ferris-wheel park. The food stalls closed. The bins were all but empty. The big duck pond where we'd found the delicious eggs and where the dogs had occasionally managed to catch a duck or two iced over. My jumper was in tatters from living in the tree for months; I had outgrown my boots. I had no coat.

Every day it was colder, and every day I said to the dogs, 'We have to leave.' But still, we stayed in our home beneath the tree.

And then, the snow came. It did not come in gentle fits and starts like the winter before. It did not do us the courtesy of coming with patience. One day it was not there and the next morning it was everywhere.

We woke to darkness. The air in the den beneath our tree was close and wet. I untangled myself from Moon and

Rip and felt my way to the opening beneath the tree limbs. My hand met snow. I felt all around the circle of the tree's wide skirt. Everywhere snow packed thick against the limbs.

My heart beat hard in my chest. Rip squeezed next to me and sniffed the snow wall. He whined, and then barked.

Another bark and then scratch scratch scratch on the other side of the snow wall.

Little Mother and her children began digging on our side of the wall. Snow flew in all directions, and then...

Light! Light and a big black nose pushed against my face. We shoved and tumbled our way out of the den and into the grey light.

Lucky jumped up and down, his plumed tail wagging, his tongue swiping the side of my face. He chased Moon and Star through the snowy meadow. Smoke and Little Mother licked each other's faces. Rip crawled into my lap and looked up at me with smiling eyes.

The meadow was a stranger now. I could no longer see the stream's course or the rocks where I'd sat every night and watched the stars. The trails that I knew as well as I knew each of the dogs were gone. The deer skull was mostly covered in snow. Only the black holes of the eyes were visible. I stared at the holes. They stared back.

Rip nudged my hand and whined. I tore my eyes away from the skull and looked into his worried eyes. 'I know,' I said. 'It is time.'

And so it was, the dogs and I left our home in the forest and made our way back to The City.

As always, the people of The City hurried this way and that, huddled in their coats, slipping and sliding on the ice-crusted pavements. Here, no birds sang. My eyes were hungry for trees, for open spaces. Here, the tall buildings and the tumbledown buildings pushed in on one another. I coughed and pinched my nose against the foul smells: car fumes, unwashed hair, chimneys, rotting rubbish, sewers.

We passed children and bums sleeping and begging in the shop doorways. Their eyes widened as we passed. One called, 'Hey! What are you?' Another called, 'I smelled it coming a mile away!' We did not stop; we did not look left or right. I curled my fingers around the knife in my trousers pocket.

Moon pressed close against my legs. The other dogs kept close too. A large, mangy dog growled and snapped as we approached. His ribs rippled beneath patches of fur and sores. The dog stood in our path, daring us to pass.

Smoke and Lucky closed in front and stopped. They raised their tails and narrowed their eyes and growled. I took out my knife, narrowed my eyes and pulled my lips back from my teeth. A long, low warning growl rumbled in my throat.

The dog blinked. He looked from Smoke and Lucky to me. I growled again. The dog dropped his tail and slunk away into the shadows.

I rubbed Lucky and Smoke's sides. They licked my hands and wagged their tails. Then we sauntered down the pavement to Sokolniki station.

At first I was so busy raiding the bins in the station, I didn't notice the people staring at me. 'There must be more in here,' I muttered to myself. 'If only I were a little taller.'

'What is that?' I heard a voice say.

I pulled my head out of a bin to see what the problem might be.

Two women stared at me, their eyes wide with disbelief. One pressed a handkerchief to her nose and mouth. 'It almost looks like a child,' she said.

The other woman shook her head and pinched her nose. 'No child ever smelled like that. Certainly no human. It looks like a demon!'

'I am a boy,' I said, my voice croaky from disuse.

Their eyes widened again.

I held out my hand. 'I am just a boy,' I said again, my voice clearer this time. 'And I am hungry.' Lucky wagged his tail hopefully; Rip tried to dance on his back legs but toppled over.

The women clutched their handbags against their sides and hurried away.

Their words rang in my ears as I looked for more food. *It looks like a demon! No child ever smelled like that!* I sniffed my clothes and my skin. I smelled like the dogs and the earth and the trees. 'I smell good to me,' I said to Moon and Star. Still, the people coming and going to the trains pinched their noses and looked at me in disgust when they passed. No one would give me money to buy food this way.

That evening when the station was quiet, I slipped into the bathroom for a drink of water. I almost fled in fear from the wild beast glaring at me from above the sink.

I bared my teeth. It bared its teeth.

I narrowed my eyes. It narrowed its eyes.

'What are you?' I demanded. Its mouth moved in time with mine.

I gasped and touched my face. It touched its face too. I stepped closer and touched the cold glass of the mirror. 'You're *me*,' I whispered.

This was not a mother's little Mishka staring back at me. This was not a boy who slept curled into a mother's side and hid in pantries. This was not a little mouse who cowered in fear of the tall boys in chains and black.

This boy staring back from the mirror had slept beneath a tree with his pack; a boy who ran through the forest swift as a deer and rolled with delight in mud and the sweet scent of dead things. This boy carried a club and killed a giant pig and howled at the moon with his family.

This boy was Smoke's brave boy, his Malchik. I smiled.

'Still, we need to eat,' I said to myself in the mirror.

I stripped off my clothes and scrubbed. The water turned black and my skin turned pink. The scar on my leg from the pig's tusk glowed red.

The clothes were in tatters, it was true. 'I need to find the Christian Ladies and get new clothes,' I said to the boy in the mirror.

Clothes, food and a warm place to be safe. That was all we needed to get through another winter. 'And then we'll return to the forest,' I said. My mind whirred with a plan as I slipped on my clothes, my too-small boots. 'Clothes from the Christian Ladies. More people mean more money and more food.' I took the knife from my pocket and pulled open the blade. I pried twigs and dead leaves from the long snarls in my hair. I grabbed a greasy lock covering my eyes and sawed back and forth with the knife. I grabbed another and another and another until hair blanketed my feet.

'And to keep warm and safe, we will again ride the trains,' I said to the brown eyes in the mirror.

The eyes that stared back from the mirror did not belong to a demon or to a wild beast or to a mother's little bear. They were the wary, cunning eyes of Malchik.

Chapter 39

THE RETURN OF RUDY

'Lord save us,' the Christian Lady said, as she looked me up and down, her beefy fists planted on her round hips.

I did not look down at my shoes. I rested one hand on Smoke's shoulder and stared straight back at her. 'I need clothes,' I said. Her brow furrowed. Something pushed from far back in my memory. 'Please,' I added.

She shook her head. 'You need more than clothes, I daresay.' She reached a hand out to touch my chopped hair. I stepped back. Smoke growled.

The Christian Lady's eyes darted from Smoke to me. She licked her lips. 'I mean you no harm, boy. But if you want anything from me, you'll call off that dog of yours.'

Back, I said to Smoke. He grumbled a complaint even as he trotted a metre away.

'You really could do with a bath and a haircut...'

I shook my head. 'Just clothes and shoes.'

The Christian Lady sighed. 'Wait here.' She bent over tall cardboard boxes filled with clothes and shoes and blankets. Other children of all sizes tried on this and that. Some took only blankets. Some followed other Christian Ladies to a long white van. It would not take long for the boxes to empty. I knew the Christian Ladies would leave the bigger cardboard boxes for the children to use for shelters. I did not think a cardboard box could make as wonderful a home as a den beneath the generous limbs of an evergreen.

'Here you go.'

I blinked.

'See if these fit. I don't have things much smaller.'

I frowned. 'I am not a little boy,' I said, standing up tall. A little boy could not kill a giant pig with one blow.

A tiny smile tugged at the corner of the Christian Lady's mouth. 'I see,' she said.

On went the new old clothes and battered boots. I pulled a hat down over my chopped-up hair and my ears. Now I looked like any other unwanted child on the streets. Once again, I was invisible.

And so we rode the trains that long snowy winter. Always, we rode the last train of the evening, clacking nose to tail down the track and into the station. At night, few people rode the last train, so we often had it to ourselves. The few passengers on the late-night trains stayed clear of a boy and his pack. I had no use for people except the leftovers they provided for food. Seldom had they not meant me harm or betrayed me. The dogs were always with me.

Moon and Star invented a game with the trains. They dared each other to wait until the last possible moment to leap from the station platform, through the whooshing doors, and into the train – without getting a tail caught. Little Mother watched their game with alarm and then irritation. Lucky, of course, joined in the fun. Smoke just watched. I held my breath each time they played this game and clapped when they tumbled aboard, tails held high – and whole.

I did my best to avoid the other children of the street. I watched them beg; I watched them fight and cry. I watched them stick their noses in brown paper bags, breathe in, and breathe out. I watched them get drunk and get sick. They froze in helpless heaps inside cardboard boxes and doorways, on top of heat vents. The police came and poked the body with their batons; an ambulance wailed its way up the street and took the body away down the street. That winter, they took many bodies away.

We rode the trains.

Once, as we waited for the last evening train, a gang of Crow Boys sauntered down the long, overlit corridor of the station. The heels of their boots clicked on the marble floor. One smashed out lights with a long stick as he walked along. Another demanded money from the few people waiting for the train. Then they spotted me.

The one with the long stick stopped and pointed it at me. 'Hey, you're that boy. That boy who lives with dogs.'

I shrugged and looked away.

They stepped closer. The tallest took a cigarette from behind his ear and put it to his lips. 'Yeah, I heard about you. The boy who lives with dogs.' He lit the cigarette and flicked the match at my feet. Rip backed away in terror. I growled and flashed my teeth. The Crow Boys hooted with laughter.

'He thinks he's a dog!' One pulled out a knife and flicked open the blade. His eyes grew hard as ice. 'Let's see if you can beg like a dog.'

I barked one high, commanding bark. From the shadows came the other dogs, surrounding the Crow Boys. The dogs crouched and crept in closer to the boys, their voices growling and grumbling with hate. My hand itched for my club. What was left of it was far away in the forest, buried beneath the snow. So instead I said simply, 'They will kill you if you come closer.'

243

One said, 'You think we're afraid of a little kid and his dogs?' but their eyes said something different. The one with the long stick said, 'Just give us what money you have and we'll leave you and your mangy mutts alone.'

I slipped my hand into my pocket. I felt the smooth lump of my baby tooth and the length of knife. I curled my fingers around my knife. 'OK,' I said.

Just then, a cold, lazy voice said, 'Is this all you have to do, play with little boys and dogs?'

There in the light of an oncoming train, smoke drifting from his nostrils, a small black gun hanging in one hand, stood Rudy.

I gasped.

Rudy did not look at me. Instead he said to the cowering Crow Boys, 'I know who you work for. I wonder how he'd like it if I told him you were no better than rats pestering a flea?'

'We were just having a little fun, Rudy,' one of the boys said. His Adam's apple bobbed up and down in his throat as he gulped.

The train hissed to a stop. Rudy tossed his cigarette to the floor and crushed it beneath the toe of his shiny black boot.

The train doors opened. Rudy flicked his eyes in my

direction. He waved the small gun. 'Go,' he said.

The dogs and I hurried down to the last train compartment and threw ourselves in. My heart was hammering in my ears when I heard a voice say, 'Why is it I keep saving your skin?'

Rudy slumped down on the floor of the train across from us. Smoke growled and Moon flashed her teeth.

'Call off your hounds,' he said in a weary voice as he tucked the gun inside his coat.

I murmured to the dogs. The growls and flashing teeth stopped but their eyes never left Rudy's hands.

We rode in silence for a bit. Then Rudy shook his head and said, 'I never would have placed my bets on you.'

I shrugged and stroked Rip's chest.

Rudy leaned his head back and closed his eyes. The train clicked and clacked along. Slowly, I relaxed.

'How did you do it?' he asked.

'Do what?'

'Survive.' He opened his eyes and looked at me. 'How did you survive the winter and the militsiya and the gangs of boys like me?'

Rip sighed and laid his head in my lap. Star shifted his warm weight into mine. The others never took their eyes off Rudy.

'The dogs,' I said.

Rudy nodded. 'The dogs.'

The train sighed to a stop. Rudy stood. He dug into the pocket of his black jeans and tossed a wad of rubles at my feet. 'You still have those fairy tales you used to read to us?' he asked. His voice sounded old but his face looked younger than I remembered.

I shook my head. 'I lost them.'

Rudy looked away. 'Ah,' he said. 'Too bad.'

The doors to the train whisked open. Rudy touched two fingers to the brim of his hat, then turned and walked onto the train platform and down the corridor without a backwards glance.

I never saw him again.

Chapter 40

BROKEN

Day after day, the snow fell. The militsiya drove the children and the bomzhi from the stations. The street kids disappeared beneath the city streets to the warm water pipes below. The bomzhi slept in doorways and apartment building entrances. The bins behind the restaurants where I found our food now filled with snow. Everything we ate that winter was frozen solid.

I tried to remember summer. What had it felt like to be warm day after day? How had grass felt under my bare feet? I could not picture the green meadow dotted with yellow flowers. I could not remember the sheltering arms of the great tree we slept beneath. I did not believe in Summer or Warmth or Angels. All I believed in was Cold.

We were all tired and snappish. Some days, all I wanted to do was sleep on the warm, rocking train. The thought of spending another day in the bitter cold and wind and snow trying to find enough food to feed the seven of us brought me to tears and made me turn on my family.

'Why can't you find your own food?' I shouted at the dogs one afternoon as I dug my way through a snow-filled bin. Rip whined. Lucky just wagged his tail.

'If it weren't for you, I would be fat,' I said. I pulled a rotten potato from the snow and hurled it at Rip. It bounced in front of him and then skittered away. Star pounced on the potato. Lucky woofed with excitement at the new game I had invented.

'I'm not kidding!' I shouted. Little Mother and Moon looked up at me on top of the snow-covered rubbish with worried eyes. 'You're lazy! You're stupid, lazy dogs!' I hurled frozen carrots, onions, chunks of bread and bones down upon the dogs. The dogs quickly realised this was no game. They crouched and cowered beneath my anger, their eyes pleading.

Stop, Smoke said.

'Oh, now you speak to me!' I cried. 'You haven't spoken to me for months and now you boss me around!' I threw a frozen cabbage as hard as I could and hit Smoke squarely in the side of his head. He yelped in pain and staggered. The dogs all looked at me like I was some red-eyed beast. I was not their boy; I was not one of them. I was an Other.

Smoke shook himself and then gave me a cold look. 'I'm . . .' The words were a frozen lump in my throat.

Smoke barked once and trotted to the end of the alley. The dogs looked from Smoke to me, standing on top of a small mountain of rubbish and snow, red-faced and shivering.

Despair and the days behind us and ahead of us swept over me. 'Go,' I cried. 'Just go! I don't need you!'

The dogs flattened their ears and tucked their tails and disappeared with Smoke.

I stared at the huge, empty, dog-shaped hole where they no longer were. I dropped to my knees and panted. I waited and watched. Surely they would be back any minute: Lucky smiling his Lucky smile and wagging his tail; Little Mother washing the snot and tears from my face; Rip snuggling against me – their eyes, even Smoke's eyes, saying All is forgiven.

I climbed down from the bin as the wind swirled up the alley. The sky grew leaden and close. Any minute now, they'll be back, I told myself over and over.

The skies opened and great sheets of snow fell. I climbed inside an empty cardboard box and curled up on my side. I hugged my knees to my chest and rocked back and forth.

I heard soft footfalls in the snow. They were back! I stuck my head out into the snow. 'I am so sorry! I—'

A large black cat looked at me with cold green eyes. A rat hung from his mouth.

I pulled back inside the box and buried my face in my hands. 'I am alone,' I moaned. 'I belong nowhere and to no one in the whole world.' I cried and shivered and rubbed the tooth in my pocket over and over and over. Day faded to night.

I woke to something warm and wet stroking my face. 'Mother,' I said through chattering teeth. I reached up my arms to the warmth of Little Mother's neck. I buried my frozen hands and face in her deep fur. Rip pushed into my lap and snuffled my neck. Moon and Star did their best to curl themselves into the box, but it was not big enough for a small boy and four dogs. I crawled out of the box. The alley was lit with snow and moonlight. I stood in drifts above my knees.

The dogs crowded around my legs and licked my hands and fingers. 'I am sorry,' I whispered in the moonlight. 'I never meant to hurt you,' I said, stroking heads and shoulders. 'You are the best dogs, the best family.' Lucky dropped a fat sausage at my feet. I laughed. 'Who did you steal this from, my little thief?' He wagged his tail. His eyes glinted with mischief.

Malchik.

I turned.

Smoke shimmered and shifted as a cloud passed over the moon.

Smoke. I held out my hand. For the first time in all the many months we had been together, he pushed his head into my hand. I stroked the top of his silver and black head and the thick ruff around his neck. His eyes were yellow in the moonlight.

Our Malchik, he said again. Our boy.

And I knew my place in the world.

Chapter 41

HOME

And then, as suddenly as it had come, winter was gone. The great rafts of ice in the river broke up and floated away. The children emerged from the underworld, blinking and pale in the spring sun. The banks of snow piled in the alleyways and against buildings, tall as any man, melted and revealed those who had not been so lucky to survive one of the worst winters in the last twenty years.

Leaves unfolded and hands unfolded. Perhaps it was everyone's relief at having survived, perhaps it was the return of true sunshine, but the people of The City were generous – for a time, anyway. The passers-by dropped coins and rubles in outstretched hands with a quick smile. The shopkeepers handed out day-old bread every morning. The militsiya once again patrolled the streets and the parks, leaving the stations to us. Even the gangs of black-clad, chain-wearing Crow Boys left the smaller children alone. The *bomzhi* were not so lucky.

One day, we found more Christian Ladies than we'd ever seen at Komsomolskaya Ploshchad. Their tables and boxes filled the square. Lines and lines of ragged children snaked round and about the benches and statues. Some stood swaying on their feet, others hopped from one foot to the other. Little boys wrestled like Moon and Star had when they were just silly puppies. Girls clung to one another or to older boys. Some of the small children cried, and others chased the army of pigeons.

The dogs and I watched the street children and the Christian Ladies from the top steps at the feet of a statue. A man carved of marble clutched the lapel of his coat, his other hand thrust in his marble pocket. He studied the crowd of homeless children with eyes that said *How did it come to this?*

A woman stopped at the bottom of the statue. 'Come and get something to eat,' she said.

'Is there food for them too?' I asked, motioning to the dogs.

The woman shook her head. She waved to the never-ending line of children. 'We barely have enough food for them. You think we would feed dogs too?' And then she stalked away.

I hopped down off the perch at the feet of the marble man. A fight broke out between three boys over a piece of bread. Two more boys jumped in just for the fun of the fight. The Christian Ladies shouted, 'Stop this foolishness or none of you will get one bite to eat!'

'Come,' I said to the dogs. We trotted across the wide square, away from the marble man with his stern, cold face and away from the crying, fighting children.

We rode the escalator down and down and down into Yaroslavl station. As always, we slipped into the last train car. The dogs sprawled on the floor of the rocking car with a sigh. All their ribs showed through their dull coats. Lucky had received a wound that refused to heal from a fight with another street dog. I had a cough that rattled deep in my chest and kept me awake at night.

I leaned my head against the sun-warmed window. It was time to go home.

We would return to the woods. The dogs would once again become fat. I would grow brown in the sun that stretched into the late evening hours. We would race through the woods and the meadows with soft grass and leaves beneath our feet instead of concrete. We would fly as if we all had wings.

*

We rode and rode the train until we came to the park with the Ferris wheel on the edge of the great wood.

We waited until dark. After the few people who were there trailed away, we made our way into the park. We said hello to the Ferris wheel, the wooden stalls selling beer and shashlyk, and the stage where the bands played. The ducks floated on the pond. Rip and I found a nest of eggs and ate them. Smoke snapped a fat duck's neck and carried it off into the woods to share with Little Mother. This year, I did not need to drag a chair over to the bin to climb in. All I had to do was stand on my toes and reach up.

I filled plastic bags with food. We set off for our home beneath the tree. Would I remember how to get there? It did not matter. Once we crossed the boulevard to the edge of the great forest, my feet remembered the way. We ran and ran along the trails we knew so well. Patches of snow still pooled beneath some of the trees. Finally, we burst free of the forest and into our meadow. Here the grass was green and dotted with yellow flowers. The creek overran its banks and sprawled this way and that.

And there, on the far side of the meadow, stood our tree.

Moon and Star galloped happily over to our den and wiggled beneath the branches.

'Let's go home,' I said to the dogs.

It was still quite wet in the well beneath the tree – too wet for us to live in for now, anyway.

I crawled out and sighed. Smoke watched me as I thought and thought what to do. Rip and Lucky rolled with joy in the grass and mud.

I crawled up onto the big flat rocks where I'd watched the stars last summer, the place where we howled together at the moon. Little Mother climbed up beside me and laid her head on my leg.

'We need to make another home until our den dries out,' I said, stroking her head. 'We could go to Rubbish Mountain and get things to make a home.' Little Mother sneezed.

'I know,' I said. 'I do not want to go back there, either. There are bad people there.'

Star barked from the boulders at the top of the gentle rise above the meadow. He sat at the foot of the tree stump – the stump on top of which the giant deer skull still rested, shining white in the moonlight.

Smoke and I trotted up the rise to the boulders and the skull. Up here, the ground was dry. Next to the boulders, it was warm.

I scraped together a bed of dry leaves. 'We will sleep

here tonight. Tomorrow, I will find a way to make us a shelter until our den is dry.'

We all piled together on the bed of leaves. I picked burrs and twigs from Rip's fur while Lucky scrubbed my face with his tongue. The wind shifted and sighed around us. Clouds sailed over the moon and beyond.

Chapter 42

TREES

The days grew longer, and the dogs grew stronger. Ribs and hip bones and knobbly backbones disappeared beneath glossy fur and fat.

Week by week, I shed first the coat, then the jumper, then the boots and socks and hat. I took my knife to the legs of my raggedy trousers and cut them off just above the knee. I scrubbed and scrubbed my lice-filled hair with mud and rinsed it in water so cold it made my teeth ache. The sun healed the sores on my face and feet.

Like the summer before, we explored the border regions of the forest. We found rotting carcasses of the old and weak animals that had not made it through the terrible winter – deer, a fox, birds and even a dog.

I squatted beside the body of the dog and studied what was left. A back leg was bent at an angle it should not be. Many of the teeth were missing. I touched the brown fur still covering the ribs.

Smoke ran his nose along the bones and fur. *Them,* he said.

My heart shuddered. Could this have been one of the dogs I had hit with my club during the fight at the House of Bones? 'I am sorry,' I said.

Smoke snorted and trotted away, his tail held stiff and high.

We did not return to the House of Bones, but we did find the skeleton of the Biggest Pig in All of Russia. The leg bones were not long enough to make another club, but I took the longest of the curved ribs just the same. It felt good in my hand and worked just fine for knocking off the heads of dandelions. I invented a game of hockey – a pine cone for a puck, the rib bone for my hockey stick – like the street hockey I had seen the bigger boys play. Star and Lucky were the best players, next to me.

One day, just after the second full moon, I climbed our tree to retrieve a bag of food. I climbed first one branch, then up to another and another. I climbed past the bag of food. I climbed higher than I had ever been – higher than the longest escalator in the train stations.

I heard a bark and a yip from below. I stopped and looked down. All six dogs sat at the bottom of the tree, their heads tilted all the way back.

I laughed and waved. 'Come on up,' I said.

Lucky wagged his tail and woofed. Little Mother whimpered and whined with worry. Rip and Moon barked. Star rolled onto his back.

Down, said Smoke.

'No,' I said, but I climbed down anyway. The dogs mobbed me, jumping and licking and crying. Smoke sat off to the side, watching me with worried eyes. *It is not right*, he said.

I tossed a pine cone in the air for Lucky to catch. 'You're just jealous because you can't climb trees,' I said. 'You are earthbound,' I said.

So are you.

Smoke and I looked at each other for a long moment. 'I am not always like you,' I said.

And so, I climbed the trees. I climbed every tree that would let me. I climbed higher and higher to the swaying tops. If I could just climb high enough, I could fly and not have to ride the trains. If I could climb high enough, I could touch the sun and never be cold again.

One hot, still evening, I bathed in a cold pool of water at the bottom of a concrete chute near the road separating the forest from the Ferris-wheel park. Never had we come this close to the park and the people when there was still light. Like the summer before, I raided the rubbish bins in the early morning hours during the short time of real darkness.

I pulled on my cutoff trousers. The dogs shook the water from their coats and sprawled in the shade of a large oak tree. I could see, just up at the top, a wonderful breeze moving the leaves of the tree. There, if I could just get up there...

I pulled myself up and up, branch by branch, until I reached the topmost limbs. I settled in the forking arms of the branches and closed my eyes. The breeze lifted my wet hair off my face. I smiled. 'Thank you,' I said.

Tweet tweet, toodle-loo, the breeze sang back.

I opened my eyes. What was that? I peered down through the branches to the dogs. They were fast asleep.

And then it came again, a beautiful sound, a sweet soaring sound, drifting across the road from the Ferris-wheel park and up to my branches.

I climbed a little higher and looked towards the park. And, oh! The giant wheel turned slowly in the strange light of the summer evening. The Ferris-wheel seats dangled from the wheel like shivering drops of water. The music carried by the breeze came from the great wheel.

I clapped my hands and laughed. How clever the wheel was! I drew my knees up to my chest, rested my chin on my knees, and listened. Sometimes the music was sad and sometimes it was happy. For the first time in many months, I thought of my mother humming at the kitchen sink. I saw her hands slipping in and out of the steaming hot water as she washed the dishes. I thought about the blind man in the train station with his beautiful accordion, how the air sang in and out of its chest like a dragon. I bowed my head. The music pulled hard on my heart from a place I had long forgotten. I wiped at the tears trickling down my cheeks.

Every evening as the sun slipped low, I returned to the oak tree at the edge of the forest. I climbed the tree and listened.

Soon, I crept closer to the road. The dogs whimpered and shifted nervously around my legs. 'I need to get closer to the music,' I said. Their eyes begged me to go back to the shelter of the woods.

'What can you understand of music?' I said with a snort as I climbed a tree. The dogs woofed and whined.

It wasn't long before I had to cross the road.

'Come,' I commanded the dogs. Only Lucky and Star followed me across. The other dogs melted into the shadows with their eyes fixed like lasers on us.

I crouched between the two dogs, my shoulders level with theirs. We eased from shadow to shadow. The music grew louder. The voices of people laughed and rose and fell. These were not angry voices, yelling voices, voices that hit and spat. These were happy voices.

We skirted the edge of the stalls with their smells of roasting meat, and the plastic tables and chairs. Always when I came here, the tables sat empty and the chairs over-turned and scattered. Now men and women and children were at the tables eating and drinking and laughing. Children sat in their mother's and father's laps sleeping or bouncing up and down. One small boy was in an old woman's lap, his head resting against the pillow of her large chest, one hand fingering the cross hanging from her neck, the other hand curled under his chin, his eyes half closed. The old woman rocked him back and forth. A scarf covered her head.

I had sat in my Babushka Ina's lap like that once, so very long ago. She had rocked me and sung to me and all the world was safe. I had food enough and I was rarely cold. The world turned as I lay curled in her lap without a care.

And then one day she died, and everything changed.

'Get out of here, you mangy cur!'

I blinked. I was crouched next to Star with my thumb in my mouth.

Glass shattered. Lucky yelped and dashed away from the tables with his tail tucked between his legs and his ears flat against his head. Clamped between his jaws was a stick of roasted meat and vegetables. Lucky, the thief.

He ran to our hiding place in the shadows. Someone called, 'Look, there's more of them!'

I wanted to stand up on my two legs and walk out into the light and call to them, 'See, I am just a boy.' I wanted to climb into that babushka's lap and rest my head against her chest.

A bottle exploded above my head. Beer and glass rained down. Laughter. Shouts. More bottles and cans. Lucky stood in front of us, shielding me with his strong shoulders and fierce teeth. He barked and growled. All the fur stood up on his back.

'It's mad!' a woman cried. 'It's a mad dog!'

'There's three of them!' someone else shouted.

There were not three. There were Lucky and Star and a boy.

A bottle hit Lucky, almost knocking him to the ground.

I sprang to my feet. 'No!'

For a split second, the yabbering crowd fell silent. Eyes peered into the shadows. Arms ready to throw, froze. The music from the Ferris wheel toot-tootled as it always did.

'No,' I whispered.

The dogs and I whirled and ran back across the road and into the darkening forest until we were far away. I washed the blood from Lucky's head and stroked his side. 'I am sorry,' I said. He shivered under my hands. His eyes said Why?

Star dropped the prized stick with its meat and vegetables. He had managed to lose only a few pieces on the race through the woods.

I took the stick and slid one, then two pieces off for Star. Everything else I gave to Lucky.

Chapter 43

THE WOMAN IN THE HAT

In the far north of the Border Lands where the wild pig had lived, we came across a trail of blood glowing in the light of the full moon. The blood made me uneasy. The blood trail made the dogs crazy with excitement.

They ran and ran, their noses pressed to the ground, Smoke in the lead. What if one of the Others trailed this blood too? I knew we were far from their territory, but that didn't mean they wouldn't venture this far. Like us.

The pack stopped at the edge of a stream. They searched up and down the banks for the blood trail. I trotted up next to Smoke.

'Let's go back,' I said.

No, Malchik.

I growled hard. 'I said—'

Moon yipped and bounded across the creek. The rest of the pack streamed behind her and disappeared into the woods beyond the moonlight.

Rip pawed my leg and panted with excitement.

'OK, OK,' I said.

By the time I found the dogs, it was over.

A small deer lay at the feet of the pack. Its big brown eyes gazed out at nothing.

I pushed my way through the dogs. 'Get back.' I growled and raised the rib bone above my head. All the dogs stepped away except Smoke. He watched as I knelt next to the deer.

I could see where the dogs had torn its back leg and its throat. But on the side of its neck, blood flowed from a perfectly round hole. It was not the shape of teeth or claws or even the tusk of the Biggest Pig in All of Russia. I poked my finger into the hole as far as it would go until it bumped against something hard and flat and small. That was where the blood trail had come from.

I stood and wiped my hand on my shirt. 'Eat,' I said.

Growling, smacking, the crunch of bone, the tear of skin.

I turned my back on the dogs and returned to the creek. I sat beside the moon-silver water and rocked myself back and forth, feeling small.

A twig snapped. Warm breath on the back of my arm.

Smoke dropped something at my feet.

I picked it up and brushed it off. It fit warm and egg-shaped in the palm of my hand.

Eat, Smoke said.

I did.

In the golden haze of late summer, I rested in a tree. This tree was a fine birch not too close to the Ferris-wheel park but just close enough for the wind to bring voices and music.

I was trying to remember a song my mother used to sing to me, when I heard a voice below say, 'This will do nicely.'

I peered down through the branches. A woman in a wide-brimmed hat and skirt covered with flowers stood a metre from my tree. She smiled at the small stream I had bathed in earlier to rid myself of fleas. All of us were covered with bites.

The woman unfolded a small stool, just like the one the blind Accordion Man had used to sit on. From a large bag, she pulled out and unfolded a wooden stand, a big pad of paper and a box. She settled herself on the stool and propped the pad of white paper on the stand. She hummed and opened the box.

Quietly, quietly, I eased myself down one limb and then another to see what she might have to eat in that box. Rip and Moon and Little Mother stuck their noses out from under the brush where they'd been napping in the cool dirt. Their noses wiggled back and forth.

She lifted the lid. The box did not hold food. The box held sticks of bright colour. She picked up a stick the colour of the late-summer grass and scribbled it over the paper. Then she picked up another colour stick and another. Her hand moved this way and that across the page.

I lowered myself one more time. I gasped. The woman had drawn the grass and the stream and the blue, blue sky and the flowers and the brushy brush with three black noses peeking out.

The woman's hand froze. She looked all around. 'Is someone there?' she whispered. I held my breath and kept very still. The birds sang. A squirrel scolded me for being in his tree.

The woman sighed. She put her picture and her colour sticks and her wooden stand back in her big bag. She folded up her stool and looked around the small meadow one last time. And then, humming a little tune, she walked back towards the Ferris-wheel park.

I dropped to the ground. The dogs wiggled from under the brush and danced with relief, as they always did, that I had come down from where they could not follow.

'Did you see?' I asked them. 'Did you see what was in that box?'

The dogs stretched and yawned.

I hugged myself. 'Oh, I know it wasn't food, but it was amazing. It made something beautiful.'

The woman came back the next day and the next, always in the late afternoon. I waited for her in the tree and I watched.

Sometimes she drew the light on the stream; sometimes she drew the dying flowers. Always she hummed while she drew.

My fingers itched to draw too. How I had loved to draw when I was just a little boy. I drew the stories my mother read to me from the book of fairy tales. I remembered drawing to pass the time when my mother left me alone after Babushka Ina died. I remembered drawing on any little scrap of paper I could find during those long, cold and lonely nights after he came. How long had it been since I had held a pencil in my hand?

On the third day, the woman appeared. And as always, she wore her big hat and her skirt with flowers. She set up her stool and her stand and set about drawing.

After a time, I saw something from the corner of one eye. Lucky crept towards the woman on his belly. His eyes were fixed on a plastic bag next to her chair.

I sniffed. Something wonderful rested in that bag, and Lucky meant to steal it.

My heart hammered in my chest. I hissed at Lucky.

The woman stopped and looked around.

The woman went back to humming her tune and drawing a squirrel chattering in a tree.

Lucky eased forward, his tongue flicking his nose. He stretched his neck as far as it would go and pulled back his lips.

'No!' I shouted from the tree.

The woman jumped up from her stool. Her eyes darted from Lucky to me. 'Oh!' she gasped.

Lucky flattened his ears against his skull and rolled his eyes apologetically. Then he whirled and shot into the underbrush.

The woman looked up at me, her eyes wide and blue. Her hair was white beneath the wide brim of her hat.

I dropped out of the tree and crouched in front of her.

Her wrinkled face went white. Her mouth opened and closed.

I could not bear to hear her cry, 'It's a demon!' or 'Get away!'

We locked eyes. Her face flushed. Her eyes softened.

As I dashed after Lucky, I heard her call, 'Boy! Boy!'

I ran and ran, my feet just skimming the grass. I flew across our stream and burst into our meadow. I wrestled Lucky to the ground and play-nipped at his ears. His eyes danced with relief.

'Me!' I said to Lucky and the rest who'd gathered around, their tails wagging. 'She saw me!'

Chapter 44

MOWGLI

For two days, it rained. I knew the Woman in the Hat would not come when it rained. Still, every day I went to the birch tree and waited.

Finally, the sun shone. I raced to the tree and climbed just a few limbs up. Again, she would see me – *me*. She did not look through me like a ghost; she did not confuse me for a mad dog. She did not see me digging through rubbish bins for food or eating the still-warm heart of a deer. Because her eyes had softened, hadn't they? I hugged myself and smiled.

The sun rose high to the top of the tree. She did not come. The sun slipped to the side, then sank below the outstretched limbs. Still she did not come.

When the first star appeared in the fading light, I climbed down from the tree. The dogs leapt in a frenzy.

'You,' I shouted at Lucky. 'It's all your fault!'

Lucky tucked his tail and turned his head away from me. I stood over him, my fists clenched. 'If you hadn't been so greedy, if you hadn't tried to steal her food, she'd have come back!'

Tears stung my eyes. I raised my fist. Lucky cowered.

Smoke stepped between us. He lifted one corner of his lip. Stop.

Lucky looked up, his eyes pleading.

All the anger drained away.

I dropped to my knees and threw my arms around his big neck. 'I'm sorry,' I whispered into his scarred ear. He licked the tears off my face.

I did not go back to the birch tree the next day. Instead, I explored with the dogs.

But the day after, I could not keep from going.

I had just hoisted myself onto a limb when she, the Woman in the Hat, walked into the sunlight. She hummed as she set up her stool and her drawing frame, just as she always had. She took out her wonderful box of colour sticks.

I squirmed on the limb. Why had she not looked for me? Had she forgotten? Was I just a ghost to her now?

She took another plastic bag from her very big bag and set it on the stool. Then, without turning or looking up, she called, 'I brought you food.'

My heart skipped once and then again. Perhaps she was talking to Lucky?

'But you have to come down from that silly tree to get it,' she said, her voice smiling.

Slowly, I slid down from the tree. Just as slowly, she picked up the plastic bag. She held it out. 'Here,' she said. 'Take it.'

I wanted to scamper around her in circles like Moon and Star had when they were excited, silly puppies. I wanted to roll on my back and show her my belly. Instead, I walked over to her with my eyes downcast and took the bag. I retreated to the base of my tree and squatted on the ground. The smell from the bag made my mouth water. Inside the bag: bread, a boiled egg, sausage roll and, most wonderfully, a red apple. I held the apple to my nose and sniffed in its appleness. I would share the bread and sausage roll with the dogs, but the apple and the egg were mine.

'Eat,' she said.

I opened my eyes, startled. She watched me. The wrinkles around her eyes smiled like Babushka Ina's had.

I broke off a small piece of bread and chewed. My throat was too dry to swallow. How long had it been since I'd been this close to another person?

'Do you live near here?' she asked, tucking her white hair into a bun.

I nodded.

Her summer-blue eyes took in my long, matted hair, my torn-off trousers, and the shirt that was really just rags now. 'Do you have parents?'

I shook my head.

She cocked her head to one side. 'What's your name, then?' I coughed and looked away, ashamed. What would I tell her? Dog Boy? Cockroach? She sighed. 'You're just like Mowgli in *The Jungle Book*.' I looked across to her. Mowgli. A tiny memory that I could not catch came with that name.

She sat on her stool and placed her pad of white paper on the frame. She looked over her shoulder and said, 'You're welcome to stay and keep me company, Mowgli.'

And I did.

Can you draw a firebird?' I asked. Rip licked the grease of roasted chicken from my fingers. I shifted him in my lap to better see what the Woman in the Hat was drawing. Lucky lay with his head by her foot. Sometimes Lucky and Star came with me to the birch tree. Rip always came. Never did Smoke or Little Mother or Moon let the Woman in the Hat see them.

She gave me a curious, sideways look. 'How does Mowgli know about firebirds?'

'From my fairy-tale book,' I said.

'You can read?'

I shrugged and pulled a tick from Rip's good ear.

'How old are you, Mowgli?'

I sighed. I had been meeting her at the birch tree for many days. I was tired of her questions.

I pointed to her box of colour sticks. 'What are those?'

'Pastels,' she said. She held up a pastel the colour of blood. 'Want to try one?'

I shook my head, but I could not take my eyes off the red, glowing stick.

She smiled. 'Come here, Mowgli, and show this old woman how to draw a firebird.'

I took the pad of white paper. My filthy fingers smudged the edges. I cringed.

'It's OK,' she said. She handed me the red pastel. 'Draw,' she said.

I closed my eyes and searched my memory for the great firebird, and then I drew. When I was finished, I handed her the pad, not looking at her.

She gasped. 'Why, Mowgli, this is very good!' She looked from the firebird, to me, then back at the paper.

I wrestled with the smile pulling at my face. My heart soared like the firebird over The City. I buried my face against my hands.

She touched my shoulder. I jerked away and covered my face.

'It's OK,' she said. I heard a ripping sound. My drawing was rubbish. I huddled deeper in my knees and hands.

'Here,' she said. 'You keep it.'

I looked up. She had torn my firebird from her pad and held it out to me. 'You can hang it up,' she said.

I leapt to my feet. The smile won over my face. 'You keep it,' I said. 'It will get wet and ruined where we live.'

And before she could ask the question already marching from her mouth, I dashed with Rip into the forest.

That night, I sat on the flat boulder at the far edge of the meadow and gazed at the night sky. Moon lay on one side of me, her feet twitching in her sleep. The rest of the pack lay scattered about the meadow.

I pulled my knees to my chest and rocked myself back and forth. My blood sang in my body like the music in the Ferris-wheel park.

'This is very good,' she had said. She had not said, 'You are a small pathetic boy.' She had not said, 'You are no better than a cockroach.' She had said, 'Very good.'

I cupped Moon's face in my hands and put my nose close to hers. 'I am very good,' I said. 'I am a very good Mowgli.'

Moon wagged her tail and kissed the end of my nose.

I took the piece of newspaper my sausage had been wrapped in from my pocket. I smoothed it out on my knees. Star nibbled at one corner.

'Stop that,' I said, pushing him away.

I searched the piece of newspaper hungrily for words I knew.

'The. Man. Ran. Away,' I read out loud to the dogs. 'The man ran away,' I said. I laughed. 'He ran away!'

I grabbed Lucky by his front paws and danced with him in the moonlight.

Chapter 45

DRAWING TALES

I no longer waited in the limbs of the birch tree for the Woman in the Hat. I sat at the base of the tree and listened. I knew now the sound of her footfall and the rustle of her skirt. Rip and I would meet her halfway to the tree and carry her big bag of everything, which always included food.

Now she brought me my own pad of clean white paper and a box of crayons.

After I tired of drawing pictures of the firebird and Baba Yaga, I drew a picture of the Biggest Pig in All of Russia.

I handed her the drawing of the pig with its glowing red eyes and cruel tusks. I'd drawn how the hair bristled on its back like the spiked hair of the Crow Boys in The City.

She pressed her hand to her chest. 'My goodness,' she said. 'That's a fine boar.'

'We killed it,' I said, puffing out my chest with pride.

'Who killed it?' she asked.

'We did,' I said. 'The dogs and I.'

She frowned. 'I don't think a little boy and a couple of dogs could kill a creature like that.'

I leapt to my feet. 'But we did! These are not all the dogs, and besides, I am not a little boy.'

She smiled. 'No, indeed not.'

I could tell she did not believe me.

I snatched the pad of white paper back and drew furiously. I drew the dogs leaping on the back of the boar and grabbing its ear. I drew the boar throwing Smoke aside with one toss of his tusk. I drew myself, arm raised high overhead, smashing the club on the skull of the boar. I drew the boar lying on its side, blood trickling from its mouth.

I thrust the pad in the woman's face. 'See here and here,' I said, pointing to each picture. 'This is how we killed it.'

She peered closely at my drawings, touched them one by one with her finger. 'These are remarkable,' she said. 'You've moved from drawing fairy tales to drawing picture tales.'

She pointed to the club in the drawing. 'That's quite the weapon.'

I nodded. 'It came from the leg of a huge deer.' I held my hand level with my waist. 'It was this big.'

'My,' she said. 'And did you and the dogs kill it too?' she asked with a little smile.

I shook my head. 'The Others killed it.'

She laughed and shook her head. 'You do have quite the imagination. Can you draw me a picture of this giant deer?'

I hesitated. I only knew it from its bones. And then I remembered the beautiful animal we had seen in the forest once, with its long legs and great spread of antlers.

I bent over my pad and drew. I held out the picture when I was finished.

'Ah,' she said with surprise. 'I'd heard there were elk here. That's why they call this park Elk Island.' She shook her head. 'But I can't imagine what could kill a creature that big.'

'The Others could,' I said.

She shook her head again. 'You and your picture tales.'

She looked up at the sky and sighed. 'The days are getting short again.' She pulled a jumper from her bottomless bag and draped it over her shoulders. 'Soon it will be too cold to come.'

My mouth went dry. I did not want to think about the

cold and the snow and not seeing the Woman in the Hat or hearing the beautiful music every night in the Ferris-wheel park.

'It is not too cold yet,' I said.

But all too soon, it did turn cold. The leaves fell from the trees. The limbs of the birch tree spread like black fingers. 'Mowgli,' the woman said, 'where do you go in the winter? Do you have a warm place to go?'

I concentrated on drawing Smoke's eyes. I could not seem to get the colour just right.

For only the second time, the woman touched my shoulder. I did not pull away. 'Mowgli, child. You cannot live here in this cold.'

Not looking at her, I said, 'We will stay here until the snow comes. We keep each other warm,' I explained.

She threw up her hands. 'Who is we?'

I threw my hands up too. 'I've told you! The dogs.' I showed her the drawing. 'This is Smoke.'

She looked at the drawing for a long time. Then in a sad voice, she asked, 'And where do you and the dogs go when the snow comes?'

I did not mean to make her sad. 'The City,' I said. 'We ride the trains all over The City. It's warm on the trains and mostly safe.'

She frowned. She pointed at Smoke's eyes on the white page. 'Child, is this another one of your fairy tales?'

I frowned. 'I have never told you a tale.'

The next day, I hurried along the path to the birch tree. Food was getting harder to find in the park and I was hungry. Every day was colder; every day there were fewer people.

Lucky stopped just before the thicket on the other side of the birch tree. He raised his head, his nose searching the air. The fur rose on the back of his neck.

I listened. Yes, that was the sound of the old woman's skirt and her footfall on the dead leaves, but another walked with her. This one's footsteps were heavy and impatient. I smelled a cigarette.

I wriggled under the thicket and listened.

'Here, this is where we always meet,' the Woman in the Hat said. I could see only her skirt and her feet. A pair of grey trousers and shiny boots stood next to her skirt and legs.

'Well, I certainly don't see anyone, Mother,' a deep voice said.

'He *always* comes.' The old woman's voice was fretful. 'You'll see.'

Her son sighed and flicked his cigarette onto the ground, right in front of my nose.

'It's too cold for a child to be playing in the woods, Mother. He's probably gone back to wherever he lives.'

'I'm telling you, he lives here! He and those smelly dogs,' the old woman snapped. 'He doesn't play here like some schoolboy. And of course it's too cold. That's why I'm so worried about him.'

I smiled.

The man in the trousers and boots paced back and forth. He lit another cigarette.

'Oh dear,' the woman said. 'Where could he be?'

I closed my eyes and imagined wriggling out from the bushes and standing up straight and tall. I would smile and she would hug me to her in relief.

'We've waited long enough, Mother. It's too cold for you to be out here and I have to get back to work.'

She would show me to her son, her eyes filled with pride. She would say, 'This is Mowgli. He's a very good boy. Very good.'

I opened my eyes, my heart light. I pushed myself out from under the bushes and stood.

The clearing beneath the birch tree was empty.

Chapter 46

WILD CHILD

The next day, snow dusted the ground. Still, just as the sun topped the trees, I went to the birch tree. The Woman in the Hat did not come. More snow fell the next day and the next.

Then, as sometimes happens in late autumn, the weather warmed. A salty breeze came from the ocean. The dogs played and hunted. I took the path to the tree.

I smelled his cigarette before I even got to the thicket. I crouched in the shadow of a tall pine and listened.

I heard voices rising and falling. I heard rough laughter. I did not hear the old woman's voice.

I climbed the pine tree. It still had its needles and hid me well. From a branch high up, I could see over to the small clearing with the stream and the birch tree.

Three men in tall black boots, grey coats with shiny buttons, and red and black hats stood in the clearing.

Militsiya! One of the men was the son of the Woman in the Hat.

'So your mother's been having trysts in the woods with a wild child?' the shortest of the three laughed.

'She's not having "trysts,"' her son snapped. 'She comes here to paint and she says he comes here too, with a pack of mangy dogs.'

'Probably one of those kids from over at that dump,' the third man said. 'It's disgusting how many bomzhi live over there with their kids.'

'I say we round up all the filthy bomzhi and their children and ship them off to Siberia,' the shortest one said.

The Woman's son said, 'I told her no child could live out here with a pack of wild dogs, but you know how mothers are. She won't let it alone until I find this boy.' The other two men nodded.

'There's thousands of them street children,' one of the men said. 'They're everywhere, like fleas on a dog.'

The three policemen smoked in silence and scuffed their shiny boots in the dead leaves as if I might be hiding underneath.

The old woman wanted to find me! She had sent her son and militsiya to look for me. But why hadn't she come? Perhaps it was too cold for her now with the snow on the ground. Perhaps, like Babushka Ina, she was afraid of falling on the ice.

Then a thought seized me and wouldn't let go: perhaps she was readying her house for us! Yes, she must live in a very big house if her son is a policeman! She would bring the dogs and me to live with her. She would clean us and feed us and cook porridge on her stove. I would have real books to read. I would again sleep in a bed (which I would, of course, share with the dogs) and eat out of a bowl. And I would be the very best boy.

A cold wind set the branch I perched on swaying. 'Well,' the old woman's son said. 'Let's go and disturb some bomzhi over at the dump and ask around about the boy.' They flicked their cigarettes into the snow.

The short one asked, 'How are we going to know which one he is?'

The son took a piece of paper from his coat pocket and unfolded it. 'Here,' he said. 'She drew a picture of him.' The men looked down at the paper.

The third policeman shook his head and said, 'He does look like a wild child.'

The short man hooted with laughter.

I frowned. We'd see who'd be laughing when I had a bath and new clothes.

The son folded the paper over and over. 'She calls him Mowgli. It's driving my wife crazy. I don't know what I was thinking, bringing her to live with us.' He clamped his hat to his head against the wind. 'Three adults plus two kids in a two-bedroom apartment . . .' He shook his head.

My heart fell. 'What do we do with him if we find him?' the third militsiya asked.

The old woman's son stuffed the drawing of me – her Mowgli – into his pocket. 'An orphanage, of course,' he said. 'What do you think? He'd come live with us?'

The men howled with laughter as they walked away.

I held tight to the tree limb as the word dropped like a stone into my stomach.

Orphanage.

That night I cuddled closer with the dogs than I had in a long time underneath our tree. 'You were right about the Woman in the Hat,' I whispered to Little Mother. 'You and Smoke and Moon were all right. I should have listened.' Little Mother washed and washed my face as if saying, Never mind that now.

I stroked Moon's face. 'It was just so nice to have someone to talk to, who talked back,' I said.

Smoke shifted against Rip. *She did not love you, Malchik.*

'I know,' I whispered. 'I thought perhaps she would love us and give us a home where we would be warm and safe.'

I felt Smoke's breath on my face. *We are where you belong.*

I did not return to the birch tree. Mowgli was gone.

Chapter 47

HUNTED

I dug through the bins in the Ferris-wheel park. For the first time in weeks, the bins were full. Perhaps the bin men were once again on strike; perhaps there had been a holiday I had forgotten about. I had forgotten many things in my years of living with the dogs.

I remembered the old woman asking me how old I was. I couldn't say. Six? Seven? Was my birthday in the late spring or early summer?

Rip trotted along beside me as I crossed the place where the people had danced on the long summer evenings. 'I think I am seven now,' I said. 'I could even be almost eight.' I liked the sound of being eight. Eight-year-olds got to do many things five-year-olds did not.

A shadow swept across the concrete. I stopped. Was it just a cloud passing across the face of the full moon?

'There he is!' someone shouted.

Rip growled.

Militsiya came from everywhere!

I crouched and growled.

A voice I recognised as the old woman's son said, 'Take it slow. Don't scare him off.'

I dropped my bags of food and backed away from the men.

The old woman's son held out a hand to me. 'It's OK, boy. We're here to help you.'

I looked from the men to the side of the park with the duck pond. That was where the other dogs had gone in search of rats. I threw back my head and howled. Rip joined in.

One of the men laughed. 'We should take him to the circus instead of the orphanage.'

'Shut up,' the son snapped. Then he stepped closer and said, 'Come now. I have a nice lolly for a good boy.'

I pulled back my lips and snarled even as I felt the other dogs circling quietly behind me.

One of the policemen said, 'Let's just use the net and be done with it.'

The old woman's son nodded his head ever so slightly.

My heart pounded in my chest. It was time to run. I flicked my hand. Moon, Star, Smoke, Lucky, Little

Mother and, of course, Rip, surged forward snapping and snarling.

'Holy mother of God!' one of the militsiya cried. 'Look how many!'

Smoke and Lucky drew themselves up tall with their tails held high and stiff. Smoke's eyes glowed yellow and cold in the moonlight.

'What're we supposed to do now?' the policeman with the net asked, stepping back.

Smoke and Lucky lowered their haunches and gathered their muscles, readying to spring.

Run, Malchik!

I ran and ran and ran as fast as I could. The sound of snarling and screaming and shouting and yelping grew fainter. A sick feeling rose from my stomach and filled my lungs.

Soon, I heard the running feet of the dogs behind me. They ran, swift and silent in the moonlight. I listened over my hammering heart for the sound of boots. The dogs splashed through the stream and into the birch grove. I counted as they came – one, two, three, four, there were only four!

I whistled low. The dogs gathered around me – Lucky, Little Mother, Moon, Star. Where were Smoke and Rip?

Of course! How could I be so stupid! Rip couldn't run as fast as the rest. Smoke must be with him.

'Stay here,' I said. I touched Lucky's head. 'You come,' I said.

We ran back the way we came, through the stream and past the big birch tree and across the small meadow. Soon we would be at the road to the Ferris-wheel park. I heard running boots and heavy breathing. Someone called, 'I can't see a thing.'

Lucky woofed low and raised his tail.

Into the moonlit meadow ran Rip with Smoke.

I dashed across the meadow and scooped up Rip in my arms. The sound of boots grew closer. Car horns honked. Someone swore.

'Run!' I said to Smoke and Lucky. 'The others are ahead.'

Lucky dashed off into the forest. Smoke said, I will stay.

'No,' I said. 'Run.'

I ran as fast as I could, Rip bouncing in my arms. Smoke ran next to me. He threw his ears back. They come. I stopped and looked around. I spotted just what I needed: a pine rose tall and black in the moonlight.

'Run,' I said. I hurried to the bottom of the great pine. I pulled myself up with one hand while the other clutched

Rip to my chest. He kept perfectly still. I worked my way into a thick tangle of branches and stopped. I looked down. I could just see the eyes of Smoke watching from beneath a cluster of bushes.

I bowed my head against Rip's ragged ear. 'Shhhh . . .' I whispered as I tried to quiet my breathing.

The militsiya entered the clearing. One limped and another had a torn sleeve. Yet another held a hand to his chest as if it were injured. The old woman's son had lost his hat. They panted in the cold night air.

Rip trembled against me.

'Now where?' one of the men grumbled.

'It's crazy, hunting that kid in this forest at night. We can't see a thing,' another said.

'We'll have to come back in the daylight,' the woman's son agreed.

The man with the limp said, 'And just where are we going to look? Do you know how many hundreds of acres this forest is? He could be anywhere.'

The woman's son lit a cigarette. The other men followed suit. 'The bomzhi over at the dump gave me a pretty good idea where he and those dogs live out there.'

'All I know is,' the policeman with the hurt hand said,

'we won't be able to get to that kid with the dogs protecting him.'

'There are ways to deal with them,' the old woman's son replied.

'Bah,' one of the men said. 'Why are we even bothering with him? There's lots of these street kids and no one cares.'

The son of the Woman in the Hat tightened his scarf around his neck. 'It's not just my mother driving me crazy now. She's got all her old crones riled up about it, all because he lives with those dogs.' He coughed and spat on the ground. 'Let's get out of this damned cold.'

I stayed in the tree long after the militsiya left.

Smoke crept from under the thicket and followed their trail. After a bit, he returned and barked the all clear. I lowered myself and Rip to the ground. My legs and arms shook.

My face bled from tree scratches. I stroked Rip's ears. 'You were the best boy.'

I was tired, so tired. I half slept on my feet as Smoke led us back a different way to our home beneath the tree. As we entered our meadow, the rest of the pack hurried out to meet us, whining and licking and sniffing us all over. We crawled beneath the tree and piled together. The heat from the dogs' bodies slowly stopped my shivering.

'We will rest now,' I said. 'But we must leave very early in the morning and go back to The City. They will not find us there.' There, we would be just one of many fleas upon the dog.

Chapter 48

FLEAS ON THE DOG

As always, we rode the train. And for a time, we were safe.

I begged for money, bought food, scoured the bins behind restaurants. The people in their winter coats hurrying to and from the trains dropped coins and rubles in my hand without a word or a second glance.

Then one day, as I stepped into the bright sunlight from the train station below, I saw a policeman talking to the woman I bought bread from at the stalls outside the station entrance.

He pulled a piece of paper from his pocket and showed it to her. My heart dropped to my knees. I pulled myself and Lucky and Rip into the shadows. My ears – keen from the months in the forest – picked up their words.

'This is a street boy we're looking for,' the militsiya said.

'Bah,' the woman said. 'There are too many of these to

count, these children with no home. How would I know one from the other?'

'This one is very young and travels with a pack of dogs.'

The woman hesitated. My mouth went dry. She had seen me several times with the dogs when I bought bread from her.

'You think I have nothing better to do than watch boys and dogs?' the woman snapped. But I could hear a sliver of doubt in her voice.

'Yes, yes,' the policeman said. 'But my boss is driving us crazy with this boy. He won't let us alone until we catch him.'

Could his boss be the Woman in the Hat's son?

'Here's my card,' the militsiya said. 'When you see him, let me know. You'll be rewarded, I promise.'

'Let's go,' I whispered to Lucky and Rip. We found the others sleeping in the train station. Together, we slipped into the last car in the next train and travelled to a different part of The City.

After that, it seemed everywhere we turned, militsiya watched for us. Sometimes I saw them as they showed the drawing of my face to a shop owner. Sometimes I saw them watching on the train-station platforms as people and dogs came and went on the trains. We could not rest. It was getting harder to find food. We were always on the run.

One unusually warm winter day, I napped with the dogs in a patch of sun between two big bins at the end of an alley. My hand rested on Little Mother's round belly. Her belly was not round from food, for there had been precious little of that. I'd felt something move in her belly when I stroked her the night before.

'It's him,' a loud whisper said.

The dogs leapt to their feet – all but Little Mother – and growled.

Two dirty faces looked down at me.

I sat up and rubbed my eyes. They were only street children like me.

'I told you it was the Dog Boy,' one said, jabbing the other with his elbow.

Smoke stood in front of Little Mother and me and flashed his teeth and growled louder. The children's eyes grew big in their thin, dirty faces.

I stood and placed a hand on Smoke's back.

The taller of the two licked his lips and said, 'They're looking for you, you know. The militsiya.'

I nodded. 'I know.'

'Yes,' the other said. He scratched at a sore on his

hand. 'They say you're a wild child. We're invisible, but you with those dogs...' His voice trailed off into a shrug. 'They're offering vodka and cigarettes to any of us who help catch you.'

Fear raced through me like the fire that took our Glass House. The dogs whined and pressed around me. The children stepped back.

The taller one waved his hand and said, 'You don't have to worry about us, but you better be careful of the older kids and the bomzhi. They'll do anything for a drink or a smoke.'

'You won't tell?' I asked.

They shook their heads. 'But I'd stay away from the train stations if I were you,' the taller one said.

Fat flakes of snow wheeled down from the sky. I shivered in what was left of my coat and watched them walk away.

I pressed my face against Lucky's warm neck and tried not to cry.

For days, we followed the great river winding its way through The City until we came to Komsomolskaya Ploshchad. This was the place we had seen the Christian Ladies last spring, months and months before. We would wait here until they came again. I desperately needed a new coat, boots, gloves and a hat if I was going to survive a winter not riding the trains.

So we waited, and one day they arrived.

They set up their tables and boxes in the central square near the statue of the man with the marble face. He watched, standing high above the snow, as a few children drifted from doorways and from under boxes. He watched, one marble hand still clutching his lapel, as they lined up for food and clothes. No one fought this time. It was the cold now they had to fight to survive, not one another.

Finally, the last of the children left. I crossed the square with Rip, Lucky, Moon and Star. 'Please,' I said to a big woman with her back to me. 'I need a coat.'

She turned round. Her eyes widened. 'Olina,' she called without taking her eyes off the dogs and me. 'I don't think we have any clothes left to fit this young man, do we?'

The woman called Olina bent over a box. She straightened up and looked at us, then looked again. Olina touched a piece of paper on the table. She came over and stood next to the big woman. She licked her lips. 'No, I don't think we do. Not right now.'

'But certainly we can bring some for you,' the big

woman said. 'Would you like that, for us to bring clothes just for a boy your size?'

I nodded.

The woman called Olina rubbed her gloved hands together and said, 'We can bring them tomorrow, right here – a fine warm coat, boots, jumper and as many socks and gloves and hats as a boy could need. Blankets too. Would you like that?'

I nodded, smiling. I felt warmer already. I stroked Star's head.

The big woman smiled. 'Olina, I do think we have a bit of porridge and bread left, don't we?'

My mouth watered.

The woman called Olina bobbed her head and hurried to another table. She returned with a bowl of steaming porridge and a hunk of black bread.

'Here,' she said, handing it to me.

Before she could hand me the spoon, I shovelled the hot gruel into my mouth with my hands. Finally, I broke off pieces of bread for each of the dogs and stuffed two more pieces in my pocket for Smoke and Little Mother. I let Rip lick the porridge from my fingers.

'Now when you come back tomorrow for your clothes, you must leave those dogs behind.'

I looked up at the big woman. 'Why?' I asked.

'They have fleas,' she said. Her face was screwed up in disgust.

'I'm allergic to dogs,' the woman called Olina said.

Something whispered in the back of my mind.

'We'll bring you lots of food, though,' the big woman said. 'Enough for them too.'

If I had not been so cold, if I had not been so hungry, I would not have listened to them; instead I would have listened to that voice in the back of my mind. I would have wondered about that piece of paper on the table.

I returned the next day in the middle of a snowstorm. The flags circling the Ploshchad snapped and slapped in the howling wind. Snow buried the steps at the bottom of the marble man's statue.

'They won't come,' I said to the dogs crouched in the doorway with me. 'Even Christian Ladies won't keep a promise in a storm like this.'

But soon, I saw them pushing through the wind and snow, the big woman and the one called Olina. She carried a bag in her arms. A bag full of warm clothes and food.

I yipped and jumped up. The dogs danced around me. All but Smoke and Little Mother.

'You must all stay here,' I said above the wind. 'You must stay here and I will be back with food.'

The dogs whimpered and rolled their eyes.

No, Malchik, Smoke said.

'I have to go,' I said. 'I do not have a warm coat like you, and we all need food!'

Smoke grumbled.

'Stay here!' I barked in my firmest pack-leader voice, and then trotted across the snow-covered square. The big woman waved me over. I waved back. Coat, gloves, hat, food, I sang under my breath in time with my footsteps.

'You came!' I panted in the cold.

'Yes, child,' the big woman said. 'Just as we promised.'

Wind cut through my ragtag clothes. I hopped from one foot to the other, trying to peer into the bag. 'What did you bring?' I asked. 'A coat? Food? I didn't bring the dogs, just like you asked.'

'Here,' the big woman said. 'Come and see.'

I walked over to the bag. I did not see a coat. I did not smell food.

'I have a blanket for you!' the woman called Olina said.

'But I don't need—'

She threw the blanket over my head and wrapped her

arms tightly around me. Everything went dark. I couldn't breathe!

'We have him! We have him!' the women cried.

Boots crunched in the snow. A man's voice called, 'Hold tight to him! He's a wily one.'

I was trapped! I wriggled and struggled against the woman's arms and the blanket's grasp. Another hand grabbed my shoulder. I bit as hard as I could through the blanket.

'Ow!' someone cried. 'The little beggar bit me!'

For an instant, hands fell away. I threw off the blanket and froze. I was surrounded by the militsiya.

'Holy mother,' one of the policemen said. 'Look at it.'

I crouched and looked for a way round or through them.

'He's not an "it,"' the woman named Olina said. 'He's a child.'

The big woman held out a bag. 'See here, boy, I have some food for you. Sausages, just like I promised.' She smiled. Her teeth were yellow and pointed.

I shuddered. Baba Yaga. I was not her boy.

I threw back my head and barked.

'What's he—?'

Before the policeman could finish his question,

Smoke leapt upon his back and knocked him to the ground. The Christian Ladies screamed as dogs came from every direction.

Lucky sailed through the snow-filled air. Rip darted in and out from between my legs, snapping and growling.

I grabbed the bag of food that had fallen from the big woman's hands. 'Run!' I cried.

I ran as fast as I have ever run in my life across the Ploshchad, the dogs fanning out in front. Little Mother joined us and ran as fast as her big belly would allow.

Behind us I heard the *tweet tweet!* of the *militsiya's* whistles.

'Stop him! Stop him!' the Christian Ladies cried.

But we would not be stopped that day.

Chapter 49

LITTLE MOTHER

'Once upon a time,' I said to the dogs in our cold, dark den beneath an abandoned warehouse, 'there was a ghost who very much wanted to be a boy. He thought if he were a boy – the very best boy – he would be loved and protected. He did not want people to look past him and through him because he was just a little ghost and he was lonely and afraid.'

Little Mother groaned and panted. Smoke watched her and so did I. Something was not right with Little Mother and it frightened me.

I stroked Little Mother's ears. 'And once upon another time – a time much later than before – there was a boy who wanted very much to be a ghost ...'

I sighed. Now I would bargain with Baba Yaga herself to be invisible again.

Later, something woke me in the dark.

One of the dogs pawed at my arm. I sat up. 'What's wrong?'

I heard panting and moaning on the other side of the tiny den. I crawled across on hands and knees to Little Mother. I could barely make out the glow of her wide eyes in the dark. 'Oh, Little Mother,' I said, reaching out a hand to stroke her.

She snapped at my hand, just barely missing my fingers. I gasped in surprise. Never had she threatened me before!

She whimpered in apology but still, I crawled back across the rubble away from her. I cuddled Rip to my chest and pulled Moon and Star next to me. Only Smoke was allowed to be close to Little Mother.

I buried my face in Lucky's flank. 'Nothing is right anymore,' I said. 'I do not know what I have done, but everything is wrong.'

A tiny sound woke me in the grey hours of morning – the tiniest of cries. The dogs quivered next to me with excitement.

On the other side of the den, Little Mother lay on her side licking something. Smoke hovered over her protectively.

I held my breath, hardly daring to move. I looked from Little Mother to Smoke. *Is it what I think it is?* I asked in our silent way.

Smoke's eyes smiled. *Come and see, Malchik.*

Slowly, I crept over to Little Mother. She grumbled a warning. I stopped and turned my eyes away. Smoke snorted.

I crept a little closer. This time, Little Mother did not growl. She busied herself licking the just-born puppies nestled against her belly.

'Oh, puppies!' I breathed. I counted three. Later I would find the body of a fourth that had not survived the birth.

Suddenly, the world was full of hope. We had puppies to care for! For the rest of the day, I made plans.

'We'll wait until they get a little bigger,' I said to Little Mother, 'and then find a better place for the winter. Maybe we'll go back to the den where you had Moon and Star.'

That day, Lucky and I left only long enough to find food. Smoke would not leave her side.

'I'll get us lots of food, I promise,' I told Little Mother and the others as I fed them from what I'd found. 'The puppies will grow big and strong.'

We listened to the snow-scraping machines out on

the streets. 'And when spring comes, we will return to the forest and never, *ever* come back.'

And so day after day, I hunted food with Lucky, Moon and Star. Smoke brought Little Mother food too, but he didn't like leaving her alone for very long. And Rip had taken on the role of the puppies' babushka.

At first, I tried going out only when it was dark so as not to be seen by the militsiya, if they were even still hunting me.

But I could not bear the cold long enough to find the food we needed, especially for Little Mother as she nursed her puppies; and the night belonged to the tall, skinny Crow Boys in their black leathers and chains, and the bomzhi, who would do anything for a drink.

So the dogs and I devised what we thought was a clever plan: We hunted food separately but together. The dogs would saunter along like any pack of street strays and investigate the bins at the back of certain restaurants. I stayed behind, pretending to sleep in a doorway, an old newspaper covering my face, and listened. If the dogs found food in the bins, they yipped. I waited until the pavement was empty of people and then I dashed behind the building and joined the dogs. I grabbed what food I could and ran back to our den. Some days, even after visiting several bins, there was not much food to show for our efforts. But at least it was something.

And so it was, on this particular snowy afternoon, we had found a restaurant whose bins overflowed with food. We came back again and again to fill our bags.

Lucky and Moon and Star disappeared round the corner without a backwards glance. I curled up in the shivery doorway and waited for their signal.

And waited and waited.

I sat up. The newspaper covering my face fluttered to the ground. My stomach groaned and my hands ached in the cold. 'They must be filling their bellies first,' I grumbled. I'd caught Star and Lucky doing that before, gorging themselves before calling me.

I ground my teeth. Anger filled my belly.

And then I heard a sharp, panic-stricken bark. This was not the usual we've-found-food yip, this was a call that said they were in trouble. I heard the bark again.

I ran round to the back of the building and skidded to a stop in the snow. Their paw prints led to the bin, yes, but then they continued on.

I followed the prints with my head down. I heard another bark – Lucky's deep, angry woof. The prints and the bark led to the back door of the restaurant. I stopped to listen. 'Lucky?' I called in a loud whisper. 'Moon? Star?'

Moon's answering whimper came from inside the restaurant!

Panic raced through me. How had they got inside? I grabbed the door handle and turned it.

It was locked.

I pulled and pulled on the door handle with all my might. I banged on it with my fists until they turned bloody. 'Lucky!' I cried. 'Moon!'

'They can't help you now, little Mowgli.'

Every part of me turned to ice at the sound of that voice. I lowered my fists and turned my head.

There, with falling snow resting on his wide shoulders, and a cigarette dangling from his bottom lip, stood the Woman in the Hat's son. Many other militsiya stood on either side of him in their grey coats and tall black boots.

I looked frantically to the door and then to the way in and out of the alley. Militsiya were everywhere.

'Come with us quietly, now.' He stepped closer. 'Don't give us any trouble, and your dogs won't get hurt.'

My mind raced as fast as a train. Little Mother and Rip and the puppies needed me to bring food but they also had Smoke to protect them and take care of them;

Moon and Lucky and Star were trapped inside the restaurant with no way to get out except me doing what the militsiya said. And how did I know the dogs were unharmed even now?

I flicked out my knife. One of the policemen gasped. Another sniggered.

I stuck my chin in the air and made myself tall as I could. 'Let the dogs go and I'll come with you,' I demanded, looking directly into the dark eyes of the Woman in the Hat's son.

A short, fat policeman laughed. 'So the wild child is not dumb!'

The old woman's son narrowed his eyes and studied me. A smile played at the corner of his mouth. 'OK, Mowgli, it's a deal. But you must step away from the door first.'

Once I moved aside, he signalled to one of the policemen. 'Open it.'

I readied myself for what would come next. The dogs would burst through the door and knock down every one of the policemen. Then we would run away. I knew I could outrun any militsiya. I didn't need shiny black boots to run fast; I didn't need Famous Basketball Player shoes. Like the dogs, my feet had wings.

The door swung open. There on the cement floor of the storeroom, wrapped in a thick black net, lay the dogs, helpless. They locked their pleading eyes on my face and moaned.

'No!' I cried. I lunged for the dogs and attacked the net with my knife.

Arms grabbed me from behind and pulled me back.

'Let me go!' I screamed. I slashed with my knife at anything I could find.

Someone cried out and cursed. But even as those hands fell away, more hands grabbed and hit and twisted. My knife fell to the ground.

The dogs barked and snapped and growled from their place on the floor. I snarled and snapped and sank teeth.

I was knocked to the ground. Gloved hands shoved my face into the snow and twisted my neck sideways.

Hands grabbed my legs and my feet and tied them with rope. Another pair wrenched my arms behind my back and tied them too.

'Give him the shot,' someone said above me. 'We can't carry him screaming and biting through the streets.'

I rubbed blood from my face in the snow. My eyes searched and found Lucky. His dark brown eyes poured into mine. I am sorry, he said.

'Oh, Lucky,' I moaned. He'd never spoken before.

Something sharp stung the back of my neck. A sick warm sweetness flooded my head and my stomach. The last thing I saw was Lucky's eyes.

Chapter 50

REUTOV

'Good God, he's a filthy little beggar,' a voice from somewhere above me said.

'Stinks too,' another voice said.

My head, my legs, every part of my body thrummed with pain. Why couldn't they just leave me alone?

A hand grabbed my boot and started to pull it off.

'No!' I snapped. My eyes flew open. I could not survive the winter without my boots. I could not find food for myself and the dogs without my boots!

But I was not on the streets of The City. I was in a too-bright, too-warm room that stank of soap and desperation. I was not surrounded by my family of dogs but by people in green uniforms and white coats.

I panted and snarled and looked about wildly for a way out. No busy streets to run down, no trees to climb, no tumbledown buildings to hide in – only one tiny window high above my head.

I gathered my legs beneath me and shot across the room for the only door.

'Look out!' a woman in a green uniform cried.

'Grab him!' a man in a white coat commanded.

I clawed and scrabbled at the door handle. It would not turn. I span to face down my captors. I bared my teeth and reached into my pocket for my knife. It was gone.

And then I remembered: the restaurant and the militsiya and Lucky and Moon and Star all trapped in that net and trying to cut them loose with my knife and the fist to my face and the gloved hand on my neck and Lucky's eyes.

I sobbed. Did they survive?

A hand reached out for me. I bit as hard as I could. Blood filled my mouth. The man in the white coat screamed in pain. Eyes filled with horror and disgust.

I scrambled beneath the camp bed on the far side of the tiny room and made myself as small as possible. I watched the feet scurry back and forth. I covered my ears to block out the angry words. I shook and shivered with fear. I wet myself.

Finally, the door opened, and then clicked shut. No feet, no angry voices.

I cried and rocked myself to sleep.

Later, a smell woke me. The door eased open just a bit, and a hand pushed a tray of food through the opening, then the door slammed shut.

I watched the bottom of the door and the tray of food. When no one came back, I crept out from the safety of the cot and crawled over to the tray. I lowered my head and sniffed. The hair rose on the back of my neck and along my arms. There was something very wrong with this food.

I backed away.

A noise on the other side of the door.

I looked up.

A face with glasses watched me through the small window in the door.

I flashed my teeth and retreated to my hiding place beneath the cot.

A day passed and then another, and another. During the day, people came and went. If hands tried to grab me from beneath the bed, I bit and clawed and kicked. Once I almost escaped through the door when food was brought – food that still held the bad smell – but I was knocked to the ground.

The man in the white coat, one hand bandaged, pinned my arms behind my back. 'Don't you know we're trying to help you?' he shouted in my face.

I wanted to say if he wanted to help me, he would return me to my family. Instead, I spat in his face.

That night, I paced back and forth, back and forth in my tiny room, trying to outrun my despair. I sat on the cot and rocked and cried and pulled at my hair. I rubbed the little tooth still in my pocket until my thumb hurt.

And then, like a dream, I heard it: first a bark and then a questioning γip. I sat still as stone and listened.

One howl rose and then another and another. I gasped. There was no mistaking the deep rumbling of Lucky, the high, soaring song of Moon, the γip, γip of Star.

I pulled the bed over to the window that was barely a window and climbed up. If I stood on the tips of my toes, I could just see outside. My eyes searched the shadows for the dogs but I could not see them.

I *am* here! I *am* here! I yipped.

There, on the other side of a high wire fence surrounding the courtyard, I saw them.

I laughed and cried. They had come for me! I threw back my head and howled.

The dogs barked and howled in a frenzy of excitement. I could just make out Lucky standing tall on his back legs, clawing at the wire fence.

I barked louder and beat my fists against the glass

pane separating us. Moon and Star dug frantically beneath the fence.

A bright light flooded the courtyard. The dogs froze. People ran out into the courtyard shouting and waving their arms. Moon and Star cowered before their angry voices. Lucky snarled and growled.

Someone picked up rocks and threw them at the dogs through the fence. One of the dogs yelped in pain, but I could not see which one.

Moon and Star fled into the street.

Lucky looked from the people to my window.

Don't leave me! I howled.

'Get out of here!' someone yelled, and threw part of a brick at the wire fence.

Lucky hesitated, then he loped out of sight, his head and tail low in defeat.

I pounded my fists against the glass. 'No!' I cried. 'Come back! Come back!'

But no matter how loud I howled and called, they did not come back.

Finally, exhausted, I curled up under my bed and comforted myself with the knowledge that somehow, Lucky and Moon and Star had got free of the awful net and they were alive.

They returned the next night and the next. They howled and they dug and I called to them in return, I *am here! I am here!* And every night, the people ran them off.

During the day, I heard the women in the green uniforms wonder at the dogs. 'How did they find him?' 'Why do they keep coming back?' 'What do they want of him?' One woman whispered, 'It is not normal, the way the dogs and the boy are bound.'

I smiled to myself as I listened to them from the den beneath the bed. I wanted to say to them, *They found me and they wanted me because I belong to them; we are bound because we are family, we are each other's place in the world.* But I did not waste my words on them. They were human.

And then came the night when the moon was full and bright upon the snow; I saw him. He stood silver and black and grey and proud, shifting in the moonlight. His amber eyes glowed. His voice – deep and wild as our summer forest – said, *I have come, Malchik.*

Smoke howled our story long into the night and into the next. He told of how we found one another and how he had saved me and I had saved them. He howled of the Glass House and the death of Grandmother and running free in the forest. He sang of the House of Bones and the battle with the boar and nights beneath moon and stars and city lights; of cold that almost killed us if it were not for one another.

I howled back and pounded my fists harder and harder against the glass window.

'I am here!' I cried. 'Don't leave me!'

Dark forms inky against the moonlit snow stomped across the courtyard. They shouted at the dogs. Lucky hurled himself against the wire fence. One of the humans raised something in his hand. A *crack*, and a light flashed in the night. A gun!

'No!' I screamed, pounding my fist against the glass. 'Don't shoot!'

The dogs scattered. They regrouped a short distance from the fence and barked and howled even more.

The gun fired again. A sharp yelp.

'No!' I screamed. I slammed my fist against the glass. It shattered. I gasped from the pain. Blood spattered everywhere. It ran down my arm and onto my bare feet.

I tore my eyes away from my blood and searched the night for the dogs. There they were, milling about, all of them moving. I panted in pain.

I saw the arm raise the gun again and take careful aim. 'No, no...' I moaned. My head swam and my legs shook. With the last bit of strength I had, I screamed, 'Run!' The last thing I saw was the dogs disappearing into the night.

Chapter 51

FEVER DREAMS

I dreamed I flew far above the earth. Below passed the village and the brown, squat apartment building where my mother and I had lived. I soared high above the round, golden domes of The City like a firebird. Below I saw dogs and children and *militsiya* and *bomzhi*. I flew low over Rubbish Mountain and the great forest.

I saw the dogs – Smoke, Lucky, Rip, Little Mother, Moon, Star and even Grandmother – running through the meadow, their heads tilted back, watching me.

'Come and join me,' I called, 'it is beautiful up here,' even though I knew they could not leave the earth.

I swooped across the Ferris-wheel park. The dogs ran below, barking and barking. Then, I saw them, each in a Ferris-wheel seat. They rose higher. Just as each reached the top of the wheel's great arc, they flew into the air. Wide wings unfurled from their backs as the music from the Ferris wheel toot tooted.

I clapped my hands and laughed. 'You are such clever dogs.'

I dreamed of Little Mother's tongue washing my hot face. A brilliant light shone behind her. I reached out to stroke her head. She pushed my hand away and said, There there, my little puppy.

I dreamed of climbing the tallest tree in all of Russia and fighting giant pigs. I dreamed of Rudy with his grey eyes and Tanya with her bruised and swollen face. I dreamed of seeing the little schoolgirl, Anya, in the great Red Square. She did not recognise me. She said, 'Go away, you mangy dog.'

I dreamed of Smoke singing the song of our life together in the cold winter night. I dreamed of sitting in my Babushka Ina's lap as she sang songs to me older than the earth. And I dreamed of my mother, humming this song and that as she rocked me to sleep. Her voice wove in and out with the voices of Smoke and Babushka Ina and the Ferris wheel and the Accordion Man and the cry of the trains and the laughter and the cries of all the homeless children, to make the most beautiful music in the world.

Chapter 52

I opened my eyes. I smelled something sharp and soapy. I also smelled vomit and pee like it sometimes smelled in the train stations. Was I back with Rudy and Tanya and Pasha? Had my life with the dogs been all a dream?

I tried to sit up. Someone fluttered over to me. 'No, child, no. You must be still.' All in white she was dressed, and from the side of her head lifted wings like the seagulls along the Great River.

I wanted to ask her if she was an angel or perhaps a Sister of Mercy. I ran my tongue over my cracked lips. I needed water. I opened my mouth to speak. The word I managed to croak surprised us both: 'Dogs.'

I do not know how long they kept me in the children's ward of the hospital. They said I had lost a great deal of blood when I broke the window that night. 'Whoever would

327

imagine so much blood could come from such a little boy,' the nurse said as she clucked and fussed around me. My arm became infected and my fever so high they thought I would die.

As I grew stronger, they assaulted me with questions: 'What is your name?' 'How old are you?' 'Why were you living on the streets?' 'Where is your family?'

I answered none of these questions. Instead, I watched and I listened. I was no longer in the orphanage, I knew that. I was in a hospital in The City. If I was still in The City, then I could find the dogs. I had to find the dogs. Little Mother had new puppies. They needed me and I would take care of them.

If I could escape.

I learned the comings and goings of the nurses and doctors. One night, at the time when the doctors had all gone to their homes and the nurses were sleepy, I pulled the needle hooked to the bag beside my bed from my arm and slipped out of bed. My clothes were gone, my boots were gone. My baby tooth was gone. I did not care. I wrapped a blanket around my body and slid open the glass door of my room.

I crouched in the doorway and listened. No sound. I scurried down the hallway and past the big desk where a nurse slept. I flew down the corridor, my bare feet slapping on the cold floor and the blanket flapping around me. There, at the end of the corridor, were two tall doors with bars across them.

I hurled myself against the doors. The doors did not open. Instead, a siren screamed and lights flashed. I covered my ears with my hands against the screeching and squinted against the flashing lights.

Hands grabbed. I kicked and bit. Too many hands. Something stung my arm. Everything fell away.

After that, I was tied to the bed. It did not matter if I had to relieve myself, I was kept tied. They fed me with a spoon like a little baby. At first I refused to eat. I spat the food back in their faces. But then I realised as long as I was in The City, there was hope of getting away. It would not be an easy escape, I told myself. I would have to be as smart as Smoke and as strong as Lucky and as swift as Star. For that, I needed to eat, and so I did. I even pretended to be a good boy. Soon, they untied me. I did not bite, not even once, even though I wanted to.

One day, as the snow fell outside, a tall man in shiny black boots and militsiya clothes came into my room.

I dropped to the floor and scurried under my bed. My stomach felt sick.

'Hello, Mowgli,' he said.

The voice. I knew that voice. I plucked at my eyebrows.

'I've brought someone to see you,' he said. 'Someone I think you'll be very happy to see.'

The door whispered open. Soft furred boots the colour of Lucky's brown and black coat walked into the room. A flowered skirt brushed the tops of the boots.

'Hello, child,' the Woman in the Hat said. I growled and pushed against the wall.

'Oh, child.' She stooped down. Her eyes searched for me under the bed. 'Please come out,' she said, holding out her hand. 'You know I won't hurt you.'

I growled a little louder and flashed my teeth.

She gasped. The shiny black boots moved next to her.

'Go away,' I ordered.

'Now, boy,' her son said, 'we're only trying to help you.'

I felt anger burning up through my legs and stomach. My hand itched for my bone club or my knife.

'Yes, dear,' the Woman in the Hat said, rubbing her hands. 'They're going to take you to a better place, a safer place than—'

The burning anger flew up my throat and burst out of my mouth. 'You!' I screamed. 'It's all your fault!' I shot from under the bed and stood before her, my fists clenched. The Woman in the Hat's eyes widened. Her mouth opened and closed around words she could not say. I stepped towards her. 'My place is with the dogs,' I said in a low growl. I never saw the Woman in the Hat or her son again.

Two days later, the doctor entered my room.

He listened to my heart and my lungs. He unwrapped the bandages on my arm and studied the long lines of gashes.

He looked at me for a long moment. His eyes were full of questions. He reached out a hand as if to touch me, then stopped. He put the hand in his white coat pocket. He sighed and nodded to the nurse and left the room.

'Well,' the nurse with the winged hat said, bustling around me. 'This is fine, then. You'll be off tomorrow.'

Off? But where? I wanted to ask her. It did not matter. Tomorrow, they would take me out of here and I could escape. My body tingled all over. I grinned inside myself. I wriggled my toes. Get ready, I told my feet and my legs.

But there was nothing to get ready for. They dressed me in a coat that was not like any coat I had ever seen. It pinned my arms and crisscrossed this way and that so I could not move. They bound my legs and wheeled me in a chair to a van like the ones I had seen children taken away in before.

They strapped me in a seat in the van beside a window.

'Goodbye, child,' the nurse with the winged hat said. Tears ran down her cheeks.

My heart pounded. Sick rose up from my stomach and burned my throat. I swallowed it down. The van pulled into the traffic of The City. I leaned my head against the window and I watched The City – the beggars and the children and the dogs and the Crow Boys and the police and the bins and the grand stations and the great golden domes – pass by, and finally, away and away from everything I had ever known.

Chapter 53

I dream of dogs. I dream of warm backs pressed against mine beneath a tall pine tree. I dream of flashing teeth, warm, wet tongues and amber eyes, watching. Always watching.

I dream I run and run and run with the dogs through forests thick with birch trees and giant pigs. I dream we run through winter streets and across frozen rivers. I dream we fly.

A hand touches my arm and shakes me awake. A voice – the same voice that has said this same thing every morning – says, 'Wake up, Little Bear.'

I open my eyes to this kind face, these eyes almost, but not quite, the colour of amber. She switches on the tape player on my small desk and music fills the tiny room.

'Today is your day,' she says as I sit up and scratch my head.

She leaves and I look around this room I have lived in for five years. It is small and unremarkable. There is no window. There is my narrow bed and a small desk and chair and a wardrobe for my few clothes and two pairs of shoes – more shoes than I have ever had in my life. But the walls – oh the walls! Covering every centimetre are paintings and drawings of the dogs. Dogs with wings, dogs riding Ferris wheels, dogs with torn ears, dogs the colour of the moon, dogs made of smoke. Eyes watching, always watching.

I hear the other boys on my floor yelling and laughing. I know that behind closed doors, some are crying. When I open my door, I will smell breakfast in the dining hall.

I pull on my shirt. I roll down the sleeves to cover the scars on my right arm. I put one leg in my jeans and glance at the crescent-shaped scar on my other leg before I shove it in. I carry many scars. She was the first to understand.

When I first came to The Children's Recovery Home and School on the outskirts of St Petersburg, I was not a boy. I was Wild Child. That is what they called me.

I hid under my bed. I hit and bit and barked and howled. I threw whatever I could get my hands on, so they took everything but my bed out of my room. I terrified the other children, so they tried feeding me in my room. I used the forks, even the spoons as weapons; once again I ate with my hands. They had to sedate me to give me a bath and shave off my hair.

I cried and rocked myself for days after under my bed. Everything was lost: the mother, the button, the stories, the tooth and my only family. I was lost. I was again a ghost.

I think they had all but given up on me, until she came.

One day, the door to my room opened as it did several times during the day. I pressed my back against the wall and watched from under my bed. I growled low as I always did so they would go away.

But the feet that stood in front of my bed were not the usual feet in heavy work shoes or scuffed leather boots. These shoes were made of some kind of black cloth almost like fur. Coloured thread swirled across the toes.

I sniffed. This person did not smell like cigarettes or cooked cabbage like the other women who came into my room. This person did not smell like beer and vodka. I took a deep sniff even as I growled and grumbled. This person smelled like the forest and clean smoke and there, just there, the tiny yet distinct smell of dog. My heart quivered.

She dropped to her knees and peered under my bed. I growled louder.

She laughed.

I stopped mid-growl. How long had it been since I had heard laughter?

I plucked anxiously at my hair and my eyebrows, and I rocked myself. I woofed at her to go away.

She did not. Instead, she sat cross-legged on the floor and did the most miraculous, mysterious thing: she began to hum!

I stopped rocking and I stopped growling and I listened. Her humming was beautiful. I closed my eyes and let it touch first my hand and then my face and then my chest.

The humming stopped. I opened my eyes. Her face and her eyes – especially her eyes – smiled at me.

In the softest of voices, she said, 'Look at you there, you little bear, in your dark den. Come out, little Mishka.'

Her words, that name, slipped like a key into an unused lock. Mishka.

It was then that I stopped being the Wild Child and I once again became a boy.

She came every day after that. She said she was a special teacher for very special children. She said I was the most special boy she had ever met. I frowned at her and looked away, but inside I smiled.

She brought a tape player and played music. Some-times, she sat with her back against the wall and her eyes closed, listening. Sometimes I closed my eyes too, but mostly I watched her.

She talked about herself. She said her name was Anuva and she loved music and art and books and dogs and walking in the woods.

'What do you love, Mishka?' she asked one day. I wanted so badly to tell her that, yes, yes, I too loved those things. But I did not trust my voice so I only looked away.

The next day, she brought not only music, but a pad of white paper and colour sticks the Woman in the Hat had called pastels.

Anuva slid the pad and pastels under the bed and said, 'Here, draw for me what you love.'

And so I did. I'd finish one drawing, shove it out to her, and start another. I drew and drew in a fever until all the sheets of paper in the thick pad were gone.

She studied each drawing with care and said, 'Ah yes, I see,' and 'I love that too.' And then, before she left, she carefully taped each and every drawing on my wall.

One day when she handed me the pad and colours, she said, 'Draw for me what you hate,' and then the next day, 'Draw for me what makes you afraid,' and then, 'Draw what makes you sad.' Up on the wall, along with the firebirds and dogs and trees, went a drawing of him in his scuffed boots and shiny pants and hard fists; up went a drawing of a red stain behind the door, big, pulsing; up went a drawing of a red coat and a black button; up went a drawing of militsiya and Baba Yaga with her fence of bones and skulls.

And with each of the drawings, she said, 'I understand,' and 'I am sorry.'

She brought me these things – music, drawing – and she brought books. She read out loud to me as I drew and as the music played.

One day she read to me a fairy tale I had never heard before.

'Once upon a time,' she read, 'in a certain czardom of the thirtieth realm, beyond the sea-ocean, there lived an old peasant with his wife. They were indeed very poor and had no children.'

I concentrated on drawing a perfect Ferris wheel.

'One day, the old peasant tracked a bear to its den and killed it for its fur and meat.'

I frowned.

'Much to his astonishment,' she continued, 'he found a naked little boy in the darkest corner of the cave, a child the bear had stolen and reared as its own.'

I put my pastel down and listened.

'The old peasant took the boy home and called the village priest. He had the child baptized Ivashko Mishka – Ivan Little Bear.' The hair rose on the back of my neck.

She smiled at me.

'He would have been better off with the bear,' I said.

'Ah, but listen,' she said.

She read how the boy grew quickly and became strong. How by the age of twelve he was as tall as any man in the village and stronger than anyone in the whole countryside. The people grew frightened of the boy and drove him from the village.

I tore my drawing into small bits. 'They are bad, bad people,' I said. I rocked myself back and forth. 'He was better off with the bears,' I moaned.

She moved closer to me. 'Listen,' she said softly. 'Listen.'

And then she read how he, Mishka, was the only one who succeeded, of all those who had tried, to kill the witch Baba Yaga.

She touched my cheek. 'You see, Mishka, it was because he had the strength of the bear and the wisdom of man that he was able to defeat the witch.'

She put her hand on mine. I stopped rocking and

looked at her straight on for the first time. Her eyes were the colour of amber. 'It is you, Mishka. It is you.'

One day, after many months, she took me outside. I blinked against the bright spring sun. I closed my eyes and listened to the birds and the wind. I smelled the earth and the sea. We sat in the walled garden of dirt and didn't speak.

After a time, I whispered, 'My name is Ivan. Ivan Andreovich.'

She did not ask me how old I was or where I had lived before I was captured or where my mother was. She simply sighed and said, 'Thank you, Ivan Andreovich.'

Later, months later, she would ask me, 'Ivan, why did you not want to be taken from the dogs? Why did you not want to live among people again?'

I stopped drawing. I gazed at the smiling eyes of Rip and the worried eyes of Little Mother staring back at me from the paper. I said simply, 'I felt loved and protected by the dogs. I *belonged* with them.'

Anuva nodded and that was all she asked of me.

Anuva opens my door and says, 'Are you ready to go, Ivan? Everyone is waiting.'

I nod even though I am not ready. I pluck nervously

at my hair and my eyebrows, something I have not done in a long time.

She crosses the room and gently takes my hand away from my face. 'You don't have to worry, brave Mishka, I will be right there with you at the art show.'

I glance at the grainy, black and white copy of a photograph of me from an Australian newspaper. The picture was taken not long after I was sent to the shelter in Moscow. The words under the picture of the frightened little boy with haunted eyes say, *Mowgli-like child captured after living on the streets of Russia with wild dogs!*

'They just want to see me because they think I'm a freak,' I say now.

Anuva glances at the photograph too. 'That was many years ago, Ivan. Time has passed. Now they want to see you because of your art. They want to see this artist who paints dogs with wings and dogs on Ferris wheels, who signs his work *Malchik*.'

I pull on my coat. Even Anuva, who knows as much about me as any human, does not know why I sign my drawings and paintings Malchik. She does not know who gave me that name. She does not know that, even after all this time, I dream of the dogs every night. I have been given many names – Ivan, Mishka, Cockroach, Circus Mouse,

Runt, Dog Boy, Mowgli, Wild Child and then Ivan again. But it is that one name, Malchik, which I keep for my very own. It is that name that gave me a place in the world.

With one backwards look at my room, I straighten my shoulders and point my shoes forward. I close the door behind me and step, once again, out into The World.

After the fall of the Soviet Union in 1991, the social and economic fabric of Russia was left in tatters. Gone were the government-controlled systems such as health care, rent control and pensions that had provided some semblance of a safety net for families, children, the elderly and those living on the edge of economic stability. As a result, many parents (in the cities and in rural villages) could no longer afford to keep their children. Alcoholism, physical neglect and abuse tore families apart, forcing children to take refuge on the streets. By the mid-1990s, estimates of the number of homeless children in Moscow and St Petersburg were anywhere between 80,000 and two million. Most of these children formed packs, and lived in abandoned buildings and in the city's large underground train stations. The children were both ever-present and subtly invisible – a backdrop, at best, to city life.

Ivan Mishukov was one of these street children. In 1996, at the age of four, Ivan left his abusive home – or was sent away by his mother, no one knows for sure – and ended up on the streets of western Moscow. What distinguished him from the thousands of other street children was not his age or his circumstances. Ivan chose to depend on a pack of feral street dogs rather than other children for his survival and, eventually, to be his family. For the next two years, Ivan established a very close, symbiotic relationship with the dogs. He begged for food from passers-by and shopkeepers, and shared his food with the dogs. In return, the dogs protected him from roving gangs of older children and homeless adults, and helped him survive the brutal Russian temperatures in winter that can often reach minus twenty. But it was not purely a relationship of physical survival. In an article about Ivan in the *Chicago Sun-Times*, 26 July 1998, Ivan reportedly told a worker at the Reutov children's shelter, 'I was better off with the dogs. They loved and protected me.'

What became of Ivan after his separation from the dogs? This is a question that has no definitive answer. Over the years I spent researching the different aspects of Ivan's story, I came across several vague answers. Some said he remained in one orphanage or another; other accounts suggested he had been adopted. I even read that he was a student in an elite military academy. There were two things consistent in reference to Ivan's future – one gave me hope, the other was the spark that ignited my fictional account: because Ivan retained his facility for speech and he appeared exceptionally bright, social workers were optimistic that he would, over time, adjust to normal life; and in almost every account I read of Ivan after his capture from his pack, it was reported that, even after a year, he still dreamed every night of dogs.

In the years since Ivan Mishukov found himself homeless on the streets of Moscow, there has been some improvement for the street children of Russia. The biggest change has been the attention the problem of homeless children and youth in Russia has attracted – not only on the world stage but, more importantly, by the Russian state. As of 2006, the Russian government had committed almost six billion rubles to the federal child and homeless and juvenile crime prevention program. The number of orphanages in Russia has increased by more than 100% in the last decade. Still, 2007 estimates of the number of children living on the streets run between 500,000 to 800,000. UNICEF estimates 95% of these children are social orphans, meaning they have at least one living parent.

The problem of homeless children is not unique to Russia. In a recent report issued by UNICEF, there are an estimated 100 million street children worldwide. Whether these children are in Africa, India, Cambodia, Spain or the United States (where there are an estimated 1.3 million homeless and runaway street children), they all face the same problems: drug and alcohol addiction, malnutrition, violent encounters with gangs and police, HIV infection, exploitation and early death.

This is just one child's story.

ACKNOWLEDGMENTS

As always, I owe a huge thank you to my agent, Alyssa Eisner-Henkin, for opening her heart and championing Mishka's story.

My editor, Arthur A. Levine, believed in this story and my ability to tell it, from the beginning. With his respectful and compassionate guidance, he helped me write the story I had dreamed of for years.

I would not have encountered the inspiration for this book – Ivan Mishukov – without Julie Richard's article, 'The Wild Children: When Nature Replaces Nurture,' in Best Friends magazine way back in 2005. A special thank you to Best Friends Animal Society for all they do for homeless animals.

Two books in particular were vital in my research. Many thanks to Michael Newton for his excellent examination of feral children in his book, *Savage Girls and Wild*

Boys: A History of Feral Children. Margaret Winchell's memoir of her time in Russia, *Armed with Patience*, helped me understand life in Russia in the mid-1990s.

An invaluable resource that helped me see what life was (and still is) like for Russia's homeless children was Hanna Polak's critically acclaimed documentary, *The Children of Leningradsky*. Many thanks to Hanna and Active Child Aid for their continued efforts to make these invisible children not only visible, but valued.

Bottomless thanks to the patient and talented members of my pack: Chris Graham, Lora Koehler and Jean Reagan. Y'all watched me gnaw on this bone for a long time. Also thanks to Lisa Actor, Corinne Humphrey and Sydney Salter for reading early drafts and providing the two things writers need most: support and feedback.

Finally, I would like to thank my husband, Todd, who makes me feel loved and protected.

BIBLIOGRAPHY

Ivan Mishukov:

Innes, John. 'Call of the Wild Only Refuge for Russia's Mowgli.' The Scotsman, 17 July 1998.

McKie, Robin, and Tom Whitehouse. '6-Year-Old Lived with Stray Dogs.' Chicago Sun-Times, 26 July 1998.

Newton, Tom. 'Urchin Ivan Reared by Dogs, Wants Back to Pack.' The Mirror (London), 17 July 1998.

Osborn, Andrew. 'Abandoned Boy Said to Have Been Raised by a Dog.' The New Zealand Herald, 18 April 2004.

Raymond, Clare. 'Boy Raised by Dogs; Ivan, Six, Lived with Strays on the Street.' The Mirror (London), 20 July 1998.

Richard, Julie. 'The Wild Children: When Nature Replaces Nurture.' Best Friends Magazine, September/October 2005.

Tyler, Richard. 'Homeless Russian Boy Raised by Stray Dogs.' World Socialist Website, 23 July 1998.

Feral Children:

Brooke, Simon. 'Daughter of the Dog Pack...' The Times (London), 15 December 2003.

'Chilean "Dog Boy" Found Living in Cave.' Taipei Times, 20 June 2001.

Dennis, Wayne. 'A Further Analysis of Reports of Wild Children.' Child Development 22, no 2, (June 1951): 153–158.

Gardner, David. 'Boy Who Lived with a Pack of Wild Dogs; Police Find Abandoned Child.' Daily Mail (London), 20 June 2001.

Gerstein, Mordicai. 'Who the Wild Things Are: The Feral Child in Fiction.' The Horn Book Magazine, November/ December 1999.

Gold, Karen. 'Myth-Making in Silence.' Times Higher Education, 1 February 2002.

'Jungle Book Comes Alive as Wild Boy Found in Romania.' The Scotsman, 14 February 2002.

Newton, Michael. *Savage Girls and Wild Boys: a History of Feral Children*. New York: St Martin's Press, 2003.

Osborn, Andrew. 'Siberian Boy, 7, Raised by Dogs After Parents Abandon Him.' *Belfast Telegraph*, 4 August 2004.

'Russian Police Discover Teenage Girl Brought up by Dogs.' *Moscow News*, 14 July 2005.

Seymour, Miranda. 'Nature's Children.' *Sunday Times* (London), 10 February 2002.

'They Never Knew Human Touch.' *Toronto Star*, 9 June 2004.

Homeless in Russia:

Ford, Nathan et al. 'Homelessness and Hardship in Moscow.' *The Lancet* 361 (2003): 875.

Ivanov, Andrei. 'Sharp Deterioration in Nation's Health.' *Inter Press Service*, 17 July 1996.

Lodge, Robin. 'Thousands of Homeless Face Death During Russian Winter.' *Telegraph* (London), 12 October 1997.

Quinn-Judge, Paul. 'Tales from Cold Mountain.' *Time* (Europe). 02 February 2003.

Swarns, Rachel L. 'Moscow Sends Homeless to Faraway Towns.' *New York Times*, 15 October 1996.

Russian Street Children:

Aref'ev, A. L. 'The Homeless and Neglected Children of Russia.' *Sociological Research* 44 (July-August 2003): 22–44.

Hansen, Liane. 'Profile: Growing Problem of Homeless Children in Russia.' *National Public Radio Weekend Edition*, 24 February 2002.

Jones, Laura. 'Homeless and Alone: Russian Street Children.' *BBC Newsround*, 5 March 2003.

Kenneth, Christopher. 'Homeless Children Eke Out a Miserable Living on Moscow Streets.' *The Russia Journal* 415 (2002).

McMahon, Colin. 'Russia Struggles to Address Problem of Rising Number of Street Kids.' *Chicago Tribune*, 30 March 2001.

Mereu, Francesca. 'Russia: Homeless Children – Helpless Victims of Collapsing Welfare, Family Systems.' *Johnson's Russia List*, 19 June 2002.

'Moscow, 50,000 Homeless Children.' UNESCO, 5 May 2002.

'Moscow's Street Children Endure and Survive Russia's Record Low Temperatures.' *Médecins Sans Frontières*, 1 January 2006.

Paddock, Richard C. 'The Grim Face of Russia's Orphanages.' Los Angeles Times, 17 December 1998.

Parfitt, Tom. 'The Health of Russia's Children.' The Lancet 366 (2005): 357–358.

Rainsford, Sarah. 'Moscow's Street Kids Army.' BBC News, 25 January 2002.

Weir, Fred. 'Russian Runaways Find Few Willing to Help Them.' Christian Science Monitor, 19 December 2001.

Wroe, Georgina. 'Lost Children.' Sunday Herald, 14 February 1999.

Yablokova, Oksana. 'Street Children Disappear from Streets.' Moscow Times, 21 February 2002.

Street Dogs of Russia:

Antonova, Maria. 'Warning: Let Stray Sleeping Dogs Lie.' The Moscow News, 21 March 2005.

Cooley, Martha. 'Dogs: A Moscow Triptych.' AGNI, 12 October 2005.

English Russia. 'Smartest Dogs: Moscow Stray Dogs.' Accessed 9 February 2010. http://englishrussia.com/?p=2462.

Liakovich, Oleg. 'Homeless Animals Getting Smart.' The Moscow News, 13 October 2005.

Schoofs, Mark. 'In Moscow's Metro, A Stray Dog's Life is Pretty Cushy, and Zoologists Notice.' *Wall Street Journal*, 20 May 2008.

Sternthal, Susanne. 'Moscow's Stray Dogs.' *Financial Times* (London), 16 January 2010.

Additional Resources:

Children of Leningradsky, The. DVD. Directed by Hanna Polak and Andrei Celinksi. Poland: Forte Andrzej Celinkski Hanna Polak, 2005.

Wheeler, Post. *Russian Wonder Tales*. New York: The Century Company, 1912.

Winchell, Margaret. *Armed with Patience: Daily Life in Post-Soviet Russia*. New York: Hermitage Press, 1998.

Praise for *The Dogs of Winter*:

'Beautifully composed writing enhanced by Ivan's visual
acuity and depth of emotion. Terrifying, life-affirming
and memorable'
Kirkus (starred review)

'The book's emotional impact is immense'
Publishers Weekly

'Packs plenty of punch'
New York Times

If you have enjoyed *The Dogs of Winter*, you might
also enjoy these other titles, available now and
published by Andersen Press . . .

L I A R & S P Y

REBECCA STEAD

'As close to perfect as middle-grade novels come'
Publishers Weekly

Georges (the s is silent) has a lot going on. He's having
trouble with some boys at school, his dad lost his job
and so his mum has started working all the time – and
they had to sell their house and move into an apartment.

But moving into the apartment block does bring one
good thing – Safer, an unusual boy who lives on the top
floor. He runs a spy club, and is determined to teach
Georges everything he knows. Their current case is
to spy on the mysterious Mr X in the apartment above
Georges. But as Georges and Safer
go deeper into their Mr X plan,
the line between games, lies, and
reality begins to blur ...

From the author of the
multi-award-winning
When You Reach Me

9781849395076 £9.99 Hardback

The Baby and Fly Pie

MELVIN BURGESS

'Gritty and realistic . . . Can't be put down'
Books for Keeps

*'We're the rubbish kids, losers and orphans. Every day
we go out on to the Tip to sort rubbish for Mother
Shelly.'*

For Sham, Fly Pie and his sister Jane, this is the
grim reality of their lives. Then one day everything
changes when they find a baby on the Tip –
a baby worth seventeen
million pounds . . .

This discovery takes them into
a savage, lonely city and so
begins an endless fight for
survival.

9781849394550 £5.99

THE
APOTHECARY
Maile Meloy

'An absorbing and original historical thriller with
a Pullman-esque feel' *The Bookseller*

Fourteen-year-old Janie Scott is new to London and
she's finding it dull, dreary and cold – until she meets
Benjamin Burrows who dreams of becoming a spy.

When Benjamin's father, the mysterious apothecary,
is kidnapped he entrusts Janie and Benjamin with his
powerful book, full of ancient spells and magical
potions. Now the two new friends must uncover the
book's secrets in order to find him,
all while keeping it out of the
hands of their enemies – Russian
spies in possession of nuclear
weapons.

'If you read anything this summer,
this book should be the one'
Telegraph

9781849395069 £6.99

THE SNOW MERCHANT

MERCHANT

SAM GAYTON

'A germ of JK and a pinch of Pullman' *TES*

Lettie Peppercorn lives in a house on stilts near the
wind-swept coast of Albion. Nothing incredible has
ever happened to her, until one winter's night.
The night the Snow Merchant comes.
He claims to be an alchemist – the greatest that ever
lived – and in a mahogany suitcase, he carries his
newest invention.
It is an invention that will change
Lettie's life –
and the world – forever.
It is an invention called snow.

'A delightful debut . . . full of action
and invention' *Sunday Times*

Illustrated throughout
by Tomislav Tomic

9781849393348 £5.99 Paperback